Praise for

THE FAMILY CODE

The Family Code is a gritty and unflinching look at the devastating effects of intergenerational trauma. Wayne Ng has created vulnerable, damaged, and compelling characters who will resonate with me for a long time. Heartbreaking but also hopeful, this book put me through the wringer.

> —**Bianca Marais**, best-selling author of *The Witches of Moonshyne Manor*

The Family Code's intricate plotting and sizzling dialogue show us an imaginative master at work, narrating in dual points of view with authentic voices, sharp wit and deep sympathy. We live with a dysfunctional family struggling with poverty, petty crime, violence, alcohol, and sexual tension. Wayne Ng's psychological insights and ability to bring us passionately into their troubled lives make for an intense experience.

> —**Josip Novakovich**, author of *Rubble of Rubles* and *Man Booker Finalist*

Building on his years of social work, Wayne Ng has written a searing portrait of a family in crisis, the complexities of love and the pain of intergenerational trauma. Hannah, a struggling single mother trying to cope with deep levels of pain and her own skewed choices, is a complex character who readers will cheer on and abhor in equal measure. Ng's sensitive portrayal of Hannah's young son, Axel, is both heartbreaking and heartwarming. Hannah and Axel are two people trying desperately to find safety and express love in a system that is stacked against them. These characters will stay with you long after the book is over.

> —**Amy Tector**, author of *Speak for the Dead*

A heart-stoppingly vivid cast of characters awaits readers of *The Family Code*. Wayne Ng brings his masterful storytelling to every page, fearlessly examining trauma, abuse, and the often brutal complexities of family. The story of Hannah and Axel is one that will break your heart, but also one that stands as a timeless and stunningly textured testament to hope, redemption, and love. A must-read!

—**Hollay Ghadery**, author of *Fuse: Meditations on Mixed-Race Identity and Mental Illness*

Wayne Ng's brilliant novel, *The Family Code* hooked me immediately. I was deeply invested in his protagonist Hannah, desperate to know what would happen next. Ng's characterization is beautiful and utterly convincing. He writes with the perfect balance of grit and beauty, compassion and stark reality, always aware of his character's motivations, imploring the reader to observe without judgement. My favourite books explore difficult people and their psychology, and Ng's writing is sharp and insightful. Though his characters often misstep, they are all complex and three dimensional. I can't recommend it enough!

—**Danila Botha**, author of *Things that Cause Inappropriate Happiness*, and *For All the Men*

Hannah just wants to hang on to her kids. But her abusive upbringing hasn't equipped her with the parenting skills the authorities want, and her rough street smarts may not be enough. With the immediacy of a bruised throat, Wayne Ng's compelling new novel *The Family Code* confronts us with an unsympathetic character with whom we sympathize, the baffled son she struggles to care for, and the tenacity of their hope in seemingly hopeless circumstances.

—**K.R. Wilson**, author of *Call Me Stan*

THE
FAMILY CODE

Essential Prose Series 206

Canada Council   Conseil des Arts
for the Arts   du Canada

ONTARIO ARTS COUNCIL
CONSEIL DES ARTS DE L'ONTARIO
an Ontario government agency
un organisme du gouvernement de l'Ontario

Canadä

Guernica Editions Inc. acknowledges the support of the Canada Council
for the Arts and the Ontario Arts Council. The Ontario Arts Council
is an agency of the Government of Ontario.

We acknowledge the financial support of the Government of Canada.

THE
FAMILY CODE

GUERNICA
EDITIONS
TORONTO · CHICAGO · BUFFALO ·
LANCASTER (U.K.)
2023

Guernica Founder: Antonio D'Alfonso

Michael Mirolla, general editor
Margo LaPierre, editor
David Moratto, interior and cover design
Guernica Editions Inc.
287 Templemead Drive, Hamilton, ON L8W 2W4
2250 Military Road, Tonawanda, N.Y. 14150-6000 U.S.A.
www.guernicaeditions.com

Distributors:
Independent Publishers Group (IPG)
600 North Pulaski Road, Chicago IL 60624
University of Toronto Press Distribution (UTP)
5201 Dufferin Street, Toronto (ON), Canada M3H 5T8
Gazelle Book Services, White Cross Mills
High Town, Lancaster LA1 4XS U.K.

First edition.
Printed in Canada.

Legal Deposit—First Quarter
Library of Congress Catalog Card Number: 2022949890
Library and Archives Canada Cataloguing in Publication
Title: The family code / Wayne Ng.
Names: Ng, Wayne, author.
Series: Essential prose series.
Description: Series statement: Essential prose ; 206
Identifiers: Canadiana (print) 2022046765X | Canadiana (ebook)
20220467668 | ISBN 9781771837934 (softcover) |
ISBN 9781771837941 (EPUB)
Classification: LCC PS8627.G318 F36 2023 | DDC C813/.6—dc23

This book is dedicated to the many children and families who over my years as a social worker trusted me with their stories and have shown astonishing resilience, spirit and humour in the face of adversity.

Contents

SPRING 2018

1

HANNAH

I've heard it a million times: that even if mothers can't bake fancy cookies worth shit, or juggle forty things at once, they know how to protect their children. That the mother instinct will kick in like a smoke detector when you nod off with a cigarette dangling off your mouth. This is just before you burn down the couch, the whole apartment, and everyone in it.

I smashed that smoke detector long ago when I couldn't get it to shut up.

The things that come naturally to me are getting by (yes, that's debatable), getting out when the shit's hitting the fan, and getting the first punch in (unless I've been suckered). I'm good at those. References are available if you don't believe me.

Okay, maybe it was stupid to think my instincts would just come back. I banked on that until they took Faye for good. She's my eldest kid. Ax, short for Axel, was seven, a couple of years younger than he is now when it happened. It was just before Faye's ninth birthday. I shot into Ax's school to take him to visit her. I ditched my cigarette and could barely catch my breath when I stepped into the hallway, which always had this stinky kindergarten feet smell.

The secretary was on a break, leaving Principal Wilbaugh (I had to stop myself from calling her Dildo) to cover the office, which was more like a lottery terminal: people coming and going, no one

3

sticking around unless their scratch-and-lose tickets sang. You'd think I'd blow half my cheque on that lottery shit, but luck had never tapped my shoulder anytime else, so I never bothered to play. Now, I would consider rolling the dice, figuratively speaking, if I saw a good score coming. You never know.

"I need Ax. I'm taking him out," I said to Dildo.

I could feel her judgy eyes, although she'd deny being like that, they all do. I caught her checking out my tats, my crooked nose (broken by an old hookup, but I got him good), and I'm sure she had something to say about all the store-bought lunches for Ax.

"Hannah Belenko, so glad you're here ... just the person I was going to call." She didn't really say it with what you call *authenticity*. I could tell she didn't want to deal with me.

Fuck, what now?

"Axel brought a peanut butter sandwich to school today. You know we have a strict nut-free policy."

Really? That's why you needed to call? Sure you don't just have a thing for women who could rough you up and flip you around like a twin mattress? "He made his own lunch. So you're gonna nail my son for showing initiative? Most boys his age legit can't pee straight."

She phoned for Ax, then lectured me. "We want our students to be considerate of one another."

Consideration. Caring. Community. Empathy. Oh, puhleez. Every Catholic school beats you over the head with slogans. They might as well put up a billboard and sell ad space and make some money for some real playground equipment. *Party Right With Bud Light, Light Up Your World, Budweiser—True.*

"It's not enough that we cater to a generation of wimps and babies, but you want to make them rats and snitches too?" Most principals can't stand a mouthy mother, so I enjoy grinding them from time to time.

The principal sighed. "Let's not do this, okay?"

That was good with me. But I wasn't going to just stand there and do small talk, so I waited in the long corridor lined with tiny kindergarten shoes and Disney and Marvel knapsacks.

I'm sure Ax's Grade 1 teacher jumped with joy when she heard I was there to pick him up.

She held his hand as he skipped along the smooth linoleum floor. She explained that he was revved up 'cause he had been in the personal reflection space (fancy lingo for the time-out gulag) for inappropriate language against little Abigail Holzman, who was obviously teacher's pet. He'd offered some of his peanut butter sandwich to her. When she saw the offending sandwich, she shrieked, "Peanut butter—he's trying to kill me!"

The teacher made like he'd just said the N-word when really Axel was legit just being nice. "That," she said, "was when Axel announced in front of the class that Abigail was a dirty whore and screamed that he didn't do anything wrong."

I tried not to laugh.

Her knuckles rested on her hips. "I explained to Axel that nuts could make Abigail sick or even die. It wasn't until I said it was like kryptonite that he seemed to understand. But I really need you to monitor his bag and reinforce the importance of respecting our nut-free school."

"Ax, ya little shit, really, you said that?"

The principal squirmed at my language. I enjoyed that.

"Why are you here, Mom?" Ax asked.

"We're going to see your sister, remember? That's how we get her back, by playing this stupid game."

I dragged his lazy butt to the bus stop and lit one of my Indian smokes. I sucked hard and it irritated my throat, in a good way. I knew no judge would dare separate me from my children forever. At least that's what I wanted to believe.

A couple of days before that, I lost it when I told Kevin that the CAS taking Faye wasn't enough for them. They wanted to make her a crown ward, turn her into government property. That would mean, if they won, I'd lose Faye. Not for three months, or even six months. But for good. Forever. Kevin, like every guy I've ever gone out with, zoned out. But Ax has ears the size of a satellite dish. He asked if that meant she was going to become a princess and if so, he also wanted to be a crown ward so he could be a prince—better able to guard Faye and me.

I said that would be stupid, that I had it all covered.

We jumped on the Montreal Road bus cutting through Vanier. One of the ladies was out working already and the cops were shaking down a couple of panhandlers in front of the pawnshop. After a quick stop for takeout Subway and snacks, we walked into the glassed CAS building through the back door and settled into our assigned family room. I straightened Ax's shirt and re-tied his shoelaces.

"I want you looking good. Remember, they watch everything we say and do. They want to trip us up. But we won't give them anything. Faye belongs to us, and we're gonna convince that stupid judge that nothing is my fault. If he asks, say nothing about Kevin. Say you and I get along, and our house is clean and quiet. Don't forget."

I made him repeat it until his eyes and attention wandered off.

Each of the six rooms looked the same—battleship-grey walls, a table and chairs, a couch, a DVD/TV player, and a two-way mirror. It didn't matter what was in the rooms, they all felt like a 1980s Cold War interrogation room. They did have a cupboard filled with assorted toys. There was a one-eyed Cabbage Patch Kid, a Rubik's Cube (can you believe they're popular again?), some LEGO, and a checkerboard missing pieces. Almost before we sat, Laura Catano, the worker, greeted us. She's got this thick ginger hair and a goody-goody look, like Glinda the Good Witch in Ax's favourite movie, *The Wizard of Oz*. But I know what she's all about. I'll bet after watching and listening to every fucking thing behind that two-way mirror, recording every little fart and yawn, she's hitting the bars on Elgin Street, where no jerk is too low for her.

She brought in Faye, who smiled at Ax, then hugged me like I was the delicate one.

Ax thinks he's the man of the house. His first fight was when someone called Faye a terrorist. At age three he didn't know what a terrorist was, but he knew it was nasty and against Faye. Standing by the swing set, eyes ready to bust out of his head, he screamed he would kill the punk and threw himself at him. The punk was more than twice Axel's size and age and easily held off Ax's wild swings. But my Ax regrouped with spit and bites, followed by snot that he smeared onto the kid's hands. The punk ran off terrified. I watched it all from a bench. It's what you call a good day at the park with the kids.

Both of them have the dark olive complexion of their deadbeat Lebanese father. It's the only good thing he gave them. Faye has my blue eyes. Axel's eyes are hazelnut and shift with the light and his mood. It makes him seem elusive and slippery, almost complicated. He's not. He just has to be fed, kept busy, and reminded to wipe himself.

The air in the interrogation room felt canned, like we were in a submarine. Speaking of which, I divided the sub and chips. The kids babbled with food in their mouths, playfully teasing one another, exchanging silly sounds and jabs in a language only tight siblings get. He beamed as he showed her his Burger King Hulk keychain. She giggled as she launched into the splits she'd learned in dance class.

Dance class. Next she'll be selling peppermint Girl Guide cookies. They're turning her into a perfect suburban kid. I wasn't about to keep listening to her go on about the suburban dream, so I reached for my phone.

"When are you coming home?" Ax asked Faye.

For a second I stopped scrolling through Kit Harington's Instagram to see what she was gonna say.

"I don't know," she said. "But I wish you could stay with my foster parents, they're so nice. They have a pool and a cottage."

I slammed the bag of chips into the table, sending salt-and-vinegar shards everywhere. Nothing steams me like foster parents calling themselves parents, making like they know my Faye. Where were they when my kids' father walked out? Where were they when our fridge and cupboards were empty? Where were they when she was running a fever at three in the morning? Collecting a cheque, that's what they were doing. They get a nice per diem per kid. I Googled enough to know that newbie foster freaks make thirty-seven thousand dollars a year. That's decent starting money with all sorts of tax breaks. Crap, when all this is over, maybe I'll be a foster mother.

"She's not your mother," I told Faye. "She gets paid. She only cares about her cheque. You are my—"

"Hannah, Hannah?" Laura's pinched, sparkly Good Witch voice came through a tiny speaker.

All three of us stared into the mirror.

"Hannah, let's have a good visit, okay?" Laura said.

The kids looked worried.

"Okay, okay. Faye, what did you do in school today?" I could see Ax breathe a sigh of relief, but Faye was fighting back tears and stuttered out something about learning about dolphins. Then all anybody heard were her sniffles. Such a drama queen, over what— chips?

Ax broke off half a cookie and handed it to her. He said dolphins were his favourite animal 'cause they're smart and friendly.

Faye nodded. "I know you like them. You have one at home. It was mine, now it's yours."

Ax stretched his hands forward to form a V shape and pretended to swim around the room like a dolphin.

Faye copied him. "Mommy, if we can find ten more dolphins then we'd have a pod."

"Yeah, Faye, all we have to do is find ten more," Ax said.

He'd settled her down, so I returned to my phone.

For most of the next hour, the kids played, getting into the LEGO, the art supplies, and finishing the cookies.

Then they started on a *Cat in the Hat* nine-piece puzzle.

"I wish you could visit," Faye said.

"I wish too. Can we walk there?"

"I don't know. My foster parents have a van, it takes a long time. It's near a McDonald's and a dollar store."

All this talk about the foster freaks was really starting to piss me off.

"Kevin has a new car," Ax said. "It even has a touch screen except it's broken. He can drive us."

Before Ax even got to the part about the stupid screen I knew it was too late. The little shit had said too much. Laura would red-flag that offhand remark, knowing that it showed I had skipped the court order to stay away from Kevin. Fuck me. Fuck Ax.

"It's time to go," I said.

Laura stepped into the room, bending down to the kids' level. She casually fit the last piece—an ear—where it belonged, completing the puzzle. Her eyes avoided mine but her shoulders sagged. "Almost time to pack up, buds."

She turned to me. "Do you need bus tickets?"

"Yeah." I tried to read her face but she had on her standard saccharine smile.

I bent down to Faye. "Remember, no one, *no one*, loves you like your for-real mother."

Laura faked a cough, her signal that I had crossed into a visitation no-fly zone: do not slag the foster freaks.

The kids waved goodbye to one another.

I reached for Ax's hand and gave Faye one last look. My stomach cratered as though something inside had been emptied. It didn't feel natural or instinctive. I wondered if I'd ever see her again.

―――

The next time we were in court, the CAS paraded the Good Witch around. She went on and on about our last visit with Faye and bullshitted that I "continued to associate with Kevin." He wasn't living with us. He didn't tell me what to do, so it was bullshit. During her testimony, I made a long, slow slash across my throat and mouthed, "Fucking bitch, you liar," to let her know who she was dealing with. That made her flinch. Fuck with me, will you?

The judge had to nudge Catano back to her crap. She took a deep breath and refocused. She looked directly at the judge and went on about my missed visits and about how even when I was there, I wasn't present. How the hell is that even possible? For two full days, she added to the bullshit testimony already given by other "experts" that I was a horrible mother. That I couldn't step up to meet Faye's complex medical needs, and that meds weren't consistently given. Have you ever read what the side effects of epilepsy meds are? Well, Faye got them all: rashes (everywhere), grogginess (she'd fall asleep while eating), dizziness (walking made her dizzy), nausea (the smell of anything made her want to puke). Plus they hadn't been there to see how the meds turned her into a zombie, or what a bitch she became. Judge me, will you? Try living with that first.

"It's all a pack of lies," I said to my prissy (but free) lawyer.

I had half a deck of smokes but bummed one anyway from the courthouse security guard before calling Kevin to pick me up.

I told him about the CAS and how Axel had ratted us out. "You picking me up?"

"I'm not coming," he said. "The car's in the shop."

"That's what you fucking said yesterday."

He said something about a new compressor and a thousand dollars. "I'm in no mood for your shit, Hannah."

"You're such a loser," I yelled into the phone and hung up. I waved a cab down outside the courthouse. I hesitated when I saw that the driver had a Middle Eastern look. I was sure the driver, like most men, and probably a few women that day, were checking me out. My lawyer had told me to wear something respectable, which meant my leather jacket over a thin white blouse, a short skirt, nude nylons I bought just for the occasion from Shoppers, and pumps. Not the coolest gear for a warm May day but respectable. I knew I looked hot. And I know for a fact all Muslim men want a blonde trophy. Most own the taxis in Ottawa, which pisses me off. Soon they'll also control Uber. What then? Somebody should ask if we have enough immigrants.

Now, I'm no racist. My kids are half Lebanese, for Christ's sake. I'm all for good eats, like shawarmas—one of my favourite foods. Phuong is Vietnamese. She does my hair and nails cheap and does a gorgeous stiletto acrylic set. We need those kinds of people who will come in and do a good job and be grateful.

"Please, madam, this is a non-smoking car," the cabbie said.

Fuck this. I finished the smoke, exhaling into the cab just to piss him off.

It was barely ten minutes to my Vanier walk-up apartment, which I have to enter from a flight of rotting stairs in the back. Honestly, it's a miracle our place hasn't been B-and-E'd. Everybody in Vanier gets jacked eventually or knows someone who has. And if your gear *is* lifted, chances are you'll find a replacement in the pawnshop. There's no beating the cheap rent, though. Good luck finding a landlord who'll sink a dime into their place.

Boris, my part beagle, part whatever-mutt-did-his mother greeted me. He needed a walk. That would have to wait until I lit a joint and got a Red Bull into me. I downed the Red Bull in three gulps. I went through a bag of clothes in search of some summer outfits and changed into my denim short-shorts and a T-shirt. We still had unpacked bags and boxes kicking around. I'd been putting off unpacking, since you never know when you'll need to suddenly bounce anyway. I cleared a pile of clothes off the couch and turned on the TV to *The People's Court*. I love that show. I miss Judge Wapner but I gotta say, Judge Milian rocks. First, she's a woman. Two, she's Hispanic, though you wouldn't know it, and to be honest, I don't care. And three, she takes no bull and is straight-up. I'd love to take my kids' dad in front of her, and my parents for sure. It might be the only place where I'd ever find justice.

I could hear Boris drinking from the toilet bowl. He scampered out of the bathroom and jumped onto my lap, almost knocking the joint out of my fingers.

"Boris, you dumb shit, see what you almost made me do." He gave me a look with his big brown eyes, which always melts me. I planted a kiss on my fluff muffin.

My phone rang from the kitchen. I shooed Boris off and ran to it but stepped on Ax's Optimus Prime Transformer and tripped, falling hard onto my side. I cut open my leg on one of his toys and it started to bleed. Fucking shit, how many times do I have to tell him to put his stupid toys away? I picked up the Transformer and threw it at the fridge, shattering it to pieces. The missed call was from my lawyer. She'd left a message saying the judge was handing down a decision the next day. It didn't sound good.

That was on Ax. I reached for several big garbage bags of clothes and emptied them. Then I filled them with Ax's stuff. By the time the school bus with Ax arrived, I had two bags full. He was going to pay.

2

AXEL

———

"**A**XEL."

"Axel."

"Axel!"

The teacher yelled at me for daydreaming except I wasn't really dreaming. I was worried Mom would still be mad at me for saying Kevin had a new car. It's not a real secret. He drives us everywhere. Why is that bad?

I fell asleep during math. Again in French. Then I got really, really bored when I was supposed to draw a picture of ways we make the planet get hotter. It's summer, it's supposed to get hot, isn't it? So I got up and told the new student he's a transgender. Do you know what a transgender is? I don't. He got pretty mad and cried, easy. Then at recess, I got Mohamed Al-Salem in trouble by pushing him into a girl. I ran off before the teacher saw anything then grabbed a loose ball and banged it into the parking lot. But then Assi Al-Fayed got picked on by a Grade 3 I don't know. He made Assi cry and fall. Assi is my friend. I wanted to kick that mean boy in the balls, but I took Assi to the office and stayed with him. I held ice to his knee and told him he was the best at basketball and that he would be okay.

At the end of the day, I got off the bus and saw Mom with her arms folded and face like she was holding her breath. Her really mad look. My stomach did not feel so good. I had to pee. When she is

13

like this I know I have to be really good, or just run somewhere. Except I am not sure what being really good is, and I cannot go anywhere Mom will not find me. Sometimes I get so scared, I just charge like the Hulk. Except I am more like the son of Mrs. Hulk. Except I can also be a Hulk who knows how to answer the phone if Mom is still sleeping. I know how to triple-check the doors and windows at night. I never seen Hulk do that either.

"Come on, Ax, I've got something for you."

This felt like a trap. It always is when she has kind words but a mad face. I looked to see where I could run.

"You must be hungry." Mom gave me a Hot Rod. That made me think it was a false alarm, like the time I pulled the fire alarm in the winter and the whole school had to go outside and we saw the fire trucks come.

I grabbed the pepperoni stick and ripped it open. Maybe Mom is really in a good mood, I wished. But when I have to pee or poo even when I didn't eat or drink, something is going on.

Mom turned to go home. I looked back at Melina, who I sit beside on the bus. She is the slowest runner in the class and the easiest to catch when we play manhunt. She always gets picked last for teams and groups. One time she got laughed at 'cause she stutters. That's when I smacked them and got in trouble. Ever since then, she always shares her lunch and waits for me. She is my best friend.

Sometimes when Mom wants to be alone with Kevin, she lets me go to Melina's house by myself. Melina has dolls and stuffies, but they are boring. She also has MEGA Bloks. Her mom likes that Melina has a friend, so she always makes me a fried bologna sandwich when I come over. We sit beside each other on the couch, eating our sandwiches wrapped in paper towel and watching TV. Our favourite shows are Super Monsters and Beat Bugs. Melina likes the Beatles and she got me singing along to them when the bugs sing. But I still like Super Monsters more 'cause I want to learn superpowers like them and if I ever got them, then I could protect her while she sings. One time I asked if she would be my girlfriend. She said yes and then let me feed her goldfish. I think we are going to get married in Mexico then go to college.

Mom said hello to Melina and her mom. Then she pulled me away. Melina and I waved goodbye to each other except I wanted to follow her to somewhere my stomach would feel better.

When we got home, Boris smelled my pepperoni stick and jumped all over me before licking my hands, then my face. He barked, and that made me giggle, then we wrestled until I forgot I was scared. Garbage bags were all over the floor.

"Are we moving again?"

Mom ignored my question and kicked one of the bags. "This is garbage. I've been cleaning up. Look."

Mom only cleans when she is scared. Like when the CAS is around. So now the apartment is always clean, except for the bags in the middle of the floor. Mom can be really good at cleaning when she wants. She sweeps all the cockroach poo in all the kitchen cupboards, all the mice poo from under the sink and in the pantry. She got rid of the thick, dark lines around the tub. She even scrubbed Boris's poo and puke out of the carpet and threw out all the takeout food containers that were in a big pile.

I looked into the bags. My Spiderman mask, Optimus Prime, Power Rangers, and all my other toys were inside. "This is not garbage. This is mine."

Mom sucked on her cigarette. "When you ran your mouth about Kevin's new car, do you know what that did?"

All of a sudden my tummy hurt.

She walked back and forth like she was winding up to jump me.

"You know what that could mean? That could mean Faye is never coming home. You did this."

I did not move. Not even to breathe. Not even to blink.

"You couldn't keep your yap shut and now she might be gone for good, and whose fault is it? Not mine, I'm the only one holding us together. I'm all you have left, and you could be gone too, with a mouth like that."

Except sometimes Faye had seizures, like when she was really, really thirsty and hungry. Those were not my fault. And that time she got lost at the mall, when she and Kevin were buying bras, that was not my fault either.

I could not feel my feet holding my body to the floor anymore. It was like I was inside a balloon floating away but looking down at myself. I could hear Mom yell, but it sounded like she was in a bubble far away.

Then I heard the voice in my head that comes ever since they took me and Faye away. *Boy, are you ever gonna get whupped. Just shut up and say nothing.*

"Ax?" She pushed her cigarette into her Red Bull can. "I see I've spoiled you. You have everything, but I have shit. So *we're* gonna be generous. All your toys, your LEGOs, your Transformers, your Beyblades, your Air Hog, your stupid Spiderman watch, everything … is going to someone who knows how to keep their mouth shut. Someone who knows that there are people who want to take them away forever, people who don't give a shit about them, who want nothing more than to use them for a monthly cheque. That would be all the kids at the cee aye fucking ess."

She grabbed some twist ties. "Actually, it's garbage day. Let's just throw this shit out. But wait, you can keep this as a reminder." She handed me the dolphin Faye left behind, my favourite stuffed animal. His head was ripped off and split open.

From high above inside the balloon I watched Mom carry all my toys to the street. Boris licked my fingers, but I only knew 'cause I looked down and saw his pink tongue curling. I could not feel anything. The TV was on but I don't think it was in English anymore. I was stuck in that giant balloon, trapped but safe enough not to be heard, and slowly, slowly running out of air.

It's time to leave, get out, out now. Then I could feel Mom's hot cigarette breath when she got in my face.

"Take Boris out right now for a walk before he shits in the house again."

I peed in my shorts.

She laughed at me but not like it was funny. "Well, you can sit in that for a while, I'm not changing you. Take Boris out first then clean your own mess, fucking little baby. And try not to talk to anybody, can you do that?"

She threw Boris's leash at me.

I followed Boris along the street. I did not even feel the wet stickiness of my pee down my leg. And I did not care that Melina and her mom said hello and kept calling my name. They asked if everything was alright. I think they saw the wet spot on my shorts. I turned up another street where Boris, even though he's a small dog, let go a steaming pile of poo. I left it there and he followed after kicking up some grass to try to cover it. We kept moving and turned left, then I unclipped him and jumped the chain-link fence into the Islamic school. Boris whined when he saw me climbing, but when I got to the other side he wagged his tail and squeezed through a hole in the fence. I stepped around the smashed beer bottles and saw that someone painted "Die Bombers Die" on the wall by the playground. I kept going through the yard to the tiny park where Boris sniffed a broken, slimy balloon.

I sat on the grass under a tree and tied Boris's leash to my leg and took a break. A mom helped her kids up the slide. One time I walked here with Melina and sat on the swings. She pointed past the houses and said that rich people lived close and on garbage day they threw out TVs and bicycles and electric fireplaces. She also heard that the prime minister's house had four floors and that he gave out whole chocolate bars at Halloween, not the little fun-sized ones but whole ones. I never seen that before at Halloween and wanted to go there and get some new toys and maybe a Mars bar even if it wasn't Halloween yet.

I'll bet those houses have big backyards with tree houses and swing sets. I wish we lived in the houses around the park, even if they're not the rich ones. Not only do they have big backyards, but the park is right beside them too.

I do not know how long I was asleep for, but when I woke up under the tree my chest pounded like I was being chased. I had to get home before Mom found another reason to explode.

I cut through someone's backyard and almost stepped on a needle. I hate needles. Mom made me get one to stop diseases and it hurt, so I see why people would throw them away. Soon I was in front of my house. I stared up at the window where Mom would be. I did not want to go in. Then Boris pulled me to the backyard and upstairs.

Our door was unlocked. I opened it and saw Mom on the floor crying. I poured her some water and searched for her cigarettes.

Mom covered her head with her arms like somebody was going to hit her. "I'm scared, Ax. I'm scared Faye's gone for good." She reached out to me but it was her cigarettes she went for. "My little girl, my little angel's gone."

I didn't know what to say. Before when there wasn't enough money or Mom was sick I would try and keep her busy by getting her mad or happy. I was used to looking after her but not while she cried about losing Faye.

"Boris and I had a good walk, Mom." I rubbed her back while she cried. "Everything's going to be okay." I wanted to say we'll get Faye back and that everything will be better soon, but I knew not to say anything about Faye, and I really did not know what "better" looked like. Still, I wondered.

By then my pee was dried up, but I did not care.

3

HANNAH

———

I MAY HAVE ragged a bit hard on Ax, but he has to learn. Once I settled down I figured it wasn't going to be easy for a judge to separate my kids from each other for good, not to mention from me. They call it a crown wardship, like there's a prize for getting snatched away.

I could see me winning and suing the CAS for harassment and settling out of court for five thousand dollars, maybe even ten thousand. If it weren't for Trump's Muslim ban, I'd take my kids to Disneyland, but for sure they would get hassled there. Dairy Queen would have to do. Ax would order a chocolate dip and he'd peel and eat the yummy outer layer first. Faye would have a banana split with extra Smarties.

I walked into my lawyer's office expecting good news, but her grim look told me we'd lost.

"I'm so sorry, Hannah. I really thought the judge wouldn't go this far and permanently break up the children."

I sank into the closest chair and covered my head with my arms.

"The good news is he acknowledged that the concerns and risks for Faye and Axel are different, although the supervision order remains in place," she said.

"What are you saying, I should be happy I get to keep one of my two kids? How fucked up is that?"

"It is rare and fortunate you still have Axel."

So I should just shut up 'cause I still got one out of two kids? It didn't feel fortunate. At that moment Ax felt like a consolation prize. You didn't get crowned Miss America but you still get to be Miss Rhode Island. My lawyer was really starting to piss me off. "This is stupid, no, way worse. Absolute bullshit. We're going to appeal."

"I'm not sure we have grounds for appeal. But you should know there is still a possibility of seeing Faye regularly. In fact, it's encouraged for the siblings' sake. Although, if she's adopted and the family decide against it, well … they get to decide."

No appeal? That meant I could only see Faye at the discretion of the CAS, if I jumped high enough. It would never be high enough. Like, I had played their stupid game and look where it got me. Being Faye's mother shoulda been enough. But it meant nothing to them. My lawyer reminded me that I had another three months on the supervision order. The court allowed Ax to stay with me but the CAS would continue to lord over me with conditions—counselling with fancy terms like DBT or CBT. BS is what it was, straight-up bullshit.

I'd played along, kissed ass, and smiled through people lording over me like I was a lab rat. Now I had fuck all left and they wanted me to keep this up just to see my own daughter. I tore out of there.

Months ago, when Faye was in foster care, I was pretty messed up and just barely holding it together with Ax. The CAS sent me to a therapist. He actually wasn't half bad at first—real young, kinda cute, a bit stuck up with degrees in fancy IKEA frames all over his concrete walls and new-agey music playing. I mean, what kind of therapist has background music? Like was he going to massage my feet too? No doubt, he was making good money, though. To be honest, if he had made a move on me, I might have been okay with it.

"I've always respected your survival skills," he said. "You pulled yourself back from the abyss."

"I guess."

"You went through postpartum depression after Axel was born. Faye was what, three at the time?"

"Two. Faye had already turned two."

"Alright, two, and they both went into care by your choice. That must have been a frightening time for you, Hannah. Yet even at rock bottom, you were able to decide in the best interests of your children."

I nodded and reached for the tissue box. "I didn't know what they were talking about. I thought I'd never see my children again. I had nothing left, no reason to go on." I'd hid in my basement apartment for weeks. I stopped eating and couldn't give a shit that I stank. When I wasn't drinking or high I binged *Friends* and *Gilmore Girls* and had an epic pity party all by myself. The CAS kept both my kids for a year. They told me if I didn't get help and get it together, they would take them for good. I'd lose all my parenting rights forever.

"But you pulled yourself together. You started healing old wounds rather than running from them. You started a new pattern. That took courage."

There was no hiding the tear sliding down my cheek.

"Those were tough times. My children were mine. They belonged to me—they were the only thing I ever had in the world that nobody else had. All my life I've felt like a worthless piece of shit. But my kids needed me, and I needed them. I had to fight, I had to get it together."

"Yes." He said it like it was a line in a play and he'd rehearsed it perfectly and I was just another actor to him. "And you did it, you persevered, you fought the system, your family, loneliness, and the demons inside you."

"Demon?" Boy, did he use the wrong word.

Papa used to call me a demon. Like the time I got home from school and he was there early. Normally when he did that, my stomach picked up on whatever bullshit was coming. But that day he'd just come home with a bucket of KFC and that neon-green coleslaw I just couldn't get enough of. He said we were celebrating and he put in one of his favourite CDs, the Bee Gees' *Stayin' Alive*.

He moved our gym equipment aside. We had a ton of free weights and benches, boxes of protein shakes, and stacks of body-building magazines. Our family's whole apartment was a shrine to his mis-guided dream of recapturing the Olympic glory he missed when he defected to Canada from Russia.

He cranked up the volume, and he and Mama laughed as they did the bump and grind. Ivan and I exchanged glances as if to say, Have our old-fart parents been abducted by aliens?

Papa sang along as he jabbed his hands into the air. "Stayin' alive, stayin' alive."

After the song ended, he said he had "a special announcement."

I held my breath while he told us he'd quit his gym jobs and invested everything into a beater semi-tractor and the world of free-lance trucking. I didn't understand that, but I did get that he would be gone most of the time, leaving all of us in a better mood.

Money had always been tight but at least he'd had a regular paycheque. Trucking meant feast or famine. Mostly famine. Gone were trips to the McDonald's drive-throughs. We started shopping at Food Basics, and I heard them arguing about when the next cheque was coming in.

The first time Papa called me a demon was over a dinner of pierogies and sauerkraut. He had announced further cutbacks. He said he was glad I had done well this past season of competitive soc-cer, 'cause it was my last.

"But why?" I squeezed my fists beneath the table.

Papa waved me away like I was some server who had mistakenly brought over a glass of light beer instead of a shooter.

I was supposed to move onto the competitive skating program after impressing the coaches. I was damned good. But Papa said that my coach sucked, and that I should concentrate on track and field.

"You said I would be the next Tonya Harding." I dug the end of my fork into the table.

He shrugged like it was nothing. Like what I wanted was nothing.

"We all must feel some pain," he said, cutting into a cheese-filled pierogi.

I asked if my dickhead brother Ivan would still be playing

competitive basketball in the fall and winter, then tennis and football in the spring and summer.

"*Da.* He is fifteen soon. I watch. Ivan is best on all his teams. Everybody is scared of my boy."

"So what?" My fork gouged random lines into the table. "I'm thirteen next year and I'm the top-ranked skater on my team."

"*Da*, but for girls."

"I'm also a midfielder on my soccer team. You always said it was the most skilled position."

Again, he just shrugged.

My dickhead brother pouted his lips and fondled his chest to mock me and all girls.

"That's enough, Ivan," Mama finally said.

Ivan stopped laughing, but his smirk was just as loud.

"That's so not fair." I knew tears would be seen as weak, but I was about to explode.

"What is fair in this world? Fairness is for losers and whiners," Papa said.

Ivan teased me about being a crybaby.

I lost my shit. "I hate this family, I hate you all!" I got up and turned to leave.

"Sit down. You leave when I say," Papa said.

I sat, but I took my sweet time. I jabbed the sauerkraut on my plate with my fork and flung it toward Ivan. But most of it landed on Papa's face.

Ivan and Mama gasped.

Shit, I hadn't planned on that.

Papa picked bits of sauerkraut off his face and squared his body toward me.

I inched backward and was about to run when he reached out and slapped me in the face, dropping me hard onto the floor.

Stunned, I grabbed my stinging face and screamed and fucking screamed. It's not like he'd never smacked me or pushed me around before. But he'd just taken away something that I was good at that got me out of the house. Meanwhile, Dickhead still got to keep doing everything.

Papa yelled at me to shut up. When that didn't work, he hovered over me. "I do not know what kind of demon is inside you, but if I have to beat it out of you, I will." He grabbed me by my top and with one hand lifted me off the floor like I was one of my Beanie Babies. He widened his feet and shifted his weight to his back leg like he was about to shot-put me when banging on the ceiling stopped him.

We shared the house with the landlord upstairs.

"Papa," Ivan whispered. "He said he will call the police this time."

I wish he would've. I wished it then too.

The phone rang. Papa covered my mouth. "*Politsiya?*"

I could taste my own tears and snot smeared onto his hand.

Ivan reached for the phone.

It was the landlord and not the police. Ivan apologized for the noise and said that I had fallen hard while we were wrestling.

Papa mouthed to me, Shut the fuck up.

Mama wiped the slime off my face with the crusty cloth napkin she kept hanging from the oven door. "What were you thinking?" she whispered.

Silence was the only resistance I had left.

———

"Demons?" I glared at the therapist with his fancy IKEA degrees. "Nobody gets to call me that anymore."

"We all have history Hannah, some of which is very difficult to overcome. Your parents—"

My parents?

The therapist knew shit about Youri and Steffi Belenko.

"Who the fuck are you to tell me I've got demons?"

He studied me like I was a lab rat. "Let's talk about why your mood suddenly shifted so strongly."

"You think I'm mental, don't you?"

He recoiled. "No, not at all. What I mean, Hannah, is you've come a long way, and you've managed to—"

"I'm not crazy. There's no demon inside me. There's nothing wrong with me." I squeezed my fists and felt my face turning red. "My parents and the CAS have always been against me. My problem is stuck-up pricks like you thinking they know me. You're just another snitch for the CAS. Save your fancy bullshit for someone who needs it."

I went straight to his boss and flat out filed a complaint that he had made inappropriate sexual advances. Maybe it was the right thing to do. I did kinda think he flirted with me. Anyway, it was like taking a flame thrower to the counselling centre. It led to an investigation and an immediate suspension of service. That worked for me 'cause I'm pretty sure nobody wanted to touch me with a barge pole after that. I know how gossip works and I can guarantee every therapist in the city either thought he was a perv or I was a psycho. Nothing backs people off or gets them fired up like rape allegations. I'd know, trust me.

Like when I took up ringette. Mama showed some rare backbone and smarts by signing me up for it while Papa was out on his long-haul tomato run to Leamington. The equipment was donated by someone who stopped playing. I didn't care that it was secondhand—it was free, although the skates were way too small, so I had to be the only one with figure skates at the tryout. The other players laughed at me until this little *thing* named Mackenzie helped me figure out the equipment.

I didn't know fuck all about taking a pass or shooting. But I was a powerful skater and chased that donut down like I was a heat-seeking missile. Plus anyone who got near Mackenzie got a stick across their ankles from me. The coach called me on it, but I made the team anyway.

I learned the game pretty fast and I gotta say, I was good. I protected my crew and scared the crap out of the other teams. By the time our season was closing, we qualified for the provincial championships.

Before provincials, the coach threw a year-end party at his house. Maybe I was overthinking it, but I was afraid Papa would come, piss drunk, and say something dumb about the coach being gay, 'cause he was.

Ivan said he wanted to come to the party and check my teammates out. Like, *ew*. He was almost sixteen and most of us were three years younger. Mama said it'd be good for me and Ivan to hang together. If she thought he was going to even talk to me at this party, she was even dumber than she acted.

Adolescence had started early for Ivan. He'd fought a fierce but losing war with acne all through high school and was addicted to Halo. He worshipped UFC fighters and would freak out over the smallest thing, like being out of Cheerios or not having clean underwear. His obsessive bodybuilding pleased Papa, even though he did it mostly to attract girls. Papa didn't have a problem with that either.

Mama dropped Ivan and me off at Coach's house. "I'll be thirty minutes!" she said, rolling the car backward out of the driveway. Then she sped off to get a cake for us from DQ.

Coach had this interior design thing going. Tastefully renovated is what you call it. Exposed brick, a funky chandelier, mirrors everywhere. But then again, he's gay, right? Most of the party centred on the main floor, although Coach said people were welcome to explore the basement and use the upstairs bathroom if needed. None of the girls knew until then that I had a brother, so they were all googly-eyeing him in his tight muscle shirt.

"Is that Mackenzie?" Ivan whispered to me. "She's got quite a rack when she's not geared up," he said to me in Russian. What a creep. (I knew some Russian back then. I've lost most of it now, except the swear words and command words.) "Gross, don't be a perv. Mackenzie's my best friend, don't screw this up for me."

Mackenzie had also noticed him, and Ivan angled over to her when Coach called all the players over. He handed each of us a card with personalized messages we'd written to each other after the last game. I wrote my messages in purple sparkly gel pen and stuck mini holographic skate stickers on the cards for the girls I liked best. Each of the team members had her name loudly chanted as she received her card from the group. I got a real loud cheer. Everyone had to read one personal message aloud.

I teared up as I read my messages. When it was my turn to speak, I read Mackenzie's. She said she loved me and that I was her BFF. "I love you too, Mac. Really, I love you all. You guys are the best thing that's ever happened to me. You took me in. You're like a family, better than a family."

Ivan coughed, interrupting my flow.

"I just wanna say thank you." I could feel the heat of Ivan's glare on me, reminding me that we never talk shit about our family and I'd just about crossed the line. Everyone else applauded.

My teammates hugged me and encouraged me to return for a second year. Someone cranked up the Janet Jackson and we started dancing. Then it was Sir Mix-a-Lot, then TLC, then LFO, then Sugar Ray. Then J.Lo. I mean, back then she was just Jennifer Lopez. We danced and sang by the fireplace under Coach's glittery chandelier until I needed to cool down. Mackenzie was nowhere in sight by that point.

The bathroom Coach told us to use was occupied. I really need-ed to pee and headed to the one upstairs. I heard muffled cries from behind the closed door across from the bathroom. I tried the door-knob and it was unlocked. Ivan was on top of Mackenzie, his big, dry, meaty hand covering her mouth. His other hand was groping under her top. Mackenzie's eyes pleaded with me for help.

Mackenzie's whimpering sounded like Mama's when Papa would come home hammered and drag her into their bedroom. Spaced out, I turned around and closed the door and walked into a closet where I almost gagged on the smell of mothballs.

Later, according to Papa, the only time Mama ever showed any sense was when she wouldn't allow the police to interview Ivan with-out first consulting a lawyer. This gave Papa, our lawyer, and Ivan time to cook their story for the police.

"This girl, she likes you, yes?" Papa asked Ivan.

Ivan nodded.

"You touch her?"

Ivan looked at the lawyer. Papa slapped Ivan in the face. "I asked you a question, why look at him?"

The lawyer flinched. I held my breath. Part of me wished Papa had smacked Ivan way harder. I was just glad it wasn't me.

"Yes, Papa, I touched her. But she wanted me to. I did everything you taught me, she played games, she messed with my head, but she wanted it."

Papa nodded. "You rape her?"

"No, Papa. All I did was feel her up. It's what she wanted. I swear to God."

Papa placed his hand on Ivan's shoulder. I thought he was going to whack him again. Instead, he said, "If she makes eyes for you, she tricked you, then she is a liar."

"Yes, Papa, that's it, that's exactly what happened. Hannah saw everything. Then her faggot coach and that girl's mother jumped me."

That was good enough for Papa.

By then, Ivan's story was way different from Mackenzie's. He said he'd gone upstairs to use the bathroom. Mackenzie followed him. She told him how cute he was, that she wanted to feel his muscles. He told her that it wasn't cool. But she caught him off guard and off balance, pushed him into one of the bedrooms, and kicked the door shut. She ran her hands up and down his body and even bit his hand trying to be a sex freak. He said I interrupted when I walked in. I woulda seen that Mackenzie was not in any danger and was, in fact, the instigator. My opening the door gave him an out so he could finally leave and go to the bathroom. After he went downstairs and was grooving to the music, Mackenzie's mom confronted him, accusing him of raping her daughter. That's when she assaulted him, leaving a large bruise on his face. The lawyer demanded that she be charged with assault and uttering a death threat. He also insisted Coach be charged, as he had roughed Ivan up while kicking him out.

A whole room of witnesses confirmed the physical and verbal confrontation between Ivan and the adults. Still, I was the only one who had been in the bedroom. My parents were able to keep the police away from me for a couple of days and during this time they tag-teamed me, telling me I had to back up my brother, that family was everything, that Ivan's future was at stake. The Belenko name was in my hands.

"You saw that girl all over Ivan. He did nothing. You saw that."

"Who has your back, a girl with a faggot coach who wants to put your brother in jail—or your family?"

"Maybe she wanted attention. Maybe she really enjoyed it."

Finally, Papa pulled out my ringette stick. He ran his hands along the shaft and banged the butt end against the floor. He tried to bend it. He pointed it at me. I thought he was going to whip it at me.

"Two-piece construction, aspen and birch. Strong wood. Fibreglass walls for long life. Tiny rubber tip and quarter-inch dowel. Everything work together. Every piece essential. Every piece just shut up and do job. Job is not to shoot ring. *Nyet,* that is for player. Job for stick is to stick together, make strong."

He pulled a hammer out of his toolbox. "But if one piece does not do what it is made to do, or one piece attacked"—he slammed the hammer down on the stick's rubber tip against the floor, destroying it—"whole stick fail." He slammed the shaft across his thigh, breaking it in half. "Everything becomes garbage, nothing left."

He turned to me. "It is like family. Everybody does their job. Number one is protect each other. Number two is do your part. You do your good job by keeping mouth shut. That is family way, rules for family is to be strong, say and do nothing to hurt us. That means we survive."

"Everything we do," Mama said, "Papa's long hours on the road, everything we've given up—Papa's Olympic dream—is for you and Ivan. All we ask in return is you remember."

"If ever I needed you to be a sister, it's now." Ivan pleaded with sad puppy-dog eyes that just didn't belong.

Like I said, they worked me over pretty good. It didn't feel right, but I backed Ivan up.

Mackenzie tried calling a few times. Pretty ballsy of her. Ivan coulda picked up. I wanted to say something, but instead, I let Mama scare her off. I dragged my ringette gear to the ravine behind our house. I coulda donated it, but I figured why pass my bad vibes onto someone else? I used my stick to shovel a hole in the snow. When that didn't go too well, I dug with my skates. After a while, I'd created a small hole. I threw my stuff in, then covered it with snow. It was kinda stupid. A spring thaw would leave it exposed. I couldn't even trash my gear right. Burning it woulda been a better idea.

So yeah, I know a few things about rape accusations and people saying shit. Like, if you wanna drop a nuclear device? Cry rape. Wanna fuck yourself up even more? Say nothing. Just swallow that shit. If there's a slow-release pill against hope or happiness, that's it.

Maybe that's why I didn't like the idea of Ax being in therapy. He doesn't know what he's saying yet, and it'd be so easy for people to plant things in his head.

4

AXEL

ONE TIME MOM said I was stupid for wanting to die. She said I didn't know what I was talking about. I think dying is worse than Game Over 'cause you can't restart the game. You get no extra lives. There are no special credits to let you come back. But what if I could have a chance to be a different player, a new Axel? Maybe I'd get a different mom who would always love me and tell me how special I was instead of being mad all the time. I could even win a few games, and the prize would be to see Faye again.

The day I wanted to die was when Mom found out about Faye. The bus after school was late and smelled like rotten milk 'cause somebody threw up. The driver opened all the windows and yelled at anybody who didn't stay in their seat. He was so mad.

I looked out the window when the bus stopped and saw her smoking. When I got off the bus, she stomped on the cigarette. When she hugged me, her travel mug came under my nose, with a strong sour smell that I know was beer. In a really calm voice, she told me what the court said. That we lost Faye. I seen Mom sound madder when the pizza place was out of pineapple. I knew that whenever she was this kind of mad-calm, bad things were going to happen. This was a time to be quiet and stay away. I didn't want it to be my fault when the next bad thing happened.

One time she smashed the TV 'cause Faye and me were fighting over the remote. She said it was my fault she lost her temper. It was my fault she lost her job at the Mandarin for being late. She said if I wasn't watching that faggot SpongeBob, I woulda woken her up. But when someone does a sleepover with her, I know she doesn't like to get up early. Now, 'cause I could not keep my mouth shut, Faye is gone forever. I'm so stupid, stupid, stupid.

If Faye gets adopted by new parents, will she forget me? Am I an only child now? If I get taken away, I will have no mom, no daddy, no sister, nobody.

I was watching one of my favourite SpongeBob episodes. It's the one where Squidward takes over SpongeBob's body and enters a dance contest but loses to Patrick Star. Faye loves that one too. That started me thinking about her and I started to wonder how she was doing. But then Kevin came. He let himself in through the back door. Even though I don't remember my for-real dad, I used to think Kevin could be my new one. One time when I was under the table with my dolphin, and Mom and Kevin were playing cards, she told him they are kindred spirits 'cause he gets her. I think that means he buys her things and they are in love.

He liked building things with me and doing LEGO. Sometimes he brought over Pokémon cards, and for my birthday, he got me a Pokémon shirt. He said I had to toughen up and be ready for anything. He said when he was a kid he had a crew who watched out for one another. I asked if it was like the kids in *Stranger Things*. He laughed and said yes.

I used to like it when Kevin came over, and so did Mom. He would bring over things like beer, and they would stay up late together and have sleepovers. He is really tall.

He stepped through the whole apartment in only a few steps and went straight for a beer. Then he dropped a tiny plastic bag on the table and sat down on the couch before putting his feet up. Mom switched off SpongeBob and stared at him.

"Are you stupid? I said don't come during the day," Mom said to him. "Especially right after school." She grabbed the little bag and looked at me funny.

He made a sour face when he heard the word *stupid*. "Take a chill pill, woman, it's Friday."

I don't know what a chill pill is, but I knew everything else. If Kevin was around they could take me away. Dads are supposed to protect you, not put you in danger. I wanted him to go away. Instead, he took a drink of his beer.

"You don't get it," Mom said. "They took Faye and they'd like nothing more than to take Ax too. That bitch could drop in any time."

I looked at the door to see if anybody was there. They visit me at home and at school. I don't hate the CAS, but Mom does. After every meeting, she grills me about what the CAS asked and what I said. I just do what she told me to: "Everything's great. Mom's a great cook. She doesn't have any boyfriends. We get along real good. She's always home."

Kevin shrugged at Mom. "You wanted some candy, so Daddy's here." He reached for Mom's butt.

She stepped away. "Get your fucking hands off me."

"Whoa, bitch, don't be a cunt. You didn't have a problem with me the last time I was over."

Mom had her hand on her hips like she was ready to yell but just shook her head at Kevin.

"Suit yourself," Kevin said. "If you wanna be a bitch just remember your tab's up to two and a half bills. You can forget about me extending your credit again."

"This is not about—How many times do I have to tell you to stay the fuck away while the CAS is snooping around? Are you that stupid?"

He drank his beer in one long gulp and slammed the can down. "How many times do I have to tell you I don't like it when you call me stupid? Twice you just called me that."

He stood up and slapped Mom's face with the back of his hand, knocking her back against the couch.

I didn't move. Not even my eyeballs.

Mom touched the side of her face like it was on fire, then screamed and jumped at him, scratching his face and punching him on the side of the head.

Kevin turtled and took some steps back. Then it was his turn to attack. He punched Mom in the face and she fell down.

This time my screaming came out. "Mom!"

Boris barked and snarled, charging toward Kevin. But Kevin had such a mean look like he would tear Boris's legs off that Boris turned around and ran off.

Kevin dropped his knees onto Mom's chest and started to choke her. She gagged and her face changed colour, and her eyes bulged out. I looked for something to hit him with but only saw clothes and a pizza box near me. I could not move.

He let Mom go. "You fuck with me again and you're dead, and that rat son of yours becomes someone else's problem. He sure as shit ain't mine."

Mom sucked in air and tried to call me.

Kevin emptied Mom's wallet onto the table and took the baggy back. "You still owe a bill and a half, plus another two for this bull-shit, no, make that three. You got two days or you won't be able to get up the next time I'm done with you. Plus you won't have to worry about the CAS showing up. I'll call them myself. Say goodbye to Axel." He kicked over a kitchen chair when he left.

I squeezed my fists as tight as I could and closed my eyes, then screamed until my throat hurt.

Mom turned onto her tummy, propped up on her arms, and threw up on the floor. The sour smell was worse now. "Sh-shut ... shut up. Ax. Shut up."

I could not stop crying. Then I could not breathe. I was shaking like somebody covered me with a big cold, wet blanket.

"Br-breathe," Mom said. "Breathe, Ax. Deep breath, that's it, deep breath." She coughed some more.

I listened to what Mom said and my breathing got better and I crawled into her arms, careful not to touch the vomit. It felt good being in her strong arms. But I wanted to start the game all over, even if that is what some people call dying. I know I am a loser for not protecting my mom. It's my job and I failed. For that, I should die and I said so.

"Ax ... Ax ..." Mom struggled to speak. "You're being stupid. Someday, I will find us a place where no one can ever hurt us. Where no one can separate us." She wiped her mouth. "Your mother loves you and will always protect you, 'cause no one else will. Do you understand?"

I nodded. But I already heard that so many times already.

5

HANNAH

I SHOULDA KNOWN better. Kevin had lost it on me before, but never quite that bad. He'd never threatened to rat me out to the CAS. I had no doubt he could lose his shit again and mess things up for Ax and me. When I met Kevin, he came in all sweet and dangled his university degree and parents' cottage like he was a made man. But he was a poser. His parents didn't like me, but they disliked Kevin even more. I swore I wasn't going to fall for that shit again. And yes, I'd said that before. A few times.

The school phoned the day after the bullshit with Kevin. They said Ax had been informally suspended for crossing into the junior side of the yard and bloodying an older student in the nose. For fuck's sake. I said I was too busy to pick him up. Like, really, what the hell is an "informal" suspension? Plus, my throat was killing me and I really didn't want to walk around with a scarf to cover up my bruises. More importantly, I was busy emptying as much of the apartment as I thought could fit into a taxi onto the sidewalk in front of our building.

It's not easy to hide bruises on the neck. Still, I got good at it. Some foundation and concealer always worked, but I learned that too late. I fucked that up back in high school, and it cost me Jennifer. I tell myself that's my personal no-fly zone, for my own mental health, but I often drift over it like an out-of-control hot-air balloon, ready to crash.

I was fourteen when Opa Adler died of a heart attack and left some money to my parents. Papa wanted to move away from the "welfare bums" and "live like real people," so they bought a new house in Stittsville near some golf-and-country club. Yep, the Trailer Park Boylenkos were levelling up.

Stittsville is Ottawa's gated community without the gates: genteel, prissy, uptight. It's as exciting as vanilla on vanilla, where they've perfected boredom and where the biggest drama is who will outdo who with their garish, over-the-top Christmas decorations. The fact that no one spray-painted an *h* over the first *t* in Stittsville shows how fucking oppressively dull it is.

Papa used the dry van and his crew to help with the move. Once the truck was unloaded and the unpacking started, sets of neighbours came by to say hello and offer welcome baskets. One couple with matching salt-and-pepper hair, Bill and Audrey Krohn, dropped off a tray of lasagna and invited us all over for drinks and dessert after dinner. That was so weird. New neighbours ... not only talking to us but offering food. And smiling at us. Mama was startled too and didn't know how to respond.

"I've just made a Black Forest cake. It's my grandmother's secret recipe and it's to die for, really," Audrey said. "And Bill makes his own beer."

Bill grinned.

"It's better than it sounds," Audrey said. "So come over. You'd be doing us a favour. Our kids need to meet other kids."

Other kids? I figured her kids were perfect and got along with each other, baked cookies for starving African kids, and would try to teach me to play golf. Christ, I never thought I'd miss the hood rats of Carlington.

Mama's parents were a good German brand—the Brauns. So the German-heritage connection was hard for Mama to ignore. She accepted without consulting Papa or us.

Papa used to lecture about how trusting others is like letting them cheat you, and how giving your trust freely and completely is like giving away an Olympic gold medal. "People shake with one hand and with the other stab you in the back." Apparently, in his mind, it also applied to teachers, police, shopkeepers, little old ladies, and neighbours. He was pissed at Mama for agreeing to get together with the Krohns. When she pointed out that it was his idea to live in this kind of neighbourhood, Papa backed off. The Krohns were offering free beer, after all.

We unpacked some utensils and wolfed down the whole casserole of the Krohns' lasagna, which even Papa admitted was unreal. Afterward, we made our way to their corner lot. A walkway of fancy cobblestones in black and white waves wrapped around their house, a much bigger one than ours. The path led to an in-ground swimming pool in a backyard the size of a parking lot. They sure as hell hadn't cheaped out. We sat on cushy patio furniture surrounding a stone fire pit. If money had a smell it would be fresh cedar—'cause that shit hung everywhere.

Bill and Audrey showed off their main floor, then introduced their youngest kid, twelve-year-old Thomas. In the backyard, Audrey served wine, beer, homemade lemonade with the lemon rinds still in it, and Black Forest cake. The lemonade was out of this world. The Krohns chatted about their new sailboat and their management positions with the federal government. Papa's mouth was clammed shut. He'd always said boats were for snobs and that civil servants were lazy-ass, do-nothing bureaucrats of our corrupt state—but right then he looked jealous and uncomfortable. He did, however, lighten up with talk about the golf-and-country club, and when Mr. Krohn talked about some of his DIY projects.

"I'd be happy to help you whenever you're ready for some projects of your own," he told Papa.

As the conversation moved on to life in Stittsville, Jennifer glided in on her bicycle. She had just finished a shift as a customer service rep at Walmart and still had her work vest on, though it was unbuttoned over a Cranberries T-shirt, a combo she made look cool.

She pulled off her sunglasses and helmet in one fluid motion, revealing royal-blue eyes that made you want to bow without taking your eyes off her, and a full head of dirty-blonde hair. She jumped off the bike and bent down to kiss her mom.

"Jenn, you little twit, I just about spilled my drink," her mom said.

"Sorry, Mother. Any dinner left? I'm starved."

"We saved you some lasagna," Thomas said.

"And it's amazing," Mama said, nodding. "Your mother is a wonderful cook."

Jennifer shook hands with us. I felt like I shoulda curtsied.

"Yeah, well, she had help. I was on cheese detail and shredded the mozz and the parmigiana before I went to work," Jennifer said.

"And I peeled the tomatoes and chopped the onions and peppers." Thomas did a chop-chop motion.

That freaked me out a bit—seeing a bro and sister get along, and talking with grown-ups. I couldn't imagine our family cooking together without a shouting match. I wondered what they did when they were pissed at each other.

Jennifer mingled effortlessly without appearing to try. She was warm and hospitable without being showy. She was cool and poised without being remote. It's not like she was gorgeous like Pamela Anderson or Britney Spears. In fact, her nose was a bit misshapen from a break in rugby two years earlier. Her braces hadn't completely corrected her misaligned teeth. Her lips were thin like two marsh reeds. But when she blinked and smiled at me, I hoped my breathlessness wasn't obvious.

Feeling a blush creep up on me, I took my eyes off Jennifer, like calm your tits, Hannah, and noticed Ivan studying her. I just knew the perv was mentally undressing her. He jumped into the conversation and asked Jennifer about Holy Triverius, their high school, with me starting Grade 9; Jennifer, Grade 10; and Ivan, Grade 12.

"Well, Holy T is a big school, Catholic of course."

"Guess that means skirts for the girls." Ivan grinned then swatted at a mosquito.

"Believe it or not, girls can choose to wear pants." Jennifer made like she was modelling hers, in a silly way.

"Bill and I actually met at a Catholic high school," Audrey said as she lit the patio candles. "It was a marvellous experience. I wouldn't want our kids schooled without faith and values."

Papa swatted a mosquito away, as did Mama.

A few buzzed around Jennifer, but she was either oblivious to them or just too cool to be bothered. "You'll have to get used to a few things, like the school uniform if you're not already. There's always lots going on. Like any school, there are fantastic people as well as jerks, but the opportunities to learn and grow are there. It's what you put in." She went on about other stuff, but all I could hear was her calm, reassuring tone.

The evening ended with an onslaught of mosquitos and a promise from the Krohns that they'd show my parents the golf-and-country club. Ivan took it one step further and asked Jennifer if he could get a personal tour of the neighbourhood. Jennifer agreed, with one condition. "Only if Hannah comes too."

I tried to play it cool but said yes immediately.

Several days later, Jennifer knocked on our door wearing a tiny cropped T-shirt, super-oversized baggy, ripped jeans, and skater shoes. She looked chill without even trying, whereas I suddenly felt like a Value Village poster.

Ivan and I followed Jennifer through a field and along the creek before arriving at Main Street, stopping at the Showbiz Entertainment and Gift Store. It wasn't like any convenience store or Blockbuster I'd seen. They rented movies but also sold gifts, toys, popcorn, and cotton candy. She introduced us to the owners, who greeted Jennifer like a niece and welcomed us. I was shy, and Ivan laid on this gross, polite charm that *so* wasn't him. I was only too happy to move on and browse through some toys, books, and knick-knacks before checking out the DVD movies.

Ivan held up a copy of *Speed*. "It's going to be a classic, Sandra Bullock is smoking. And check this out." He picked up a copy of *Pulp Fiction*. "This guy Tarantino is awesome."

Jennifer looked at the DVD jacket and then at Ivan. "Yeah, I agree, he's a brilliant director, but I think *this* story will be timeless." She handed him a copy of *The Shawshank Redemption*.

"You have to be kidding," Ivan said. "It's like, a lot of talk. I fell asleep."

"Sure it's dialogue driven. And it's not like we need another male-bonding story, but this one is different. They kind of find peace and safety together without smashing heads or cars."

"Still sounds boring to me," Ivan said. "But I'll give it another try."

"Stick it out, be patient, that's the lesson in the story. Redemption follows." Jennifer led us to the cotton candy.

Back in elementary school, I was the one leading a posse of girls around, but that day I hung on to Jennifer's every word and seamless movement.

We took our cotton candy outside and sat on a bench. Jennifer nodded toward the grocery store and Napoli's Restaurant. "Welcome to downtown Stittsville, but wait, there's more. Rumour has it that a Tim Hortons might open up."

We cracked up.

On the way home along the creek, we talked about music. Jennifer loved Oasis and The Smiths. Until flipping through the TV the week before and landing on a documentary about The Smiths, Ivan had never heard of them. He normally listened to Van Halen and Aerosmith. But he put on his sensitive, new-age guy voice and spewed a load of regurgitated BS. "When The Smiths broke up in '87, it was supposed to have been the loss of a powerful voice that represented teen confusion, loneliness, and alienation. But honestly, they sound like crybabies and whiners, and I'm tired of people stereotyping us like that. I want to be taken seriously." What a fucking poser.

"Wow, Ivan, I didn't think you had that in you. You really mean that, don't you?"

"Damn straight I do."

Jennifer cracked a smile and placed a hand on her hip.

I didn't understand everything I'd just heard but wanted to puke. At one point we crossed the creek and Ivan took Jennifer's hand to help her leap over. Then as she landed, his big hands steadied her hips. I flashed back to the ringette party with him and Mackenzie, except now I could imagine Ivan luring Jennifer back to this creek and having his way with her. My heart started to race. I wanted to gouge his eyes out with jagged stones, push him into the water, and hold him down until he drowned. Something like that. I'd do the right thing this time, I thought, if I could have another go at it. I'd save Jennifer.

"Are you okay?" Jennifer's concerned voice snapped me out of my trance.

"Huh, yeah ... I'm good."

"She just gets a bit moody and spacey sometimes." Ivan twirled a finger around his ear.

"Well, I have to roll, Walmart awaits. I guess I'll see you around the 'hood and school sometime."

"I was thinking of maybe checking out that restaurant before school starts, want to come?" Ivan said.

"Napoli's, us?" Jennifer said with a certain lack of surprise. "Wow, I'll bet that'd be an experience."

Ivan flashed an ear-to-ear smile.

"Sure, just let me check my work schedule. In the meantime"— she turned to me—"I've got something for the feminine condition, if you catch my drift."

"Stop." Ivan raised both open hands in surrender. "That's Aunt Flo talk, I'm out of here. Gimme a call, Jennifer." He ran off.

She waited for Ivan to be out of earshot. "Hannah, I know he's your brother and all ... And you may not see how some girls might find him cute ..."

I bit into my lip.

"... and I hate to ask this favour of you since I hardly know you, but you know where he hangs and when, right?"

My chest tightened. I didn't want to fail Jennifer like I failed Mackenzie.

"And you'd know if he's going to come around. So ... if you don't keep that dick away from me, I'm going to puke all over him."

I was stunned. Then I burst out laughing. Jennifer quickly followed suit. She held a thumb and an index finger an inch apart. "Am I right?"

"Yep."

It was like she'd handed me an umbrella in a storm, temporarily blocking out the crushing sense of being alone.

School was crap at first, filled with stuck-up suburban hoes. But Jennifer gave a shit about me and once I was seen with her, I no longer ate alone in the caf. She was one of those girls who got along with everyone—the stoners, the jocks, the preps, metalheads, nerds, grunge ... you name 'em. No one ever got enough of her. She was my first love.

But even she couldn't save me from Papa. He bitched me out for anything and everything: I dressed like a slut, was gonna be a welfare bum, was gonna fail school ... He was just a fucking ass. Plus he embarrassed the shit out of me by parking his trucks on the street and strutting around in his muscle shirt, scratching his ass in front of the 'hood, including Jennifer a couple of doors away.

I ratted him out by calling bylaw, repeatedly, who ticketed him, repeatedly. Then I decided to mess with him and started leaving anonymous letters in our mailbox from a "friendly neighbour" who reminded him to properly tie up the garbage (Dickhead Ivan's job), to mow the lawn more often (also Dickhead's job), and to "not park oversized commercial vehicles so that our tranquil neighbourhood doesn't look like a trailer park." One afternoon when Papa was getting wasted in the backyard, I wrote another letter: ... *drunk and disorderly behaviour made the neighbourhood look like it was populated with goons fresh off the boat.*

Later that week, in the morning when I was still trying to drag my butt out of bed for school, he stormed into my room.

"Papa, what's going on?"

His gorilla-sized hands threw my covers off and he seized me by the neck. "How do the hands of a goon fresh off the boat feel? Or would you prefer them up your butt with a hot cigarette? Heh?"

I couldn't remember having logged off the family computer the night before. Ivan had jumped on right after me, and a creeping dread was telling me I'd forgotten to delete the document with the letter on it. Ivan musta ratted me out to Papa.

He tightened his grip. "In the army, they teached us that strangulation is like drowning, that your lungs become desperate for air."

My face was ready to explode. My fists and legs flailed at him as I fought him, but my blows bounced harmlessly off.

"The quicker way is to simply break the neck by twisting it like you see in the movies. I have to be very strong to do that. The neck muscles would resist, and even then it does not guarantee death. Still, maybe I am strong enough. Strangulation can also lead to brain injury, you could survive as a vegetable, and then I have to stare at your ugly face forever."

My vision blurred and I got light-headed. I remember seeing big black flowers like ink spilled onto a projector screen and thinking it was the last thing I'd ever see.

Papa released me. I fought for air, coughing. My entire body heaved. The blood was returning to my head, but Papa wasn't done.

He brought in the keyboard, computer tower, and monitor and threw them at the wall like pebbles. "No more letters."

He smashed the phone on my night table as though it were made of LEGO. "No more bylaw calls."

He grabbed my face and squeezed it like it was a peanut to be cracked. "And no more bullshit. Or next time I will kill you!"

For the rest of the day, I stayed in bed or over the toilet where I puked, my head still pounding. Mama placed ice packs around my neck and gave me Tylenol, but swallowing was difficult.

That was about the worst time Papa choked me. It wasn't the last, though. And where he left off, others tagged in. I coulda saved myself a lot of pain if I'd worn one of them spiked neck collars. Hahaha. That woulda taught them to keep their filthy mitts off me.

I had an hour to drop everything off at Oma Greta's garage before picking up Ax. I brought along Boris, who I promised to return for.

"Where to this time?" Oma asked. "You can't keep running. How many times do I have to ... wait, what's that?" She pointed to the bruise on my face and the dark marks on my neck.

Before waiting for an answer, she took me by the hand and led me inside. She poured me some coffee and cut me a piece of strudel. I took the coffee but pushed the strudel away.

"You used to love strudel as a child, remember?" Oma said.

"Yeah, well, I'm not a kid anymore."

"*Ja,* but you still want the same things." Oma plopped on a dollop of whipped cream.

I rolled my eyes, ready to reject anything resembling motherly advice. But I cut into the strudel and took a bite. "Oh my God, apple ..."

"Spiced apple *mit* raisins, *und* flaky, layered pastry ... the way little Hannah always liked before, *und* now, still."

Oma threw a few crumbs at Boris.

"Spoiling him already, heh, Oma?"

Oma smiled, then reached into her purse and pulled out a thin wad of bills.

I reached for the money but she pulled it back. "For Axel, understand?"

I nodded.

"So where this time?" she asked again.

"Somewhere safe." I stuffed the money into my bra.

"You always say that."

"Yeah, well, I've never said I'm heading back to Halifax."

Oma shook her head, knowing what happened the last time I left for Halifax. I met the man who fathered my children. And shitshow part two happened.

I knew what she was thinking. But I also knew Kevin—or anyone else—wouldn't think to look for me there. And if they couldn't find me, they couldn't take my Ax.

6

AXEL

MOM DIDN'T SAY anything about the fight I got into at school. When she lets me get away with things, it's 'cause she is busy. After school we went to Burger King. There are always men outside buying things from each other and Mom doesn't like taking me there, but Burger King makes the best fries.

When she told me we were moving again, I got mad and slammed a pack of ketchup onto an empty seat and it squirted all over. I asked her if I messed up again.

"No, we're gonna find your father."

"You said Daddy was gone."

"He was. But I found out he's back."

She hardly ever talks about him. She is always mad when she does, but it's almost like she's holding her breath at the same time.

"What about Faye, can she come?"

She shook her head like it was a stupid question.

I covered my fries in a blob of ketchup until they were all red. "How will we know it's him?

"We'll know. I'll know."

I added more ketchup onto my blob. "But why do we have to move?"

"Because he's far away."

"Where?"

She looked over her shoulder to see if anyone was listening. "Halifax."

"Is that in Ottawa?"

"No."

"Is it safe there?

"Very safe, okay. Very safe. Ease off the fucking ketchup, will you?"

"Are you sure it's safe?" I was thinking about Kevin finding us.

"That's why we're going."

"Do we take the bus?"

"Fuck, no."

"A taxi?"

"No."

"Then how?"

"The train, the goddamned train. Alright?" She looked around again. I know Kevin likes hanging around Montreal Road. Sometimes selling things.

"The O-Train?"

"No, not that crappy light rail. VIA Rail, two trains, we change in Montreal."

I got confused. "But we're here already."

"The city, Montreal the city. Not the road, you stupid. It's in Quebec." She was ready to blow. "We get to have a picnic on the train and sleep in big chairs and there's even a snack bar where we can buy hot chocolate."

I wanted to sneak another question in. "What if I have to pee?"

"They have a bathroom on it. It's gonna be so much fun." She didn't look excited about it.

Someone sat on the seat with the ketchup. That made me laugh, and I think that made Mom think I was okay with moving again. But I don't want to be away from Melina and Oma Greta.

7

HANNAH

For Ax, a twenty-five-hour train ride in coach was sounding like the greatest adventure ever. He'd been too young the first time we made that trip to know that he'd been on a train with a washroom and restaurant before, and that he'd been to Halifax and that he'd seen his dad. Actually, he was born in Halifax where Bashir and I met. I tore out of Halifax to Ottawa on a train with Faye and Axel when he was two years old. Community Services, the equivalent of CAS, was circling once again, and Mr. Deadbeat Bashir had already returned to Lebanon.

Bash was part of the second wave of Lebanese immigration to Halifax. I'm not sure why I had to know this but the two of us got hammered one night while watching *Jeopardy!* and he decided to give me a history lesson. Don't ask me how I remember 'cause I don't know. I have a memory for the weirdest things. Probably he gave me the greatest orgasm of my life after he went down on me and it got seared into my brain. Or maybe he just told this story a thousand times. Anyway, the first Lebanese immigration wave was in the 1880s, the second was during the civil war in Lebanon that started in 1975. It raged for fifteen years. After hopscotching through Syria, Cyprus, Greece, and France, Bash and his mother arrived in Canada in 1988, on his eighteenth birthday.

He loved rubbing in that I probably mastered the potty at about that time.

He never really went to school but could MacGyver just about anything. He was curious about most things, could speak Arabic and French, and could charm his way through English, Spanish, Italian, and Greek if necessary.

He landed a temp handyman job at the Canadian Lebanon Society, but it didn't pay enough. He needed to send money home. I'm sure he left a girl back in Beirut. He bounced around odd jobs, often juggling several—construction, driving taxis, landscaping, snow removal. He eventually settled into a part-time job at the King of Donair where donairs were the late-night rage. Partiers lined up for them and he loved showing off his guns as he sliced the meat off its skewer, slathered on sweet and spicy garlic sauce, before winking at the many gorgeous, hungry women lining up for his magic donairs and old-world charm.

That's how we met in 2009.

I wasn't sure what to expect from him in Halifax now that his seven-year-old son and I were coming after years of literal estrangement. Part of me wanted to smack him. Another part wanted to ... well, let's not go there. I didn't have the nerve to even call and tell him we were coming. Why the fuck did I even have to? He shoulda been reaching out to his kid.

Ax chatted with everyone in our train car. He looked out in amazement at the world going by. He'd never really seen the country before so even flat fields and farms excited him.

"Is that a for-real cow?"

"I'm going to Halifax. Where are you going? Is that in Ottawa?"

"*The farmer in the dell, the farmer in the dell ...* Wanna PEZ?"

"Who's your favourite superhero? I'm going to see my daddy."

"I'm seven, my mom is twenty-nine. She was thirteen when she had me."

"There goes another giant pee-pee," he said, referring to the grain silos. He woulda driven me nuts if not for the other passengers who let him climb into the vacant seats next to them and chatter away, which allowed me to zone out.

I heard Axel tell some of the passengers that I'd told him how fresh the ocean air was. That the whales were the size of school buses and that Nova Scotians were the friendliest people in the world. One of the passengers asked him if I had told him that Nova Scotia had the best seafood in the world.

"Yeeuck." Ax dropped to his knees and pretended to vomit, sending passengers into hysterics.

In the five or six years I lived there, I had never seen much of the ocean, let alone whales. I became a mother, had robbed and been robbed, had a run of loser boyfriends, and left Nova Scotia scarred from dealing with child welfare Nazis. They had me on edge all the time, thinking everyone was a potential rat. This included Bash, the pawnshop owner, my welfare worker, the bus driver, my neighbour—everybody. I hoped it would be different now. I couldn't think of any other reason for returning except that it was far away from Ottawa.

The steady lumbering of the train lulled me. The last time I was on a train, I was running away. Here I was going in the opposite direction but doing the same thing, again. At least this time I wasn't hoping some guy was going to rescue me. Across from us sat a couple of women. One had ripped jeans, and their thighs rested against one another as they gently pinched and jabbed one another. The jeans and their touchy-feeliness reminded me of Jennifer and how she'd been the one person who for a moment made me feel safe.

That day after Papa choked me and smashed the family computer, I was barely able to swallow, so I had watery oatmeal and juice for breakfast. I ignored Mama's order to stay home and went to school late. The hallway was empty as I shuffled to class.

"Hann!" Jennifer called out, startling me. "Whoa, girl, you okay?"

I nodded but looked away.

"You don't look so hot."

"Just tired," I mumbled, sounding like a thirsty truck driver.

Jennifer studied me. "Okay ... if you say so. I emailed you

yesterday and tried calling. Selena says you missed a team meeting. Hey, what's that on your neck?" She reached to tug at my scarf, but I slapped her hand away.

"What's going on?"

"Nothing. I'm late for class ..."

"Bullshit." Jennifer grabbed my hand and leaned me against the lockers.

Her hand in mine was more healing than any Tylenol or ice pack. I wanted to fully embrace her right there but knew Papa would somehow find out.

"I can tell something's wrong," she said.

"Ladies, why aren't you in class?" Vice Principal Katz suddenly appeared. "Move it along, now."

That day, I autopiloted my way through school, teetering between being a total bitch and turtling. Two of my teachers and a punky girl a year older than me asked if I was alright. I said I had a headache and a sore throat, both of which were true. I joined my friends over lunch but the cafeteria lights and the echoing noise of hundreds of students made my head pound.

I couldn't get home fast enough, but Jennifer was waiting for me outside her house. She waved me inside. My heart raced. I couldn't tell if I was excited or shit-scared.

"No one's home yet, but my mother will be soon, so let's go up to my room."

I kept my beanie, coat, and mitts on and stood rigidly while she collapsed onto her perfectly made bed. A book lay across her pillow. She put it away, but I noticed that it was by Sylvia Plath—*The Bell Jar.*

"Selena can give us a ride to the party Friday night," Jennifer said.

I shrugged.

"Okay, I can't small-talk my way into this." Jennifer squared herself to me. "You look like shit. Like you've seen a ghost, had the crap beaten out of you, then swallowed a load of pills, and had your stomach pumped."

I shook my head. "You're wrong." My voice sounded and felt like I'd swallowed broken glass.

"Wrong about what? Seeing a ghost, maybe? Look, it's killing me seeing you like this. Talk to me."

"My mom doesn't know I'm here. I gotta go." I started to get up.

She pulled me back onto the bed. "It's him—Ivan, right? No, it's your dad, I'm sure of it."

The girl knew me. She could see through me and into me. I blinked and looked away.

Jennifer leapt off the bed and faced me with her hands on her hips.

I said nothing at first, but feeling that it wasn't fair to put even the possibility of this on my brother when he had nothing to do with it, I mumbled that it wasn't Ivan.

"Jesus! Dads aren't supposed to do this. I'm sorry to say this, but he's an animal, anybody can see that. This is breaking my heart."

"He's not evil," I said without any conviction. "He drives me bananas, but I know he loves me."

"Funny way of showing it." Jennifer slowly removed my beanie and mittens, unzipped my coat, then took the scarf off, where I'd tried to hide the dark bruises on my neck. "Holy fuck," she whispered, then hugged me.

We started to cry. She sat me on her bed and reached for some tissues, drying me off, then herself. But the tears kept flowing and Jennifer soon ran out of tissues, which made us giggle.

"I'll buy you a box of Kleenex," I said.

Jennifer shook her head and used her fingers to rub my remaining tears away. I started talking about my family. I said I cringed anytime we went out together, knowing my father would be a public embarrassment and I'd be humiliated. But it was the constant red alert that messed me up even more than the actual violence and his drinking. I said it was like living in a minefield where the safe spots kept shifting. I hated him. The thought, sight, and sound of him made me want to vomit. I told her I was always scared. I often wished he'd get into an accident while out on one of his trucking long hauls. It was difficult to speak 'cause of my throat, but the pain no longer bothered me. I talked about my prank letters and calls to the bylaw office and what had happened after he found out.

When I finished, I buried my face in Jennifer's comforter. She rubbed my back in long slow circles. I lifted my head and looked into her comforting eyes. I brushed her hair back and then cradled her face with my palm, slowly drawing it toward me until I felt her warm breath on my closed mouth.

Back and forth we grazed the outlines of each other's lips with our lips until Jennifer opened her mouth slowly, just enough. We explored each other's tongues, running our fingers along each other's bare arms, then gripping at each other's hips. I found a tear in Jennifer's ripped acid-wash jeans and inched my fingers into them, massaging a tiny area of her thigh.

She fumbled with my jean button. I was ready to tear them off when we heard Jennifer's mom coming up the stairs.

"Shit," we both said, stifling giggles.

"You can't say anything to her, or to anybody." I picked my coat off the floor and put it back on.

"You can't live like this, Hann. You have to call the police or somebody. Look at yourself, your dad beat the shit out of you. This is not normal."

"It is for me. Someday I'll leave this shit, but it's my life and it's all I have right now." I threw my scarf back on, then kissed her. "Promise you won't tell."

"What if you go home tonight and he loses it again?"

"He won't, he's on his tomato run."

"His what?"

"He goes down to Leamington every once in a while and comes back with a million tomatoes. He won't be back until tomorrow night. Then he'll come in with a bag of dollar store shit like he's a cheapskate Santa Claus—like nothing bad ever happened."

Jennifer exhaled. "Well, that's good."

"So, Jenn, promise me. Promise me."

"If he hurts you again …"

"My family will kill me if our shit gets out. It's like an unwritten bullshit code to never talk about family stuff, not even with each other. Promise me."

Jennifer sighed. "I promise."

The promise did not cover up the fact that I had become the first Belenko to break the family code. Jennifer and I hugged and kissed once more as I made for the front door. But her mom just had to be the perfect, friendly Stittsville mother and stop me for a quick chat before I finished wrapping the scarf around my neck.

She glared at my neck as I covered it up but didn't say a word. She looked at Jennifer who exchanged glances with me. I forced a smile. "Oh, uh, wrestling practice. Things got carried away."

Mrs. Krohn nodded. But I wasn't sure she bought it. "Have your parents taken you to a doctor?"

I widened my smile. "We Belenkos bruise easily. It's no big deal. Anyway, I gotta go. Thanks for your help, Jenn. And remember your promise?"

Jennifer folded her arms and nodded.

———

The next morning, a CAS worker pulled me out of class and introduced himself.

"Nothing's more important than your safety," he said. "So if this report is credible, we have to do something."

"What report? Who talked to you?" I couldn't think of anybody who'd call.

He went through the details of Papa almost killing me and how he'd always roughed me up. Fuck. Could Jennifer have talked? She wouldn't do that. But who else? Still, I told the guy it was bullshit.

"If there's no substance, we can end this now. If there is and you won't talk to me, I have to contact your mother and the police."

"The police? What for?"

"Anytime an assault causing bodily harm has been committed against a child, we have to call the police. It's up to you."

"I'm not a child." I started to shake. It had to be Jennifer. How the fuck could she do that to me? Was the night before bullshit for her? I folded my hands together and placed them on the back of my head, bringing my elbows together over my forehead. I wanted to run out of the room and go as far as I could, but the CAS worker sat by the door.

I didn't know what the fuck I was doing but knew Papa was going to kill me if he thought I ran my mouth. Then it just came out, the big lie. "It was Jennifer."

"What?"

I let fear do all the talking. I shook as I said Jennifer came onto me two days ago. When I blew her off, she got physical and tried to choke me. It was so easy and I was so good at bullshitting. Queen of Bullshit. Or just, I am bullshit.

He gave a dubious look. His pager buzzed again and he excused himself as he left the office. I saw him go to another room and reach for the phone on the wall. I imagined the pager call was the police, or that Papa had pulled up. I tore out of the main office and turned into another hallway. Jennifer was walking out of her class.

"Hann, you okay ...?"

"Do you know what you've done? Some guy from the Children's Aid is all over me."

Jennifer looked around then took me by the arm. "Not here, not now."

"Papa's gonna kill me if this comes out."

"He almost already did." Jennifer lowered her voice to a hiss. "I was just trying to protect you."

The feel of Jennifer's soft hand on mine momentarily took me back to the night before. My breathing started to steady. Then, out of the corner of my eye, I saw Ivan approaching. He strutted down the hall like he owned it, like a mini Youri Belenko.

I batted Jennifer's hand away. I tore off my scarf and threw back my hood, revealing bruises and eliciting gasps among nearby students.

"This dyke attacked me after hitting on me," I shouted so everyone in the hallway could hear, pointing at Jennifer, my chest heaving with fear and my own sense of survival, "and now she's trying to blame it on my family."

I jumped on her, pinned her to the ground, and cocked my fist back, enough to scare the crap out of her for ratting me out. Several students chanted, *Dyke fight, dyke fight!* Ivan yelled at me to pound her. He sounded more and more like Papa. I so wanted to pound someone, even if it was Jennifer. I'd never seen sheer terror before until I saw her face as my punch came toward her just before someone pulled me off.

By the time we pulled into Halifax after a legit twenty-five-hour train ride, Ax was sleep-deprived but well-fed thanks to his charm with everyone in our car. It was early evening. The train had arrived on time. My original plan was to head to a family shelter, but I was afraid someone might rat me out to Nova Scotia Community Services, who might then cross-reference with their Ottawa counterparts. If they saw me collecting in Ontario, I'd be ineligible to double-dip in Nova Scotia. So I phoned my old building superintendent, Jimmy on Pinecrest Drive. I knew he rented by the week. Truthfully, he'd rent by the day. Six years ago we stayed in that soulless corridor of low-rise apartments, a few convenience stores, and the odd boarded-up, post-WWII homes.

Most of the rush-hour traffic had died by the time our taxi climbed onto the Macdonald Bridge, which connected Halifax and Dartmouth over the harbour. Ax's face pressed against the car window. "Look, Mom, we're flying over the water."

I didn't look down. The bridge is a primo suicide spot. I figured many of them came from Dartmouth North where we were heading. Crappy housing, quick and easy drug fixes, heavily strapped gangs.

Mostly single-parent families with half the take-home of the rest of the Halifax region. It was one of the seediest 'hoods east of Toronto.

Jimmy led us to the basement apartment. The previous tenant had skipped rent and quickly vacated the furnished one-bedroom. I didn't care that the stains on the futon in the bedroom resembled a map of Africa, that turning on the lights scattered an army of fat, glossy roaches, or that a small mound of unwrapped ground beef was turning grey in the fridge. My only question for Jimmy was whether I could get cellphone reception in the basement.

He shrugged. "See for yourself."

So I did. I got two bars near the window.

He waited by the front door with his hands in his pockets. "I want first and last week now, cash."

I'd expected that from Jimmy. He'd become smart with money. That wasn't usually the case when it came to Dartmouth folks I knew. He'd been working on his gold AA ring when I last saw him. I think he was trying to recruit Bash and I too. One night he'd told us bits of his life story. He'd been your typical Dartmouth Northsider: boozing it up, pissing his life away. He could get work 'cause he was good with his hands. He could build or fix anything. But he couldn't hang on to jobs—and according to some of the other tenants, he had a temper like a motherfucker. Fortunately I'd never seen it. But he hit bottom when his father died.

That's when his grandpa appeared. Jimmy discovered what he was and where he came from. His grandpa told him that back in Miramichi in the 1940s, he and his siblings (Jimmy's great-aunts and great-uncles) would hide when the agent from the residential school came to collect them. They would scatter for their lives in the woods. His grandpa was Ax's age. That kind of thing would freak Ax out. He'd shit himself then get eaten by a bear. That musta fucked Jimmy's gramps up good. You have to wonder what that does to people, like generationally too. I could see Jimmy had finally earned the gold ring, at least.

"Fuck, Jimmy, I just got here. I'll give you first now, last when welfare kicks in. You know I'm good for it."

"Like you were before? You think I've forgotten? I spent a week patching up that unit."

"That was Bash's doing, and you know it."

"Do I? Besides, your name was on the lease."

"Yeah, well, cash gives us both an out." I handed him two hundred and fifty dollars, a complete rip-off for the "furnished" hole in the basement for a week. As building manager, he definitely pocketed a good chunk of that.

Jimmy counted the bills, too slowly for my liking, then handed me the key. "Didn't you have a daughter? Farrah, Fanny ...?"

I shot him a look.

"My, aren't we some owly." He started to leave. "Tell Bash I said hello. He still makes a mean donair." He let himself out.

I had heard from Jeanine, who I'd worked with at the Dollarama and who'd recently left Halifax, that Bash was now running both King of Donair restaurants for his cousin.

"Who's Bash?" Axel asked.

I paused. "Bash is short for Bashir, your father. I've told you this before."

"Oh. Bashir Belenko?"

"No, Bashir Malik. No more questions. Let's go get some milk and smokes."

―――――

The next morning, Ax was up early and being unusually quiet. At first, I assumed he was scoping out the apartment and all the stuff left behind. There was an empty fish tank with a sunken ship I was pretty sure he'd wanna play with. Pretend he was a shark, or something. Then I discovered he had wet himself on the futon. Little fucker. I hadn't even had a coffee or smoke yet.

"Jesus Christ, Ax. Are you stupid? I don't need this shit right now."

He'd tried to hide it by covering it with a stack of clean, folded clothes, but I guess I surprised him by getting started on unpacking and putting our shit away ASAP.

"With all that I've done for you, this is the crap I get back?"

He backed himself into a corner and started to cry uncontrollably. "I'm sorry, I'm sorry, I'm sorry, Mom. I'm so stupid. Stupid, stupid, stupid …" He lowered his head and started to bang it with his palm, harder and harder.

"Enough, already. I said enough."

The forehead-banging continued until I grabbed his arms. He kicked and flailed as I carried him to the bathroom. I stripped him down and was about to turn the shower on but saw there was no thingie to switch the water flow from tub to shower. I ignored the thick layers of grime on the acrylic walls and faux-porcelain base and filled the tub with him sitting in it. I gave him a face cloth and instructions to wipe himself down.

As he cleaned up, I started on the first item of my mental to-do list: a call to the welfare office. I was put through to someone who took the usual information: social insurance and health card numbers. They put me on hold for twenty minutes and I swear I wanted to slice my ears off listening to Rod Stewart's jazz standards. I checked on Ax. He had emptied his entire knapsack onto the floor looking for something. I'd told him to only pack a few bars and what he needed. Turns out that was also rocks, some stir sticks, a magnet, batteries, some gum he'd chewed, a magnifying glass, a couple of Hot Wheels that must not have gotten thrown out when I lost my shit, and some drawings of some superheroes—or him as one.

I dug out some clothes, tore off what he'd slept in (which is what he travelled in), then dressed him. He was no help as usual, stiff as a board. Like he wanted me to baby him still.

The teleworker finally returned.

"Sorry to keep you waiting, Ms. Belenko, but your file has been flagged. I thought I'd give it a closer look."

"What are you talking about?"

"Nothing too, too serious. It seems that you last collected social assistance in this province … in July 2012. At the same time, you also received benefits in the province of Ontario. That's considered welfare fraud. But it was under a thousand dollars, so it can be treated as a misdemeanour at worse, or an overpayment at best, from your perspective, I mean."

"That's bullshit."

"Well, that's what I'm seeing on the screen. I could cross-reference with Ontario. Are you currently receiving social assistance from anywhere else?

I paused. My next automatic deposit was in three days.

"Ms. Belenko?"

"No."

"Good. We're going to need you to come in to sort this out."

"What're you saying?"

"That you're ineligible for full benefits until this here overpayment is rectified."

"You can't do this. I have my son with me. How am I supposed to feed him—"

"A son? Our database shows you have two dependent children. Faye Belenko and Axel Belenko, DOBs ..."

"No, I mean yes, I have two children. Just one dependent right now. Axel for the time being. I have been advised by legal counsel that I have a strong case for an appeal. It's my understanding—"

"I really don't need to know, Ms. Belenko. Let me just update your file here. One dependent still ... Axel ... got it. I can set things in motion with an appointment for the sixteenth, seventeenth, twentieth, nope, that's a long weekend. How about the twenty-first at ten-fifteen? Come in with all the necessary documentation. I think you know what we need."

"Fuck that. That's almost two weeks away." That was going to mean hitting the food bank, rolling my own cigs, begging someone to spot me a few bucks, loading up on peanut butter and jelly, maybe finding a quick job that can pay under the table. If Ax could get into the right school, I'd have had him do breakfast club and lunch there, maybe hit them for a grocery card.

"Don't go flipping out on me, Ms. Belenko. I'm just trying to help. If you want us to process your application, someone from the Decision Review Committee will have to sit down with you. That's my next opening for someone from upstairs to look at this, take it or leave it."

Bastards. I had to take it.

I had four hundred and twenty bucks stuffed in my tampon box and forty-five left in the bank. I would have to give Jimmy another two-fifty in a week. The ideal thing would be to scrounge up a full first and last month's rent instead of paying him weekly. That would be fourteen hundred. I'd still have to do groceries, smokes, and whatever the apartment needed. My monthly child tax benefit of a hundred and twenty would be automatically deposited in two days. I was expecting my Ontario Works deposit in three days. That was a big eight hundred and sixty-seven coming. But after that phone call, I figured that would be the last of it since I was out of province now.

I'd have to get a job, which meant putting Axel in school for a month. And then what?

—————

After Ax dried himself off and put on clean clothes, I let him explore the apartment. I'd already seen there was nothing worth pawning. I got a better look at the place. Cracked and pockmarked pale-blue walls needed a fresh coat and patching. Everything was peeling or cracked: floor tiles, paint around windowsills, baseboards, the kitchen counter. The bathroom ceiling was swollen with water stains and the caulking around the tub and sink were black with mould. I figured I'd get Jimmy to knock off a few bucks if we stuck around.

At least the mountain of filthy pots, pans, dishes, and dinnerware would save me from having to buy them new, but they would take some time to clean.

I looked at the time: nine-thirty in the morning. My son's dad would be sleeping still if he had worked the night shift. I took a deep breath and made the phone call anyway. It rang and rang.

"Yes, who is this?" Bash said in his typical quick, no-nonsense tone.

"It's me, I'm in town." I could imagine him shaking the sleep out of his head.

"So why tell *me*?"

I looked at Ax. "'Cause your son is right here and wants to see you."

Long pause.

"He looks like you, Bash, but he's a lot smarter." I chuckled.

"Fuck off, Hannah."

"And he's a shit disturber, like you, a hundred percent."

"No, no, no. Like his mother."

I lit a smoke and sucked hard. "Whatever. We're staying in Jimmy's building. One B. Come over, bring both groceries and beer."

Another long pause. "I don't have time for your bullshit. Why are you doing this?"

"Why? Because he's your fucking son." I paced the room. I could hear him light a smoke and take a deep drag.

"What about Faye? Where is Faye?"

It was my turn for a long pause. "Child warfare Nazis."

"Again?"

I bit into my tongue, a little too hard, and tasted blood. "Maybe, maybe if you manned up, things might have been different."

"My fault again? No, maybe that is a good thing for her."

"Fuck you. At least I never walked out on my kids. At least I never skipped the country, never mind town. I'm here, Bash, with my son, now, always, right, Ax? Ax, get over here, say something to your father."

Ax was sitting on the floor. He'd found some paper clips and unbent many of them, but he'd heard everything. He looked up at me, unable to move.

"Well, come on, Ax, tell your dad we're here and we need groceries."

He slowly took the phone. "Um ... hello, Daddy. This is Axel. Um ..."

"Tell him we need groceries, Ax."

"Daddy, we need groceries."

I took the phone back. "I'm not asking for six years of child support, asshole. Just man up, be a dad for a change. Is a box of cereal and a jug of milk too much? Some beer wouldn't hurt either."

"What the hell was that? You make a boy do your work. You are a crazy woman. You cannot tell me what to do." He hung up.

"Fucking asshole!"

"Is Daddy coming over?" Ax asked.

"How should I know? The loser does what he wants. Just remember I've been here for you. I didn't skip out, I didn't quit, I did this all by myself with help from no one, no one. It's just me. I'm all I've got, and I'm all you've got." I hated that I began to cry.

Ax rubbed my back and told me how I had been there for him, what a great mother I was, how I look after him. I took his suggestion and lay down while he continued to explore the apartment as though we were on a goddamned adventure.

In the afternoon, we walked to the Hester Street Food Bank, run by the United Church. While we were trying to get there, I got lost and asked a woman pushing a stroller for help. She said her name was Kim.

"The food bank? Follow me, I'm going partway. Them good people. I go down when things get low, always on a Wednesday, yes ma'am, every other Wednesday, gots to keep up to a schedule. But today, my baby bonus come in, always on the thirtieth of every month." She pointed at the stroller full of groceries then reached for her cigarettes. She could see me eyeing them and offered me one.

I had some and couldn't take hers. Sometimes I'm too proud.

"I reckon you might've said that, but you got that look like you just come from away, Upper Canada I'd say. Take a couple, honeybee, you'll pay it forward. Everyone around here does. Them good people around here." She handed me three cigarettes.

I knew she was right about Dartmouth. The cheap rent made it a magnet for the down and out, but they were the kind of people who never forgot where they came from and would share their last dollar, even if they had stolen it from you.

She reached into her stroller for some black licorice for Ax. "My son likes the red. I always said once you go black, you never go back." She smiled, revealing deeply stained, crooked teeth.

"How old you be, son?" she asked Ax.

Ax said he was almost eight.

"My Shaq's pushing ten. He wants a PS4. He don't know how much that costs. But what he really needs is a bicycle. A brand-new bicycle. The boy needs to keep moving, just like me."

Ax smiled. "Get him both. He's turning ten. That's two hands full. A PS4 and a bike will make him really happy."

"Shut it, Ax." I gave him a look. No mother wants to be guilted into poverty. "I'm sorry," I said to Kim.

She chuckled as she slapped the handle of her stroller. "That's alright. A boy gots to be a boy. Shaq would like that way of thinking."

I figured she liked talking so I told her Ax was born here but that I was from Ottawa. "Are you from Dartmouth originally?"

She was. Her great-grandparents came up through the Underground Railroad and settled in Africville, a small Black village outside of the city of Halifax. Halifax wanted that land and for years tried to push the poor but tightly knit community out. The city refused to provide sewage, clean water, or garbage disposal. They even put up a prison, an infectious disease hospital, and a toxic waste dump beside it. What assholes. It was all a game, Kim said. In 1964 the city finally started to relocate and scatter the residents of Africville. Many, including her parents, settled in Halifax, becoming dependent on social housing and the public dole for the first time.

"That is such bullshit," I said. My parents ran tight with money for a while, but I don't think they ever collected welfare. That woulda humiliated them.

Kim said she'd had three children. Two went into state care, the youngest was still with her but in school today. Fuck me. It was like running into a Black grandma version of myself. Would I age prematurely and be pushing a stroller of groceries around in my forties, fifties, whatever she was? Scary thought.

I wanted to ask if she thought about her lost kids, if she ever dreamed of getting them back. But that woulda been cruel to bring up and it seemed obvious to me already. Of course, she dreamed of her kids. Like I did about Faye. I hated those moments. They would happen when things were quiet, when I wasn't buzzed or busy. I'd grate my brain and wonder if coulda or shoulda done things differently. If I shoulda just staked out her foster witch's house and taken her to Halifax. She and Ax coulda played together on the train. We coulda hidden out for a while. Jimmy woulda covered for us. Nobody in Dartmouth was going to mind anybody else's business. We coulda started over again. I'd medicate her like a zombie and stay away from jerks, get a real job ...

Did Faye think about us? Did she remember to close the fridge door, flush the toilet? Who did she say goodnight to? Anytime something like that popped into my head, I wanted to either scream or bury myself in bed. Even if I wanted to find that bridge back into her life, I was sure I'd torched it.

How was Kim not a bitch after all she'd been through?

"Looks like rain today. But tomorrow it'll be sunny, yep. Tomorrow be sunny."

Actually, the forecast was for heavy rain all week.

That's how she did it. I get that. She would be okay spending the rest of her life clipping coupons, waiting for her next cheque, and loading up her stroller, so long as she still had hope. Hope for sunny days, for something special at the food bank, hope to see her kids again. And with that, she had found peace.

It had to be.

My head was buzzing all the time but never peaceful. I couldn't even picture what peace looked like. How the fuck did she do that?

I hated quiet moments.

"I'll be seeing you around, honeybee," Kim said as she handed Ax another stick of licorice before trundling off in her own direction.

We found the food bank and walked under the hand-painted banner: Gentle Humble Frugal. I recognized Frances, the old food bank manager, also known as St. Frances the Potty, for her drunken-sailor mouth. Still holding down the fort. You have to love that. She had to be well into her eighties. She rarely forgot a face or a name, although she used to struggle a bit with mine. But still, she gave me a gentle hug.

"It's been a while, dearie," she said.

"Sorry about that," I replied.

"Don't go being sorry for not coming. If you don't need us, that's a good thing."

"Yeah, well, I totally need you now, thanks."

"Last time I saw you, you were with that Lebanese fella who biffed you on the nose."

"Bash."

"Yeah, Bashir. I seem to recall you two bringing out the ass in each other." Frances smiled and handed me a number and invited us to join the others who were waiting and relaxing at the tables and chairs with local reading material. Two women offered coffee and donuts at the back of the room. Ax gobbled up two chocolate glazes while I picked through the clothing and footwear donations. After a few announcements and a short prayer service, some dude called my number and asked what I needed. He handed the list off to another woman in the pantry. She and others worked on our custom package of non-perishables: dried and canned soups, Kraft Dinner, cookies, beans, pasta, cereal, crackers, jam, rice, canned fruit, and juice boxes. They also included a personal package of toiletries: Tampax, a bar of Ivory soap, some shampoo, a toothbrush, some deodorant, that sort of thing. A nail file woulda been nice but we can't be too choosy sometimes.

While waiting, I approached another dude the staff had nicknamed Odd Job Tom about some part-time work. He musta been proud of the nickname as it was on his nametag. He said he could probably line me up with some serving jobs in downtown Halifax or Dartmouth. There was apparently a cleaning job for four days a week up for grabs, and there were never enough cherry and strawberry pickers given the season would soon be opening up.

I didn't like the sound of any of them but knew I had little choice. It wouldn't have mattered if I did, as I didn't have a sitter for Ax anyway. I'd have to register him in a school. Tom suggested Ocean View Elementary, which was closest to our Pinecrest apartment. I'd heard of Ocean View, the lice capital and bully pit of Nova

Scotia. I didn't want Axel going to a hole. But I also knew it was only a twelve-minute walk away.

Someone wheeled in our package while another volunteer added in perishables including apples, bread, milk, a pound of ground beef, and some veggies. One of the volunteer drivers was ready to give us a lift when Ax said he was tired and wanted to see his father.

"Not now," I said.

"When? You said we were moving to see Daddy."

"Let's get these groceries home first."

"Then we see Daddy?"

"No. I have to find you a school."

"Then when?"

"Tomorrow, maybe tomorrow."

"Daddy's coming to our house?'

"No, I don't think so. But we'll go to him."

Ax backed off for a minute, probably 'cause I was getting pissed. "Really? You know where he is?"

"I know where and I know what."

"What?"

"Donairs, it's time you tried a real donair."

SUMMER 2018

8

AXEL

WHEN YOU DON'T have a sister anymore, you need more toys than before. Except now I have no toys after Mom threw them out. I get bored fast and have to find things to do. I hope my dad will bring over a jumbo Talking Minion Dave, but a Nerf Strike Blaster with extra bullets would be even better. On the shelf at the new apartment there was a box full of paper clips that I made a necklace with. Then I saw something behind some books, a cool drinking glass shaped like a long snake with a hole for its mouth and another one on its body like a pee-pee hole.

I brought it to the kitchen and poured milk through the top hole but it spilled all over me and the floor.

"Ax, what the hell are you doing? Gimme that."

I gave her the glass and hoped she would think the mess was from the people who lived here before.

"Just drinking some milk." I put on my best innocent and cute face. It worked.

"Nice bong—good find, Ax. I didn't see that earlier, neither did Jimmy. Otherwise, it'd be gone. We can pawn that. Shit, maybe I'll keep it."

She grabbed a towel and dried my head but left my wet shirt on.

I made toast with some peanut butter and jelly left behind by the before family. We ate and looked at the mess they left in the sink.

"After breakfast, I'll do the dishes," Mom said. We looked at the pile. Every pot and pan, every glass and plate was piled in the sink or on the counter.

"Fuck." Mom shook her head. "You unpack your things into the dresser. Whatever's in the dresser now goes into the garbage bag, unless you find other treasures. If you do, tell me. Then you can watch TV till I take you to your new school."

It felt good that I did something right. "Then we go for a donair and see Daddy?"

"Yes. I mean, no. I said today or tomorrow, didn't I? Is today tomorrow?"

I didn't know how to answer that.

"Of course not. So maybe tomorrow. Just don't ask me again or we won't go. Do as I say and shut up."

I did like she said and went through the dresser. There was only men's old clothes. No money, no treasures. I threw the clothes on the floor before putting mine in the open drawer. Then I headed for the TV. It had no cable, so only a few fuzzy channels came up with a thin line like a rope across the screen. "Mom! The TV's broken!"

She poked her head out of the kitchen and saw I wasn't lying.

"Shit. I've got to call Jimmy anyway."

I got bored exploring our new apartment. Then I saw in the corner behind a table a plastic tray with some thick, gooey stuff in it. Mom had them before to catch mice. She said it wasn't poisonous but that I should never touch it 'cause it's very sticky. This time I did touch it and my finger got stuck in it. I tried to shake it off but my finger got more stuck. I used my other hand to pull the tray off, but a chunk of glue stayed on, so I wiped it off in the armpit of my shirt.

I found a bookshelf with some magazines with ladies with hardly any clothes on. I opened one and started to giggle. The ladies were smiling even though they were stretching without any clothes on. In the middle, there was someone called Miss August. I was born in August too. That makes me Mr. August. If Mom saw, I'm sure I would be in trouble, so I tried to put the magazine away, but my finger got stuck on the page and cut Miss August off at the knees.

I could hear Mom on the phone.

"Jesus, Jimmy, for two hundred and fifty we coulda found a motel where things work."

Pause.

"I don't give a shit. For fuck's sake, please, get me a goddamned TV. I can do better than stick my son with three shitty channels on a broken screen."

Pause.

"Good, not soon enough."

Another pause.

"Yeah, of course, I called him. Like everybody else, he's good for nothing. I swear I'm gonna get those maintenance enforcement workers on him."

Pause.

"He can bullshit his way out of it again, but if I can fuck up his day, I will. I'll probably track him down today or tomorrow."

I got excited hearing that. Was I really going to see my daddy?

"Hey, you know who can score me a quarter?"

Pause.

"Are you *kidding* me? He babysat for me one time. Faye loved him. The little punk's gone gangster, eh? He can't be any more than eighteen."

Pause.

"Well, send him by. Today's good, make it around noon, I have to register Ax for school this morning. And don't forget about the shower."

But we didn't go to school. Mom fell asleep in the bedroom after getting off the phone and doing some of the dishes.

I made my own tent by throwing cushions on the floor and a sheet over the couch and a chair, and had a nap. I woke up hungry but liked that it was quiet. I played some rock, paper, scissors against myself then started to think about what I wanted to do with Daddy when he came for me. I was going to make him pinky-swear that we would go to Calypso Waterpark and Canada's Wonderland. We would try all thirty-one flavours at Baskin-Robbins, play video games, and go see *How To Train Your Dragon 2*.

I already saw *How To Train Your Dragon 1* a bunch of times with Faye. I wondered what she was doing and if she missed me. Does she have new brothers and sisters yet? Will I ever see her again? If the CAS comes back and takes me like Mom said they could, how will Faye find me?

Someone banged on the door. Mom used to tell us not to open the door to strangers. Maybe that is an old rule, an Ottawa rule. The banging kept going. I was worried it would wake Mom and she'd be mad.

I put my ear against the front door and asked who it was.

"Tyler. Jimmy sent me."

I remember Jimmy from when we got the apartment when we got here, so it had to be okay. It took me a while to open the locks. I let Tyler in.

Tyler is skinny with what Mom calls a crater face and a man bun that always make me think of a butt, like he's a butthead. Kevin was a butthead too. Tyler also had tattoos of Legolas, Gollum, and my favourite, Smaug, on his forearms, except somebody didn't finish, so Smaug looked naked and not so tough without his scales.

"Jimmy sent me for Hailey."

"You mean Hannah? That's my mom."

"Whatever."

I turned around and yelled out for Mom.

"Hey, don't I know you?" Tyler asked me. "Didn't you have a sister, Fanny or something?"

"Faye. She's nine. She lives in Ottawa. But Mom says we're going to find her and get her back soon."

"I remember now. You were still a baby—wailed like a motherfucker all the time and always had the runs. But Faye was cute. What, did your mom lose her at the Quickie or something?" He laughed but it wasn't funny.

Before I could answer, Mom came out of the bedroom. "Who the hell are you?"

"Jimmy said you wanted something. He said noon."

"Fuck, yeah. I almost forgot." She turned to me. "Why didn't you wake me, Ax?"

I said I was sorry.

"What's a quarter going for now?" she asked Tyler.

"Seventy."

"Are you kidding me? For that kind of money, it better be BC Hydro."

"Nah, there was a massive bust in Langley. None of that stuff can be found around here, especially with the Quebec bikers controlling the Eastern market. But I got something even better. I'm respecting the hundred-mile diet and supporting the local economy, feel me?"

Mom didn't look like she cared.

"Hey, I'll give you a free sample. Damn straight, it'll blow your panties off or you get your money back."

Mom smiled the same way as when Kevin first started coming around. "Well, let's party, then." She handed me a cereal bar and told me to grab some toys and go play outside but to stay on the property and not talk to strangers.

I liked going out to explore but could only think of one cool thing to take outside—the sticky mouse trap. The last thing I heard before closing the door was Mom telling Tyler his Legolas tattoo was smoking hot.

I walked to the end of the parking lot. I hope the trees beside it are part of our property. I made a small pile of sticks and twigs under a tree. With the sticky tray, I made a teepee. Inside it, I put four rocks, one each for Mom, Daddy, me, and Faye. There was a popsicle stick on the ground nearby and I used that to add more glue all over the tent, then threw dirt and grass on top to make it leak-proof and safe. But I got glue all over my hands and shirt.

"Ax? Ax? Axel."

I heard Mom, but I was so good at making the house for my family that I did not answer right away.

Mom came out with Tyler. "Where were you? I was looking everywhere."

I said I was sorry. I wanted to cry, but I saw Tyler looking, so I kept my eyes wide open and didn't let any tears come out. Then I saw that Mom was in a good mood. Tyler's zipper was down, and that made me laugh inside 'cause Mom used to catch me with my zipper down and say, "Your personal air conditioner is now activated."

She was in a *really* good mood. I could tell 'cause she didn't raise her voice when she asked me a question. She had a big smile like she was ready to laugh. She and Tyler kissed. She said he knew where to find her. He unlocked his bicycle and rode away. I wonder if Tyler will move in and fix the TV. But I'm worried Daddy might find out and maybe he won't take me to do all those things I planned for us.

"Holy shit, we gotta go," Mom said.

"Where are we going?"

"To get you into school so I can get a job."

I didn't want to go. I wanted to find a playground and play there.

Mom got her wallet, double-checked for my birth certificate, and we were out the door with my hand in hers—so fast like the beer store was going to close.

"Why's your hand so sticky?"

I liked her being in a good mood. "I just built a house."

———

The students were outside for recess when we got to Ocean View. Mom did some paperwork and gave some information to the secretary. We met the principal. His name is Paul Godin. We sat in his office where I saw bins of LEGOS on the floor, cases of Coke and bottled water piled up, and on the wall, pictures of Mr. Godin holding trophies. There was a big dish of striped mints on his desk. Mom still had on her happy face and she sat back in her chair. She grabbed some mints and gave me one. The principal opened the window, letting in a breeze and the sounds of the students from the yard.

He studied the paper on his desk.

"So, Miss Belenko, says here Axel did JK, SK, and Grade 1 in Ottawa, where he's attended three schools already. This would be his fourth."

"Yep."

I didn't like the sound of her *yep*. And I could tell she didn't like the way he talked. She gave me another mint, then unwrapped one and popped it into her mouth.

"What brings you to Dartmouth?" Mr. Godin asked.

She slipped another one in her mouth. "The seafood."

Mr. Godin put the piece of paper down and looked right at Mom. "As a matter of procedure, we generally request records from previous schools. Given that you've crossed provincial boundaries, we can't request Axel's Ontario Student Record, so I'll have to call his previous school."

She straightened up. "Why?"

"Wouldn't you want us to be aware of his progress to date, to know his strengths as well as his challenges so we can program for him accordingly?"

Her teeth ground down on the mint. I heard the crackling. "You're a school. Teach him. Do your job." Mom squeezed the arms of the chair and leaned toward Principal Godin. She stopped smiling. Whatever Tyler did to make her happy wore off. I couldn't hear the yard anymore or feel the breeze. It was just Mom about to explode, nothing else.

Mr. Godin got smaller in his chair. "Well, it's already June. Are you sure—"

"You have to take him, and I have to work. And I know for a damned fact that you guys can't talk about anything with anybody without my signed consent."

Mr. Godin took a breath the way everybody at school and the CAS told me and Mom to do all the time. It's dumb, so we never do it. "Let's start again. Please call me Paul. Thank you for coming. I want to make this school experience the best possible for Axel and for you. Our pipes leak, and it gets drafty in here. But we have a great staff and wonderful children and parents. We also have early-day and after-school programming. We're geared up to make things work so you can work or do whatever it is you have to do. But sometimes, the more information I have available, the easier it—"

"He likes science, building things, recess, cheese, and pepperoni. But don't give him too much cheese. He gets wicked gas. He hates French, math, reading, writing, and mushrooms. He gets wound up if people get in his grill. That enough information? Those schools were the worst on the planet. They did nothing when Ax was bullied. Instead of giving him the help he needed, the teachers picked on him. They'd humiliate him in front of everybody. They were ruining him. Nobody walks over my Ax."

I didn't get everything Mom said. But it made me think of a movie we saw at Oma Greta's where the mother lion protects her cub from dangers everywhere and isn't afraid to get mean and fight. I like going to Oma Greta's. She is a good baker and very kind and it's the one place Mom doesn't yell at me 'cause Oma Greta shushes her and she listens.

Mr. Godin threw his hands up like he was caught by the police. "Welcome to Ocean View. I'll put him in with Andrew Spearman."

9

HANNAH

———

ONCE I FIGURED that my Ontario welfare cheque wasn't coming in, I called Odd Job Tom at the food bank. He said the Atlantic Superstore was looking for someone for their deli counter.

I'd had a deli job before. It sucked. And I'm not even talking about going home smelling like mock chicken. Weird shit happened there.

I was seventeen and had landed a summer job at the deli counter of a REAL Canadian Superstore in Westboro, a bougie, trendy Ottawa neighbourhood more than an hour away from my parents' by bus. But I was happy to sit on the long bus rides and put some distance between me and home after all that stuff with Jennifer went down. I bought one of the first MP3 players of its kind. It cost me a fortune. Otherwise, I smoked a ton of tobacco and weed, pretty much blowing most of my paycheques.

My parents took a cut from each cheque to teach me responsibility and to contribute to the family. As if I hadn't contributed anything after having given up so much already. That included the idea of family game nights, summer vacations, letting me have friends and sleepovers … the stuff regular people did. I'm not even talking about the cold war we lived under. If I had just been able to play ringette and if Ivan hadn't been a perv, I'd have been okay. Mackenzie and I would've anchored our team's defence, feeding breakout passes to our designated sniper, Meg. We'd have won the provincials and gone all the way to the nationals. Ringette would've become an Olympic sport and I woulda captained the Canadian team to a gold medal. Schools would've had assemblies with me talking about leadership and making your dreams come true and girls would be lining up to take selfies with me. I coulda been endorsing yoga pants or shit like that.

One Friday afternoon, I rushed back to the deli counter after a smoke break. A mother wearing a tiny Lululemon top was arguing with her teenaged daughter in front of my counter. The girl was probably about my age but looked older 'cause she was chunkier. I waited for them to place an order. The daughter was trying to skip out of something. You go, girl. It reminded me of something I'd do with my mom except in public she'd be more discreet.

The Lulumama stormed off in the direction of the bakery, leaving the daughter standing there awkwardly in front of the meat display to place an order.

"May I help you?" I asked, taking my place behind the counter, remembering to smile. The week before, my eighteen-year-old, crater-faced manager warned me that my "not smiling" was becoming a performance issue. What a fucking dick. I'll bet he had performance issues.

The young woman said, "Can I get some of that Italian prosciutto on sale? I'd appreciate it if you could slice it—" I saw the recognition in her eyes before she even said my name. "Hannah?"

"Mac-Mackenzie?" I took in Mackenzie's freckles, but she'd packed on some weight and sprouted. "Holy shit, I hardly recognized you."

"Yeah, well, me and food have a special relationship."

We looked at each other for a long, awkward moment. I was waiting for her to call me a lying bitch, a skank—expecting to be yelled at and humiliated. To be plunked together with my brother and Steffi and Papa as the absolute worst. I was ready for it. But it didn't happen. That made me feel even worse.

"Did you say prosciutto?" I asked, filling in the silence.

"Yeah, that really expensive kind. Mom likes it thinly sliced, please."

People who ordered prosciutto or pancetta usually came in all entitled and demanding. But Mackenzie had always been kind and decent to me, despite what Papa said about her and her family. She was my first BFF. I pulled the hunk of prosciutto out of the fridge and turned my back to her. I tried to look busy and focused on the meat slicer.

"How've you been?" she asked.

I could feel her gaze on my back, waiting for an answer. "Is this thin enough, ma'am— I mean Mackenzie?" I held up a flimsy piece of prosciutto.

"Mom's gonna want it thinner or she's gonna rag me out, please. About two hundred and twenty-five grams."

"Frig," I said to myself, then adjusted the knob to its thinnest setting and sliced away.

"So how are you?" Mackenzie just wouldn't let it go.

I took a quick peek behind her, hoping impatient customers might save me.

I wanted to say, *When I'm not high, or like slicing deli meat, which gets into every thread of whatever I wear, I want to get high and hide under my duvet, sleep forever, and disappear. Otherwise, I'm fine. How about you, Mac? Still playing ringette?*

Instead, I lied. "Great, I'm really great."

"Cool. I was worried about you after all that shit happened. I heard you moved to Kanata or something."

I'm guessing she didn't hear about what happened after the move, about Jennifer. Thank God. I didn't want to have to explain that next-level shitshow.

"Uh-huh. Is this enough?" I referred to the scale, which showed precisely two hundred and twenty-five grams, half a pound.

"No, keep it coming. Mom likes to wrap her chicken thighs with it, then she bakes them until they're crisp … it's one of her show-off meals. She has book club this Sunday. But honestly, all they do is get hammered."

I felt a jolt in my gut and stopped slicing momentarily. My last image of Mackenzie's mom was of her accusing Ivan of raping her daughter. The transformation of pain to sheer hatred and venom on her face was freaky. I've seen people pissed at me before, and I'm guessing she'd feel the same about me now, having not defended her daughter after all that shit went down. Anything less than me getting fried in dog shit would not do.

"It's not your fault, Hannah."

I paused, as I didn't want to ask what Mackenzie meant by that, then sped up my slicing.

"Sure, Mom wanted to come over and take a bat to Ivan, and then to you for not having my back."

I kept my head down.

"I kind of blamed you too, but it didn't last long. I knew Ivan and your family were—different. I kind of figured your life was a shitshow stuck on a loop."

"Wha ...?"

"Never mind. You should know, though, I tried calling you after. Your mother told me to get lost."

This time I nodded. But my slicing became feverish, the thinnest sheets of prosciutto softly piling up. It was almost to the point the movement was out of control, like slice-a-finger-off out of control.

"Mom missed out on a promotion at work, and I had to go to counselling." Mackenzie rolled up her sleeves and revealed bright parallel scars of varying lengths and stages of recovery. "So yeah, life kind of sucks." Mackenzie shrugged.

I stopped slicing. Hearing that made my knees wobble. I fought to hold it together. Focus on the task at hand. The prosciutto. I wasn't going to sit in my unhappy thoughts any longer.

The pile of meat was huge, and heavy. "Sorry, ma'am, I may have cut too much. I'll put the rest back." I removed some of the ham, bagged the order, and punched in the price sticker.

Mackenzie leaned over the counter. "I know you're a good person."

I squeezed my eyes shut but couldn't stop them from welling up.

"But you have to get out. Your family's fucked up, man, and they're going to fuck you up too."

I looked away, pretended to adjust my hairnet, and dabbed my eye with my shoulder. She wasn't ragging me out. She was saying I was a good person. No one had ever said that to me before. What was I supposed to do?

Mackenzie's mom came out from one of the aisles behind her, walking toward us with her cart. I don't think she recognized me. Mackenzie gave me a weird, stretched smile, her lips pressed tightly together. "I better go," she said quietly. "I'm sure my mum still wants you dead."

I didn't know what to say. I never thought about how much her mom might still hate me. I never thought about how all that rape stuff fucked anybody else up. In fact, I made a point of never thinking about it, period. It's not like it was a celebrated family moment. This wasn't Maslenitsa—reminiscing after pancakes about the time I covered for Ivan being a rapist. Back then, he made a big deal about having my back in the future. That never happened. It's a sub-regulation of our unwritten family rules, right after *Keep your mouth shut*. It's *Make like nothing ever happened*.

I was such a loser for letting Mac down so long ago. I looked around for my boss and when I didn't see him, stuffed the excess meat into her bag, making sure that she saw. "Will that be all, ma'am?"

Mackenzie winked and walked away but not before making a gesture for me to call her. I knew I never would.

I decided then and there that if I could help it, there was no way I was ever going to work a deli-counter job again.

Lucky for me, Odd Job said there was also a part-time job as a server available at the Double Happiness, a Chinese buffet restaurant on Wyse Road. That sounded better.

When I have to, I can really pull myself together for a job interview, and that's exactly what I did. I shaved my legs and washed my hair. I'd have loved to get some highlights but no way I had the coin—I straightened it, at least. I put on my game face and pulled out the same all-purpose knock-'em-dead outfit that I used for court. I *was* going to remove my neon-blue nail polish at home and apply a more professional blush colour but decided to splurge and get them done at the nail salon on Albro. After the crap I went through in Ottawa, then getting us back to Dartmouth, I had earned it.

It felt nice to dress up and look good for a change. I like it when men checked me out. I have nice legs. They're strong and shapely even if my skin's a bit rough and scarred in places. My hips and butt still hold together and my tits, well, I've never had any complaints in that department, I'll tell you that. Even after two kids.

I have Papa's guns, and his broad shoulders and wide back. I've always hated those. Who grows up wanting to look like a shot putter? Sure, it helped when I got into a scrap. And all I got from Mama was her dirty-blonde hair. Okay, her killer blue eyes too. Funny, I remember Mama trying to get me to go all girlie-girl but I was never into it. I wore track suits and tight jeans like Papa. Probably begging for his approval. Mama had done a good job hooking up to the Russian money-making machine, even if he was slow getting there and even if he sucked at everything else, parenting for one. Do I wish I coulda been more delicate like Mama and learned to keep my mouth shut and just blend in? I can guarantee you I wouldn't have been lining up for a job in another goddamned Chinese restaurant if I had.

I'd been a server at a Chinese restaurant once before in Ottawa and learned how to say please, thank you, hello, was it tasty?, and you are pretty in Cantonese. Some of the staff also taught me fuck you, fuck your mother, you're fat and stinky, and go fuck your mother's smelly cunt. That was fun until the owner tried to grope me.

I had to bring Ax along for the Double Happiness interview. At least we didn't have to bus anywhere. Dartmouth is pretty walkable if you're feeling energetic or just short on cash.

I told Ax to sit. "If you screw up and I don't get this job, we don't eat, and you don't get to see your dad, get it?"

He nodded. He'd actually been pretty good since we got in to Dartmouth. It isn't exactly Funhaven. Maybe 'cause I was able to dangle the daddy possibility in front of him. I wasn't being dishonest with him. I was seriously trying to get his dad to give two shits, but I can only do so much.

When Peter Hui, the owner, was ready to interview me, I nervously watched him stride up to me and glance over at Ax sitting quietly and cutesy on the chair. Ax kicked his legs up and down and gave Hui a glowing smile and waved. Ax jumped off the chair and introduced himself, then me. He shook Hui's hand and told him I could handle all his customers and to have a nice day.

Hui's chubby face gleamed. I swear he checked me out. I pulled out my standard Cantonese greetings—*lai ho, sik fun meh*—immediately impressing him. He asked where I'd learnt Chinese. I told him I ran the lunch shift at the last Chinese restaurant, omitting that I quit on the spot after the owner tried to cop a feel. He lobbed a couple of soft questions more for formality and hired me on the spot. I was to start Monday at eleven, set up for service, and work the lunch crowd. After that I'd help with the cleanup, set for dinner, and clock out by three. That left more than enough time to do the twenty-minute walk or eight-minute bus ride to pick Ax up at school. I'd get a staff meal, a share of the tips, and $10.60 an hour.

I walked out of the Double Happiness with Ax in tow, feeling pretty damned good about myself.

"Where are we going now, Mom?"

"I'm hungry. We've earned some donairs." We high-fived and then something odd but wonderful happened—Ax squeezed my hand and leaned his head into me. We skipped along in unison up Wyse, laughing as we ran for the 51 bus, barely making it. The bus meandered up Windmill, a dull roadway of car dealerships, lowrises, bungalows, and strip malls. The King of Donair was located in such a mall, sandwiched between Fan's Chinese Food and Lindy's Lucky Laundromat.

When we walked in, there were mostly men waiting in line.

"Where's Daddy?"

"I don't see him. Stay here." I took a slow walk up to the cash, feeling great that I was all done up. I butted right up to the cashier and asked where Bash was.

"Bash? If you mean Bashir, he don't usually do Saturdays, but he might come in. Marty called in sick again, some greasy-ass fuck that Marty, I'll tell ya that."

"When are you expecting him?"

"Bashir? Lady, he's the boss, he comes whenever."

It pissed me off that Bash was the boss, yet he couldn't bother to pay for some groceries for his son, forcing me to take a job cleaning up people's goddamned sweet-and-sour bo-bo balls.

"When is that?"

The cashier shrugged and gave me a look that said, I'm busy, don't bother me with your shit.

"Just tell him Hannah and his son are here, and we'll be back. In the meantime, gimme two donairs, one regular with—"

"Back of the line," several customers started saying.

"You get back of the line, assholes. I'm the mother of the man-ager's kid, right back there." I pointed at Ax, who tried to hide him-self behind another customer. Everyone looked at him like he was an orphan, but they wouldn't let up about me ordering ahead of them, so I wasn't going to let up either.

The cashier was looking at Ax, who definitely takes after his dad in the face, so he musta figured out I wasn't lying. "Okay, Henna or whatever your name is, let me take your order so you and Bashir's kid can get right out of here."

"Hannah, it's Hannah."

I grinned at the lineup behind me (haha on them, losers) then studied the menu on the wall. "Oh, man, you got donair egg rolls now? Are they filled with donair meat? No, I gotta stick with the original donair. But shit, donair poutine would be awesome too."

The customers rolled their eyes, which made me take my time even more.

With donairs and egg rolls on a tray, we sat at one of the plastic tables. I jumped right into my sandwich, meanwhile Ax only picked at the meat.

"You said Daddy would be here."

"He was. We'll stick around and wait, he'll turn up eventually. Here, try an egg roll."

After eating, I stepped out for a butt and leaned against the outside window. I watched Ax inside working on his Coke, which was more than he could drink. I could tell he still wasn't used to having a drink all to himself. He and Faye always shared.

We waited some more. I had a few more butts and bought some yummy cinnamon poppers for Ax. But he'd lost interest in food. He wanted his dad. I wished he didn't. I wanted to be enough. I gave him some plastic straws to connect and sugar packets to stack. After an hour we got up to leave. I made sure the staff knew I'd be back for Bash.

The next afternoon, a heavy knock on the door woke me from a weed nap on the couch. Ax was in the parking lot collecting rocks. I opened the door, recognizing the heavy-set man with a salt-and-pepper goatee and dark olive complexion, then noticed two carefully placed crates of groceries on my doorstep. Behind him, in the parking lot, Ax was crouched collecting rocks. This man was taller than I even remembered. Our eyes locked for an instant—we couldn't help but check each other out. There was no forgetting the out-of-this-universe sex, the all-night parties, and the never-ending laughs. And there was no forgetting the fear and excitement we shared when that first pregnancy test showed two lines, then the kids crying, our money problems, our killer fights.

"Well, well, well, if it isn't the one and only Bashir Malik. It's about fucking time." I moved past him and started rummaging through one of the two heavy crates. Bags of pita bread, tubs of hummus, cans of chickpeas.

"You almost start a riot in my restaurant, I bring you food, and that is what you have to say?"

"Excuse me, but it wasn't me who left the country and their family behind."

His hair had greyed and receded a bit since I last saw him. But his tight T-shirt showed off his body, still ripped.

"I did not come to quarrel. Wait, I have one more." He went to his car and returned with a Toys "R" Us bag. "For the boy. I also brought some things for Faye, just in case you see her. Where is he?"

"*He* is Axel, and *he* is outside." I started to carry in one of the crates. "I hope there's meat in here."

"Lots. Chicken wings, ribs, ground beef, and some donair meat, lots."

"How about some coin?"

"I can give you what I have, for now." He pulled out a few bills.

"Really? That's fucking generous considering you haven't paid child support in about, oh, six years. The maintenance enforcers will have something to say about that, now that you're a fancy manager at the KOD."

"You will get nothing that way. I have no income," he said, averting my glare.

"No income listed, you mean."

He looked away.

I knew he was likely being paid under the table. No declarable income meant no child support could be deducted. The rat bastard. I could chase him down and let the court decide. They could take his passport. That would fuck him up. But who would I also be screwing in Lebanon? And what if he someday wanted regular access to Ax? What if he ever wanted to poke his nose in Ax's schooling or have a say in his medical decisions? I was pretty confident there was zero chance he'd do that, but what if? If Bash was going to be a father, he had to be all in. Yes, that money might've been good for Ax. But I'd gotten used to nothing from Bash and having complete control. Why risk a change?

"I bet your other family wouldn't know that," I said.

"Will you just sh—"

Ax walked in and stared at Bash. It only took him a moment to realize that it was his father. Bashir looked back at him, the son he hadn't asked for.

88

"Say hello to your loving papa, the King of Donair." I doubted Ax would get my sarcasm, but Bash would.

They approached each other tentatively. For Ax, it had to be weird seeing his dad for the first time in memory. I'd told him his daddy was a fucking loser and a deadbeat and had done us a favour by going away.

One time I overheard Faye talk to him about their father. She said their daddy was big and strong and handsome. She told Ax she thought we used to fight a lot, but she wasn't sure.

Bash studied Ax's face. They share the same skin tone and the same curious, shifting hazel eyes.

They gave each other a soft hug. I lit a smoke and watched.

"Axel, I brought you some things." He handed him the gift bag and started to say he could share them with Faye, then stopped.

Ax placed the bag on the coffee table and I sat on the couch while Bash remained standing.

Ax pulled out an Elmo hand puppet, a piano-mat musical keyboard, a Disney *Toy Story* talking book, a Barbie camper, some Play-Doh, and some Hot Wheels. He liked Hot Wheels, but he had little enthusiasm for the rest. I could tell he didn't want to say that those toys were for little kids or girls. Instead, he said, "Thank you, Daddy." I realized at the same time that he'd never said that before. Bash asked Ax if he enjoyed his donair yesterday.

"Uh-huh."

"I'm glad you liked it." Bash paused. It was obvious he didn't know what to say. "School, you like school? Who is your best friend?"

Ax replied that he was going to a new school soon.

"Monday," I added. "He starts Monday. So how could he have any friends yet?"

No one seemed to know what to do next. Bash squeezed his hand into the puppet. "My name is Elmo. What is yours?"

Ax forced a smile.

I chuckled. "That's so lame. And you have another kid you actually spend time with? You'd never know it."

As soon as I said that, I realized Ax might put it together that he had another bro or sis somewhere.

Bash glared, then pulled the puppet off his hand and installed the batteries into the piano mat. He faced me. "Like you are the mother of the year?"

I exhaled smoke. "Maybe not, but at least I'm here for him."

"Are you, though? Because you are minus Faye, now."

"Fuck you, Bash. You're nothing but an ass."

"Then why did you call? Why do you take my groceries? Why do you take my money? You are nothing but a psycho. A crazy woman."

Just then our dingy living room exploded in a riot of crashing and smashing sounds. Ax was jumping all over his piano mat as though he were stomping out a fire.

"Enough, Ax, enough," I yelled. "I said *enough*."

Ax stood still.

"See the shit I have to put up with?"

"He is a little boy. Why do you yell like that?"

"What, and you're a father? How do you know nothing about kids?"

Ax pounded a few more notes.

"Ax!" I yelled.

Bash and I scowled at each other. Ax watched us, ready to jump on the piano again.

10

AXEL

I DIDN'T WANT to go to school. I wanted them to kick me out so I could be home with my new tablet. Mom got a good deal at the pawnshop because it's already cracked and the speaker doesn't work. If I didn't go to school, she would be mad at first, but then she would let me watch TV and go on the tablet as long as I did not bug her.

My new teacher, Mr. Spearman, met with Mom. I heard him say even though it was late in the year, he was looking forward to working with me. He said school years were like marathons (and he said he was training for one). You had to plan, pace yourself, and be ready for anything. He knew I would not know anybody and that many new students either don't try or try too hard. Mom said she knew that the other Grade 1 students, along with the rest of the staff, were probably ready for their summer break. But she hoped Mr. Spearman would look after me. Mr. Spearman said it was another challenge in his classroom but that he welcomed it.

On the first day he made us write something. Everybody took out their notebooks and pencils like they knew what to do, but I didn't. Everybody was going to think I was stupid. So I said out loud that it was dumb. I made people laugh, so I said it louder. More people laughed but not everyone.

Mr. Spearman counted to one and just like that, everyone got back to work. For the rest of the period, I could not get anybody to laugh.

He kept me in for recess. I was not in trouble, he just wanted to give me extra fun. It was a cold, rainy day, so I was okay about it. He shared his cheese-and-apple snack that I thought was really weird until I tried it. It was yummy.

"So, Axel, we're going to learn to spell your name today."

"I already know how, Mr. Spearman," I lied. "Can I go on the computer instead?"

"Once you can get a few words done. It's not so hard, really, watch."

Mr. Spearman took out a blank piece of paper and spelled out my name in pencil. Then he made me trace it with a red marker.

"See, that wasn't so hard. You just spelled your name. Now pick two more colours and see if you can spell it by tracing alongside what you just did." I did what he said. My letters looked good and straight.

"You just spelled your name three times. Now let's do it on a fresh sheet of paper."

I picked a yellow one.

"Except this time, I'll bet you won't need me to start you off."

I spelled out my name on the paper and fist-bumped him.

"Wow, that's amazing. You want to try another word?"

"Sure. How do you spell *bong*?"

He had to think about it, then said it was bee, oh, en, gee, but after that he said maybe we should find another word to trace out, a word that I could use every day in class. I thought of *stupid, mine,* and *dumb* but then picked *play.*

So we traced *play.* Then we did *share.*

"Do you think you're ready for six letters?"

I nodded. We did *mother.* That made me ask Mr. Spearman if he was married and had children.

I wanted to say I have a sister and another brother or sister somewhere else, but I didn't because I didn't even know their name or how old they are.

He said no.

I asked if he liked Mom.

He smiled, so I think he does, plus he said, "Yes, she seems really nice."

I told him Mom could still carry me on her shoulders and light a cigarette at the same time, but she said I was getting heavy for that.

He thought that was interesting and had never seen that before.

We just played for the rest of the recess and didn't even have to go on the computer. He said it was more important that we just get along. I like him already and want Mom to ask him out.

11

HANNAH

I NEEDED AX out of my hair during the day, so school was essential. I worried what I'd do once summer came and I had him with me full-time. There were times he'd look up at me like he wanted something but couldn't ask and I couldn't figure out what it was. Other times he'd stay away and ignore me—typical moody guy. Either way, it made me feel useless and inadequate, like I was missing something obvious that only a bad mother couldn't see. Then Paul—the principal—gave me information on subsidized summer day camps running out of the Dartmouth North Community Centre. Gotta admit that saved my ass. I signed Ax up.

Even though I wasn't thrilled about work, I needed the money. But I'd forgotten how much I hated working buffets. Buffet eaters are the most demanding, rudest, and just plain disgusting people.

"You're out of spare ribs again. I've been waiting forever for more noodles." Customers sampled food with their fingers, handled utensils with filthy hands, returned food back onto the hot table, and tried to sneak food out. Worst of all, the tips were dismal.

After a couple of weeks of that, my Decision Review welfare appointment came through. I qualified, but they'd be deducting from it for six months until the overpayment was settled. My accommodation expenses would be paid directly to Jimmy, but they refused to pre-pay my last month's rent. Things would be super tight, but I couldn't stand the buffet anymore and planned to find something else. I walked over to the cash where Peter Hui was waving goodbye to a regular, one of many locals who craved inauthentic, uncomplicated Chinese Canadian food from a restaurant whose kitchen spewed out hot beef sandwiches with canned gravy as often as it did beef with broccoli.

Peter's was smaller than the other Chinese restaurants I'd worked at and looked more like a diner going through an identity crisis. He didn't fuss with red lanterns, fish tanks, or placemats with the Chinese zodiac. (I'm an ox, by the way. Bash is a monkey. We supposedly squabble too much to be a good love match. But what do the Chinese know?) Peter had Hello Kitty and Sidney Crosby posters taped to the walls. He said he liked both.

It was harder quitting than I thought it would be.

He asked why.

I explained that I was collecting now and didn't have babysitting when Ax wasn't at school—and summer camp wouldn't start for a few weeks. "Why look so miserable," I told him, "I thought you'd be happy? You're always bitching at me for being late and yelling at the customers."

"It is because you yell at my customers for being pigs that I need you."

I laughed.

"You come work for me on the weekend, no buffet. Lunch is slower but tips are better. And I'll pay you cash."

"I could use the dough, but I have Ax, remember? School just finished and summer camps don't run on weekends."

"He could hang with Matthew and Justine. They work or do homework on weekends. He could learn to make won ton, peel snow peas—good life skills."

"Homework? School's done."

"Not Chinese language school."

"Ha ha, you're evil and that's frickin' child labour. This ain't China, Peter."

"No, but this is a Chinese restaurant."

I agreed.

He smiled and reached into a drawer and pulled out a bottle of Johnnie Walker and two tiny chipped Chinese teacups, the kind that hold maybe four ounces. He filled them halfway.

"What the fuck, Peter, you're a closet alkie, eh?"

He grinned. "Sometimes I need to relax, that's all. Or celebrate, like now. I like you." He handed me a cup.

When a guy says that, it usually means one thing. But I wasn't feeling it and I sure as heck hoped he wasn't.

I sipped the scotch. It went down harshly but the quick rush felt good.

We shot the shit for a bit. He came to Canada from somewhere in China, I forget where. His parents died during the SARS outbreak in early 2003. He said his biggest regret was that they never got to hold his kids. I thought the poor bugger was going to tear up, so I topped up our cups and asked him about his wife.

He shook his head. She'd trained as an accountant back home and was away at St. FX University in Antigonish—to get re-certified. She spent as little time in the restaurant as possible.

"Why are your kids so fricking perfect, Peter? I mean, they do as you say, they work on their homework when they're not working, and they never fight or give you lip."

He nodded and stretched his legs out. "Number one, they do homework because they don't finish it at school. Number two, when they are not here they are on their tablet all day and night. I caught Matthew watching YouTubes until two in the morning last night. Number three, they give me no lip but they don't give me anything else either. I never know what they think. I have to send them a text to find out what is going on. They are not so perfect, none of them are. But yes, they are good kids."

I nodded and shook my head. "I guess they're not perfect."

"You can do everything right, and still you cannot guarantee the results you want," Peter said.

"Or you can fuck it all up and still have a chance."

We clinked our cups before emptying them.

12

AXEL

MOM AND ME take turns sleeping in the bedroom. I know that if Tyler comes over to spend the night, I get the bedroom so Mom can stay up late and party. Usually, she sleeps on the couch until it's time for us to go to the school breakfast club. Some nights Tyler comes over with friends and beer. That's when Mom lets me play outside a little longer. Except that I usually just want to watch TV or play on the tablet inside.

One day, Mom was late picking me up from school. When she finally came, it was in a taxi. Tyler was already at home with a man wearing a Blue Jays ball cap and a woman with purple streaks in her blonde hair. A song about a jungle where there are fun and games was blasting from the woman's phone. They drank cans of beer and passed around cigarettes for the rest of the afternoon until it was past the time me and Mom usually eat. I stayed in the bedroom with my Hot Wheels.

Mom started yelling, not at me. I opened the door enough to hear her say, "Probably some stuck-up Shitsville family adopted her."

"Don't you get a say in this? You're her mother," Tyler said.

"They asked if I'd say that I agreed to the adoption. No fucking way. Then they asked if I'd be interested in contact. Contact? I'm her for-real mother, and they wanna know if I want crumbs of supervised contact. No fucking way. If they're gonna mess my Faye up, I'm not gonna rescue them."

What did it mean? Is Faye in trouble? Why isn't Mom going to the rescue?

The others raised their beers at Mom and I slowly closed my door so it wouldn't make a noise. The partying continued until the Blue Jays man got into a fight with Tyler. The man said Tyler was hitting on his woman. They yelled back and forth until Mom told them to shut the fuck up or she'd kick their asses out. She woulda, too. When they got quiet, I came out again and said I was hungry. Mom told me she was sick of my whining, and to make my own dinner.

That made me remember Faye even more. We used to have lots of days like this. Faye would cry and cry. I would try to keep her busy and cheer her up. I was good at it and liked being her brother. Now I am by myself.

"Hey, Ax," Tyler yelled over the music. "I hear you can make a mean PBJ because I got me the munchies." He put his fist in his pocket and came out with some money. There was a loonie, a quarter, a dime, and some pennies. He told me to go to the store for Cheezies and whatever I needed for the PBJs.

I did not want to go. I was hungry. Everybody was singing and dancing and they forgot I was there with my hand full of money. My stomach growled and I got very mad. I was tired of being hungry. I was tired of the parties. I was tired of being yelled at all the time.

My knapsack and shoes were in the closet. It was easy to sneak them out. I was going to run away. I gave Mom and her friends one more chance to stop me. I put on my shoes, slowly, hoping they would notice and make me dinner. I stuffed my jacket and my Hot Wheels in my knapsack. Tyler told the blonde woman to put on some Kid Rock. I put my knapsack on. Mom was lighting the bong. The others danced with beers in their hand.

I walked out to the parking lot and found the house of sticks I glued. I looked inside and saw the four stones. I took one out, then stomped on the house and the last three stones inside. I did not know where to go. When my stomach growled again, I decided I wanted a donair. Maybe Daddy would make me one. I turned in the direction of the school. When the King of Donair was not there, I turned and went in another direction. When it still wasn't there, I sat on the sidewalk. The sun started to go down and I started to cry.

A couple of teenagers smoking a pipe walked by. I asked if they knew where the donair place was. One of them said, "Donair's dope, let's get some. I'm in." I asked if I could come, but they ignored me and just kept going.

It got dark and really cold. I put my jacket on and started walking. A big truck passed, an F-150, my favourite. It was black with red fire painted on the tailgate and sides. It stopped in front of me with the motor running. The person inside was smoking a cigarette. I got scared and started walking faster. Just as I got past the truck, it moved with me. The music playing inside sounded like the people who did the jungle song at Mom's party. I speeded up. Then the truck speeded up. I stopped, then the truck stopped. I was about to run when the window opened.

"Hey ... hey, is that you, Axel?"

Out of the corner of my eye, I looked at the man behind the wheel, but it was dark and I couldn't tell who it was.

"Axel, it's me, Jimmy, I look after your building." He turned down the music.

I squinted to see better.

"What are you doing out here, where's your mom?"

"I want a donair. And I'm running away."

He looked away. "So no one knows you're out here?"

I didn't know what to say. If I said yes, Mom might get into trouble. If I said no, she might get into trouble. But I heard Mom get mad at Jimmy a few times, so maybe she didn't trust him and maybe I shouldn't either.

"Never mind." He reached over to his passenger side door and opened it. "I could use a donair too, get in."

I looked around. No other cars were coming. I was tired, and getting colder.

"Come on, I haven't got all night." Then he said, "Let's go to

KOD, maybe your dad's working tonight. I think I want some extra sauce on mine."

I didn't know what to do so I did what he said and climbed in. "I have my own money," I said.

"You do? Let's see it."

I showed him.

He counted one dollar forty-seven cents and told me to keep it 'cause he was buying. He took my knapsack off and buckled me in before driving.

"Is your mom with Tyler right now?"

I said she didn't have a boyfriend, that we got along, and she was always home—that's what Mom always told me to say. I think Jimmy knew that. He looked kind of mad, but I don't think he was mad at me. He caught me looking at the truck.

He told me he just got it, so he could pick up supplies and deliver his canoes. He told me he made big canoes for people to go on lakes and rivers. "Come by sometime and I'll show you what I'm working on. It's a good feeling, working with your hands."

I said I would like that.

My dad was not working when we got to King of Donair. We sat down at a table anyway. Jimmy said he really wasn't hungry anymore and had a coffee and watched me eat my donair.

"Great feed, eh?"

I nodded.

"So, why do you want to run away?"

I thought about it as I chewed. I was still mad at Mom. So I said I was tired of her always yelling at me, and all the parties, plus I didn't know if Tyler was going to be my new dad or if I even wanted that 'cause I wanted to be with my for-real dad. I didn't tell him my plans for me and Daddy going to rescue Faye.

He sipped his coffee. He told me he used to run away as a kid. "I even did it a few times as a grown-up," he said.

I stopped eating and stared at him even though it was rude.

"My dad had left for the big bad city. I never saw him again until I was a man." He looked away. "My mother was left with three kids and no money. This is all a secret, by the way. I've never told anybody this before, but you look like you can be trusted."

I could not believe it. He was talking to me like I was a grown-up, not like a little boy who can't hear or is too stupid to know anything. I never heard a man talk like that before to me.

He said his grandpa learned to build birchbark and cedar-strip canoes. People came from as far away as Toronto and Boston to buy them. It was a family tradition he continued once he stopped running away. "I didn't sell many at first, but I learned to be a firm businessman and building superintendent, even if it meant picking up the odd runaway."

Was he saying I was a runaway? Mom told me one time she ran away before, just like Jimmy.

"Sometimes we're so unhappy and sad we just want a fresh start. It happens to grown-ups too."

"So you ran away to your daddy?"

"No, I mean, yes, when I was a man. But running away never fixed anything for me. The answer wasn't out there, it was in here." He pointed to his head.

"What do you mean?" I rolled my eyes up, trying to see my brain from inside.

Jimmy took a breath. "It's the bees. You ever feel like there's a hive of them inside your head and you can't focus on anything because they're making all sorts of racket?"

"You mean like paying attention?"

He smiled. "Yeah, sorta. It's hard for the mind to focus and relax when it's troubled. It took forever for me to do that. I know you don't understand now—but maybe later."

"So can you take me to my daddy?"

Jimmy shook his head. "If both him and your mom said it was okay, I'd take you now. But ..."

I looked down. "So you're taking me home?"

"Axel, you know I live on the main floor, number ten. Come by sometime. I have a workshop in the garage and you can help me build a canoe. It helps calm the bees. If you feel like running away again, run to me instead, okay? Number ten." He gave me a fist bump. Kevin used to give them to me but this was different. He used to do it to me so I would like him. But I think Jimmy did it 'cause we both have bees inside our heads, plus we are for-real friends.

He took me home and walked me inside. Mom and her friends were on the couch or the floor, their eyes almost closed. They were moving in slow motion, talking slow and funny. Some of them looked over at us, and Mom waved, all happy, but no one got up from the couch.

"Ax, you have fun outside? It's time for bed. Come give your mommy a big kiss, I missed you."

I looked back at Jimmy. "Number ten, right?"

He gave me the thumbs-up. I turned to Mom and gave her a hug, not 'cause I wanted to, but I know she likes it even if I didn't like her bad breath and wet kiss.

The next day at school, when I was supposed to be working on my math, Mr. Spearman caught me drawing.

"That doesn't look like your worksheet, Axel. What is it?"

"A canoe. I'm going to make one for real."

It looked like two ants on a hot dog.

"That's really nice, Axel. I like how you look calm and are canoeing with someone. Who's your friend?"

"I can't tell you. It's a secret 'cause he ran away from home."

"What are all those dots?"

"Bees. My friend got them out of his head."

13

HANNAH

⸻

SOMETIMES MY AX is so cute, I feel bad that I mess with his head. Like the time he saw this magician Derren Brown on YouTube read people's minds. He tried to read my mind after and said I was thinking about his father. I wasn't. I was thinking about smoking up the new pineapple kush that was stashed in my purse pocket. But I knew he was thinking about his father and wanted to know when we were going to see him. So that's what I told him.

He nearly shit himself and smacked my arm and wanted to know how I could read minds like Derren Brown.

"Your daddy's a deadbeat. Now he's not even returning my calls, so you can forget about seeing him." I knew he wondered what a deadbeat was, so I explained it to him: a loser dad. I couldn't help myself, I was revving him up and enjoying it, so I kept going. "I know sometimes you sneak an extra cereal bar and eat it in bed. I know that yesterday you had to stay in for recess 'cause you threw someone's lunch in the toilet. And I know you're not so big on Tyler."

He got up and covered his ears and yelled, "Get out of my head. Stop!"

Too funny. He's not that hard to figure out. He goes around the apartment, making sure the door and windows are locked before going to bed. He's got a big stick, one that he found outside and sharpened with scissors. He told me his plan is to stab any intruder in the eye and make me proud of him. I've raised him to take no shit.

One day when I finished work, we went through the restaurant instead of out the staff door in the back. Peter and his wife were sitting with little Matthew and Justine, Peter's father, and everybody else who worked there. In the middle of the table was a big steaming pot of brown soup on a little stove.

Peter pulled up two chairs and said it was a hot pot and that we should join them. Ax and me looked at the tabletop and everything on it like it was some strange planet.

Justine pointed to the different things. "Beef tenderloin, lamb, fishballs, baby cabbage, rice noodles, black wood-ear mushrooms, tofu, soya sprouts, lotus root …"

"We pick it up and cook it in the hot pot, it's good," Matthew said. "Then we drink the soup." Matthew put raw meat in a spoon like a cage and put it in the soup for a minute, then dropped it in Justine's bowl.

"Hot pot, huh, won't the table burn down?" Ax asked.

Matthew showed him that the fuel was in a can under the pot and how safe the burner was. To Ax, fire out of a can musta seemed like magic.

The grandfather looked pretty old and worn out but was happily wolfing down the meal.

"Thanks, but we're late, come on, Ax." I pulled him away. We were free for the rest of the day, but I just didn't like the scene. It's just weird people sitting down and eating and talking together without a TV for entertainment. Like what do these people talk about? And doesn't their grandfather have anything better to do, like bingo?

Papa's father—Ax's great-grandfather, Leonid—never wanted anything to do with me or my brother. The one and only time I ever met Dedushka Leonid, I was about ten. He came to visit from Volgograd. He hugged and kissed my parents, then greeted Ivan and me with monster hugs. Once he realized we didn't speak much Russian, his interest cooled.

Papa and Dedushka spent their first two weeks of the visit

non-stop fighting in their native language. I knew a few words and phrases and put together that Dedushka thought Russian children who don't speak Russian are a disgrace.

Papa defended us. Yep, you heard that right. Youri Belenko, father-protector. "They are also German, and Canadian. Here they can be both. I know this sounds strange, but they—"

"Know nothing about Russia except we destroy them in hockey," Dedushka said.

The only thing that got him stoked was visiting the Hockey Hall of Fame in Toronto on the way to Niagara Falls. He complained the whole way. "This humidity is like a jungle, and the swarming mosquitos—how does anyone live here?" On the Maid of the Mist, he was especially bitchy about Papa's dead-end jobs. "For this, my son disgraced me?"

I assume he meant Papa's defection. Papa was once a world-class shot putter on track for the Olympics. Juicing had a lot to do with that. When he landed in Canada and could no longer cheat his way to glory, he became a bitter has-been. Or maybe he already was. When we were little, the only work he could find was as a trainer, bouncing from gym to gym. Occasionally he took landscaping jobs.

Papa was quiet the long drive back from the honeymoon capital. His father complained about our small apartment, the cost of everything, weak and stupid Canadians, and the terrible food. No one had to say aloud how happy we were to see him go. Afterward, Papa disappeared on a days-long bender. Until then I'd always assumed Papa defected from a communist hellhole like he said. But maybe what he'd really done was escape from his father. I actually get that.

One time I asked Ivan why Papa and Dedushka didn't get along. Ivan said Dedushka was weak. When it was obvious to Ivan I didn't understand what he meant, he sighed. "The Germans captured him at Stalingrad. And he talked."

I knew what Stalingrad was. While most people watched *Family Matters* and *Full House*, we watched war porn: every possible show and documentary about World War Two and the glories of Mother Russia—over and over again. Two million casualties in Stalingrad alone. That's just one of the thousands of stupid bits of information Papa drilled into us.

If Dedushka Leonid had double-crossed Mother Russia, even under torture, our family woulda been forever blacklisted. I can only imagine how fucked up Dedushka was and how little respect he got after betraying his family and country. And I can see how he might've taken it out on Papa and everyone else around him

"You bring this up again, I'll kill you," Ivan said. "You tell anyone I told you, I'll kill you. Got it?"

I understood. Ivan and I weren't exactly Matthew and Justine. There were no family hot pots for us. Peter and his old lady were not some war re-enacted—unlike my parents. I think Papa took a German wife so he could single-handedly win the war over and over again. The Nazis fought harder than Mama.

14

AXEL

MOM SAID **I** had to go with her to work on weekends at Peter's restaurant 'cause she couldn't pay a babysitter. What was I supposed to do at the restaurant? I wanted to ask if Daddy could look after me instead, but she was still mad at him.

She said I had to stay out of people's way but that it would be fun and I could bring some toys and my tablet. But the tablet ran out of power and I got bored anyway. Justine and Matthew have for-real jobs and I wanted one too. They're bigger than me but are nice and never mean. Justine is nine and Matthew is ten. Their daddy gave them the same mushroom haircuts. I want one too.

I followed them around the restaurant and swept the floors and wiped tables and filled the soya sauce bottles—I made a mess by accident, but Justine cleaned up after for me. Then she showed me how to stuff won-ton wrappers. I made some shaped like poo and pretended that I had an accident in my pants. Matthew and Justine laughed so hard, Peter came over and yelled at them for goofing around. I waited for him to smack them, but he just walked away. I thought for sure Matthew and Justine would beat me up—two against one, plus Justine's a girl and I would never hit a girl. Instead, they whisper-laughed and said maybe I shouldn't help, but we could play later.

Mom came around with some children's menus and crayons.

But that was really boring too, so I went into the room where they keep all the supplies. I counted all the cans and jars and jugs, then started to stack them and the packages into straight lines so the labels were pointing the same way. When Peter came in and saw what I was doing, he smiled and said he had other jobs for me. He got me to count and organize all the toilet paper and paper towels, the soaps, and everything else. He got Justine to show me how to change the toilet paper and paper towel. Jimmy won't believe me but they let me go in the girl's washroom to do it. And you know what? The girls' washroom is way cleaner than the boys. No lie.

When Mom saw what was going on, she told Peter she didn't want me to be like some Chinese child slave gluing Nikes together. But Justine said I was good at it and to let me keep working 'cause I made it fun for them too. The next day they showed me how to set the tables for dinner and put candles on the table. Every day they showed me a different job. Justine and Matthew each gave me fifty cents. Peter matched that, and on top of that, let me order anything on the menu for free. I went for the sweet-and-sour bo-bo balls and chicken chow mein.

I like making money. I can save in case Mom goes broke. Plus it's fun. But the best part is hanging with Justine and Matthew. Justine is not a girlfriend like Melina, so Melina doesn't have to be jealous. I know one day I'll go back to Ottawa and marry Melina. I don't have a big brother, so Matthew is like my big brother. Faye needs me to protect her even though she is the same age as Justine. But now it's like Justine is a sister who looks after me.

If Mom married Peter, then Justine and Matthew would be my new sister and brother. Cool. Except their mom would have to say it's okay and move out.

I heard Justine say she was having a sleepover with some friends from school. I have never done a sleepover or a birthday party so maybe she will invite me even though I don't go to her school. In our house, Faye and I used to play together, but when we fought, Mom would lose it on us. I wonder if Justine's family is like that and if they have a house or an apartment.

FALL 2018

15

HANNAH

B Y THE END of the summer, Ax and I had a routine going. I'd dump him at summer camp and if he didn't get sent home for bad behaviour, I'd call Tyler, we'd smoke up and have sex—if he didn't have deliveries—then sleep, watch TV, pick Ax up, feed him, watch TV. On weekends, we'd go to the Double Happiness. Afterward, if I made decent tips, we'd try and catch that asshole Bash at the KOD, and then to the dollar store for a treat on the way home. Cheque days were always dope. It meant loading up with groceries by day and party at night. By the middle of the month I'd hit the food bank then cab it over to the beer store on Windmill.

One afternoon, when Tyler and I were lying in bed, fully baked and naked, Tyler caught me having a moment. "What're you grinning at, babes?"

I let his question sink in. Dartmouth was a long way from my family, which made me feel like I could let my guard down a bit, although I missed Oma. Then I thought about Faye.

"You remember me saying how CAS took my daughter for good a few months back?"

"Such bullshit."

"Yeah, I was ready to murder somebody. I didn't think I could ever get my shit together again. But you know, I'm good. Sure, I could always use more coin, but I got me set up here pretty good, welfare coming in, no CAS bullshit, I got a regular supply of killer bud and a gigolo who delivers it …"

Tyler flexed a bicep. "And I got me a randy cougar."

A memory arose: the jerking movements of Faye's arms and legs. Her falling for no reason, her constant accidents—total loss of bladder and bowel control. It scared me back then that I would be judged. That they'd see me as a fuckup of a mother and take the children. And when you really look at things straight, that's exactly what happened. When the kindergarten staff at Faye's school ratted me to the CAS, her seizures got diagnosed and I was suddenly a "negligent parent," as if I ever let them alone. For long, anyway.

I let the weed numb all that bad stuff away. "I'm just so … chill for the first time since I can remember."

"That's because you're high as a kite and you just got banged."

"Fuck off, ya malebait."

"Fuck you, grandma."

We laughed.

"Seriously, you won't find anybody close to my age pulling in the coin I am. I mean look at me." He showed off his gold chain and Apple Watch. "It's all fucking gravy. Everybody wants the budtender, man. To be honest, I spend most of my time working the grow-op and still can't keep up with the orders."

"What's gonna happen to you when the government makes good on their promise to legalize weed? Everybody's gonna be growing it."

"Let 'em. Government weed will be shit—and expensive. Most home growers don't know what they're doing. No one, absolutely no one, will be able to compete with my quality. That's my jam."

I had to agree and thought of my part-time job. Peter Hui loved me, but the job didn't pay enough. I was always behind on bills, and Bash had contributed next to nothing. I kicked myself for ever thinking he would. "I could work for you," I blurted out.

Tyler shot me a bug-eyed stare, then laughed hard.

"No, I mean it. You're doing three jobs, you grow, you sell, and you deliver on a fucking bicycle. What's up with that, why aren't you in a sweet ride?

He covered his head with the bedsheet. "I keep failing my driving test."

"What? Even I passed that, at sixteen." I hit him with a pillow.

He unburied himself. "I've got some learning issues, okay?"

"It's amazing you haven't gotten jacked."

He shrugged. "I'm an owner-operator leading a charmed life, what can I say?"

"It's stupid, I know, but my old man, the dumb fuck that he is, freelanced as a trucker. It was such bullshit until he, or should I say my mom, figured out how he could cut costs, increase output, and grow steady revenue."

"Aren't we Elon Musk?"

I was indeed wasted. But it was so clear to me. "I'm serious. We could buy a shitbox car and I could take orders and do the deliveries while your green thumb works its magic. You have a gift, man, I'm telling you. You're thinking small time. You could expand, this could get real."

He hesitated. "I don't know, I mean, I don't have the space ..."

If anybody shoulda been hesitant, it shoulda been me. After Kevin, I swore I'd never let anybody run me over again. But Tyler was different. He was a boy. He rode a bicycle. He couldn't hurt me if he fell off a building and landed on top of me.

"What do you mean you don't have space, where's your grow-op?"

"What are you, a cop? I'm not going to tell you that."

"I just sucked your dick, dude."

Tyler giggled. "I'm pretty fucked up right now."

We cracked up.

"What do you mean you can't expand?"

"It's my grandmother's. In her basement."

"Wha ...? It's your grandmother's basement?" I broke off into hysterics, laughing so hard my abs hurt.

"She's half-deaf, blind as a bat, and lives alone. I come by with groceries, tend her garden, read her the newspaper. Her neighbours think I'm a saint—"

"Who grows weed in granny's basement."

"For sure, got me six little ladies of Mother's Milk down there, each bringing in a pound and a quarter of quality smoke."

"Bullshit! Nobody I know who's grown has ever had a quality yield like that."

"I'm being damn straight."

"Jesus, how do you move that?"

"I can't, not all of it, that's why my counts are so generous and I can afford to smoke it away with you and my buddies. Shit, I even put it in salads."

I got him to agree to show me his grow-op—and at least think about my idea. He wasn't buying right away, but I thought I could turn him around.

The summer ended, thank God. Ax hated camp. He whined and whined about how boring it was. Now he'd have Andrew Spearman again, this time for Grade 2. He bitched about school, but sometimes I think he enjoyed the break from home. Spearman—for a man, anyway—seemed to get Ax. And I have to admit he knows how to teach. He knew I was scraping by and didn't harass me about reading to Ax, bedtime routines, or healthy snacks. On days I was feeling social, I'd chat up some of the other moms waiting outside the school at dismissal. They all said Spearman kept his lesson plans short, gave lots of breaks, juggled individual reward programs with class-wide stuff, and really got to know the students. I'm not sure if this is why Ax was making progress, but not getting daily calls about him exploding was gravy.

I stayed working at the Double Happiness while I scouted for a grow-op location. I asked Jimmy about renting out one of his garages, but the man wanted five grand a month and twenty percent of gross sales. I didn't tell Tyler this, knowing the paranoid little shit woulda freaked—and maybe backed out. I wondered if Jimmy purposely priced himself out as he lectured me about the risks and losing Ax.

On a good day at the restaurant, I could pull in a hundred bucks, sometimes a hundred and twenty all in after splitting tips with kitchen staff. Plus we were well-fed. During the October Thanksgiving long weekend, I hoped it would be busy enough for me to break two hundred dollars. So when Bash surprised Ax and me at the apartment with a visit and offered to take Ax to the Bluenose Ghosts Festival on Saturday afternoon, I was all in. The timing was sweet. I had a grow-op site I wanted to check out after work. It was going to be a perfect day.

16

AXEL

I DON'T LIKE ghosts, I don't like vampires and witches, and I don't like scary monsters. Except *Monsters, Inc.* monsters 'cause they're friendly and Mom got me a *Monsters, Inc.* lunchbox.

So when Mom said my daddy was going to take me to a ghost festival I didn't know what to do. It was my first time with Daddy. I wanted to make him like me, but I didn't want to sound like a wimp already by saying I didn't want to go.

Mom said she was going to have a busy Thanksgiving shift and make lots of money. She said I was going to have fun with my daddy and to not blow it for her. I wanted her to have a good day, so I smiled even though I got more scared just thinking about it.

Daddy picked me up and we high-fived. We playfighted and I got some good shots in. That made me feel better. His beard was shaved off and he let me feel how smooth his face was, but it wasn't that smooth, not like Mom's, anyway. He said that's how men are. That made me wonder when could I shave and when could I look and smell like a man, like tea and flowers and leaves and socks mixed together. Will I be as big and strong as him? Could I be as smart as him and own two restaurants? Maybe we can work togeth-er. That would be cool. He could make the food and I could count the money. I can count to a thousand million now.

He said we were going to have some man time. He said his

friends at work brought their kids to the ghost festival last year and it was going to be loads of fun and after, we could go for lunch. He was really excited.

The festival was near the water. All the children and grown-ups wore costumes. There were zombies, ghosts, vampires, werewolves, goblins, and beasts, but no friendly *Monsters, Inc.* monsters. Some of them had blood that looked real. I wanted to ask Daddy if it was. Some of them roared and hissed at me. A vampire tried to bite me, but Daddy laughed and shooed him away by making a cross. I didn't think it was funny.

Daddy bought me some cotton candy and a big Coke. I finished it really fast 'cause I was nervous. Then we went on the casket ride, which is like a coffin except it moves around instead of going underground. That was fun and I wanted to go again, but Daddy said that would be another five dollars and we should save it for the escape room or the haunted house. I woulda rather gone on a ride than inside a haunted house but I did not want to look scared 'cause we were doing our man time.

"Where do you want to go first, my son. The escape room or the haunted house?"

I wanted to go pee first but I was going to try and hold it until he had to go too. "What's an escape room?"

Daddy smiled. "They are so much fun. We are trapped in room, like a castle or a prison. Here, I think it is a cavern."

"What's a cavern?"

"It is a cave, like for pirates. Then we have to find clues and solve puzzles fast, very fast, or the fire-breathing beast will roast us alive and eat us." He laughed. "Fun, no?"

That didn't sound fun.

But last year I went to a farm on Halloween with my class. They did a haunted barn with black pigs and black sheep and gave out candies. It was fun, so I asked to do the haunted house, not the cave.

The lineup for the haunted house took a long time. A tall skeleton in a black hooded robe carrying a pole with a blade took our tickets. Daddy asked him what was taking so long. The skeleton man said many souls had been sentenced to damnation but they could only take so many 'cause of the fire regulations in hell. Then he asked Daddy if he was sure I could handle this.

I wanted to say I didn't know but I didn't want Daddy to think I was chicken, so I said yes.

I was really holding in my pee when they let us into a black hallway with red lights on the ceiling. The sounds of people running came from in front of us, but then screams came from every direction. Then quiet. All of a sudden, a swamp monster with green goo dripping from his arms came out of the wall and reached for us.

"Daddy, Daddy!"

He dragged me into the next room, a dining room where skeletons with cobwebs sat at a dinner table.

"It looks like they've been dead a long time," Daddy said. He wondered who or what killed them. One of the skeletons took a swipe at another person closer to the table and the person screamed and we ran out of there as fast as we could.

I squeezed my hand into his. The next room was the kitchen. On the stove was a big pot with a head inside and worms, lots of worms. Maybe a million worms. Someone was by the kitchen counter with their back to us. A man with a melted face and a chainsaw turned around, but his arm stayed cut off with all the pieces on the counter. Some teenagers screamed and laughed and then ran into us. I lost Daddy's hand. I looked behind and the melted-face man got closer. He started his chainsaw. He said he was hungry and a small snack was exactly what he needed. The teenagers started to run and they pushed me out of the kitchen, leaving Daddy behind.

"Daddy, Daddy ..."

I was in a bedroom. My tummy really started to hurt and I needed to pee and poo. Floating above the bed, a boy was watching me, but it was like he wasn't there. I could see the ceiling through him. He said someone strangled him to death in his sleep and that he would haunt me forever until he could find the killer. Then he asked if it was me.

"No, no, it wasn't me," I said in my outside voice.

The ghost called me a liar and said he was coming for me.

I ran and ran through all the last rooms and pushed through other people until I got outside. I kept running, past the escape room, past the casket ride, past the cotton candy man, until I ran out of breath down by the water with boats everywhere. I had to go to the bathroom and couldn't hold it in anymore. There was nowhere to go except the boats, so I climbed into one and took my pants off and peed. I tried to aim over the wall but it was too high, so I peed on the floor and then my tummy hurt really bad so I started to poo and it felt better.

"Hey. Hey, kid. What the hell do you think you're doing?"

A lady carrying a bucket climbed into the boat.

I didn't finish but pulled up my pants anyway.

She looked really mad and grabbed my arm and pulled me away. I think she was about to push me off the boat when Daddy and a man in a yellow vest found me.

"Get your hands off my son!"

She and Daddy stared at each other the way Mom and her boyfriends always do before they get into a fight. I didn't think Daddy would beat the lady. I didn't want him to 'cause then he'd go to jail. Mom says men who lay a finger on women are the lowest of low-lifes and should be locked up. If that happens to Daddy then who will be my Daddy? Tyler?

She let go of me.

"This your son? Do you know what he just did?" She showed Daddy my accident.

Daddy looked at me like I had an accident on him instead of the boat. He turned back to her and apologized.

"Sorry? Sorry doesn't cut it. This is teak deck, I just had it oiled. What your kid did is disgusting. What I want to know is where were *you*?"

"What do you mean *where was I*? I was looking for him."

"I want a name. A boy leaves a negligent parent and vandalizes my boat. I want your name and his"—she pointed at me—"and I'm calling the child welfare authorities and the police."

They yelled at each other until the man in the yellow vest said they would send someone over from the festival to clean it up as good as new.

When we walked back, Daddy asked if I was crazy. "Why did you run off? Did you not hear me? Now look at what you've done." He sniffed me and made a look like I was disgusting. I could tell he was sorry he took me out. I was sorry too.

I did not know what to say. I was scared to say the wrong thing and he wouldn't be my daddy anymore and we would not run the restaurant together. I held my tears 'cause I knew that would make him madder. I'm so stupid. I wished I could die then come back and start all over again.

He asked me what I wanted to do now, but I didn't know. He tried to call Mom, but she was too busy. So we drove back to the Double Happiness and said nothing to each other. Daddy squeezing the steering wheel was scary. He was so mad he stopped looking at me, like I was invisible, like a ghost.

The restaurant was busier than I ever seen it. Daddy and me stood in front of the bussing station. When Mom saw us I could see her confused face.

Daddy told Mom I was out of control, that I knocked some people over in the haunted house and hurt them. He said I wouldn't listen and ran off and he had to call security to help find me. They saw me climb into a boat where I crapped all over the deck.

"Really, Ax? That's what happened?"

I looked away. "I was scared ..."

"I paid three dollars for parking, fifteen dollars for the tickets," Daddy said, peeling back one finger at a time. "I bought cotton candy and a jumbo drink, that's ten dollars, I take him on casket ride, another ten dollars, haunted house, twenty ... I did everything. Then he runs off like a crazy boy and embarrasses me. That boat owner was ready to sue me. I cannot blame her. It was disgusting."

"He was scared, you idiot. You shoulda been on him every second."

"If you had raised him properly, none of this would have happened."

"That's legit hysterical, you judging me. Really, really fucking hysterical."

Customers dropped their forks and looked.

Peter came over and called for Justine to take me into the stockroom and for Mom and Daddy to take it outside.

"We're done here anyway," Mom said to Peter, but she was looking at Daddy with one eye. "Asshole here can't handle an hour alone with his kid for the first time in seven years and I have to rescue him."

They went outside, but I could still hear them. The whole restaurant could.

"You are the asshole and he is a maniac like his mother. No respect for anybody. He cannot listen," Bash yelled. "Have you taught him nothing?"

Justine told me to just wait in the storage room.

I saw the cans of fuel for the hot pot and remembered that Matthew said it was safe. I took the lid off and smelled it. It didn't smell like anything and looked like Mom's hair gel. I couldn't see how it could burn. There was a long lighter nearby. I sparked it on and stuck it inside the can. The can went on fire so fast that it scared me and I dropped it. It fell on an apron that was on the ground, and the apron caught on fire. I tried to put it out with some paper menus, but then they caught on fire too. I got on my hands and knees to put out all the sparks. The smoke detector in the room went off and soon the whole room filled with smoke.

I heard Justine scream, "Axel's in there!"

I started to cough and crawled out of the room. The smell of burning filled the restaurant.

Peter, Daddy, and Mom found me with my head down, crouched on the floor just outside the stockroom. Mom hugged me and said she was glad to see me cough out the bad stuff. One of the cooks came with a fire extinguisher and put out the fire and sparks.

The police and firefighters arrived. A paramedic came to check on me. Once I stopped coughing, he checked to see if my breathing was okay, then he said I could go.

Peter was talking to a firefighter, then came to see Mom and

Daddy and me by his car in the parking lot. "We were very, very lucky. No one was hurt."

Mom nodded and took a deep drag of her cigarette.

Peter was talking fast. "The police asked questions about Axel. How did he get hold of fire-making material? Why was he not supervised? And they say sprinklers should have gone off, but they did not. The fire marshal will come. The police think he will close me down for how long I do not know. Everybody will be out of work. My insurance is going to skyrocket."

"Fuck, Peter, you shouldn't leave stuff like that around, especially if kids are around."

"Now you say this? Justine and Matthew never make trouble. My children are good kids. Axel is a good kid too."

"So why are you blaming me?" She wrapped an arm around me.

"I'm not, the police are. They said they're supposed to call Community Services."

17

HANNAH

————

As soon as we rounded the corner from the Double Happiness, I reached into the backseat of Bash's shitbox Neon and smacked Ax in the head. Not hard, just enough to let him know I was pissed as all hell. "What the fuck were you doing, Ax?"

"Sorry, Mom." His head hung low. "But the voice inside made me do it."

"Stop with this bullshit about this voice." I took another swing at him, but Bash blocked me.

"You stop, are you crazy?" Bash shouted. "Leave him alone, he is just a little boy."

"You couldn't get rid of him fast enough, so just stay out of this."

"But I never smacked him and neither should you."

"Don't tell me what to do. Peter says the police will notify Community Services. It's going to start all over again."

Ax kept his mouth shut, but I saw in the rear-view mirror that he was fighting back tears.

"He could've burned the whole restaurant down." Bash slapped the steering wheel.

"But he didn't, he wrecked a few aprons, so don't get so fucking dramatic. If you had been a normal dad and just had a normal visit, none of this woulda happened."

"You don't know what you're doing. That is why they took Faye. Obviously you—"

"Don't you dare tell me losing Faye is on me. You were fucking nowhere when she had her seizures. Then she turned evil after they made me medicate her. I got stuck with the work and all the blame. Meanwhile, you drop off a few crates of food every six years and fall flat on your face trying to play the hero to my son."

"Maybe Faye just wanted a mother who was not crazy. And maybe"—he banged the steering wheel again—"if you taught them how to obey, none of this would have happened."

A cop car pulled alongside us at a red light and scoped us out. Racist bastard. I smiled at him, then told Bash to take us to the north end of Halifax. There was an apartment I wanted to check out, one with a basement.

I glanced back at Ax, who curled in his lips. I coulda told Bash that Ax doesn't like strangers and that he still wasn't much more than that to his son. Ax also doesn't like ghosts or monster stuff, and crowds and noise trigger him. But I didn't say anything. I wanted Ax out. Away. Gone. And it was about time he sucked it up and hung with his father. And Bash doesn't listen to anything I say anyway.

I told Bash he was driving too fast. He told me to fuck off. As we climbed onto the Macdonald Bridge, traffic slowed. Just then, Ax unbuckled his seat belt and opened the car door and yelled, "I just want to die!"

"Bash, stop the car, stop the car."

Bash slammed the brakes. "Axel, what are you doing?"

I jumped out of the passenger seat and pulled Ax out of the car. A bunch of drivers leaned on their horns.

"Jesus, Ax, what were you thinking, do you know you coulda killed yourself? Do you know what that woulda done to me? You're all I have. Don't you get it?"

Ax looked like he'd just played a good UNO reverse card. I buckled him in and sat in the back beside him. I squeezed his hand and glanced nervously at him for the rest of the drive. He calmed down a little.

Bash pulled the Neon into the driveway of the North Halifax address I had given him. It was a small standalone one-storey home in need of a complete makeover. I got out, telling Axel to stay where he was, an order I also gave Bash.

"This is stupid, you cannot find anything cheaper than Jimmy's, why would you want to live here?"

I ignored Bash's question, then thought how much better it would look to the landlord if I had Ax with me. I waved to Ax to get out of the car.

Bash followed.

"I don't need you. Just stay in the car."

"I am not your chauffeur. You do not get to order me around like one."

I wanted to call him an ass, then decided to leave it be. I knocked on the door and a middle-aged woman opened it. I asked about the apartment while she checked me out. She chilled once she saw Ax and then Bash—our Hallmark Canadian mixed-race family.

The apartment was even smaller than our current one. It was unfurnished, but more expensive than the rent we were paying for Jimmy's basement—this was Halifax, not Dartmouth. It had a garage, which was what really interested me. Tyler had said he could set up climate-controlled indoor grow-op tents complete with grow lights, exhaust kits, and filtration. Because he already had the clone plants, he could guarantee a consistent product. He'd made clear it was on me to find a safe location and to front the start-up cost: a thousand dollars. Plus I'd need first and last month's rent as well as money to outfit the new apartment.

Bash left Ax to play on the lopsided swing set in the parkette across the street and joined me in the garage.

Clusters of spiders hung everywhere. Half-filled paint cans, unclaimed junk, wooden pallets, and broken furniture littered every inch of the garage. "This place is a dump, like the apartment," said Bash. The woman was out of earshot inside the house.

"It's perfect."

"What the hell do you need a garage for? You don't even have a car."

"I'll get one. My boyfriend's gonna buy it for me."

Bash laughed. "Yeah, Jimmy told me about your jailbait skateboarder. He even know how to drive?"

"He rides a bicycle."

"Wow, I underestimated him. Is he off training wheels yet?"

"Piss off." I bit my lip. "I need two thousand bucks, Bash."

Bash eyeballed me. "What?"

"You heard me, I need two grand."

I could tell he wasn't sure how serious I was, but his tone changed. "You are crazy. Whatever you are thinking, I know it is crazy."

"Two grand doesn't even pay for a year of child support for Ax. That's all I'm asking, then we're even. I'll walk away. I'll lose your number."

"Two thousand dollars and you will be out of my life forever?" Bash rubbed his chin. "That sounds too good to be true. What is really going on?"

"It's a business venture."

"A business venture?" He laughed again. "Nothing good will come of this."

"You don't even know what it is."

"I do not need to know—it is a Hannah Belenko plan. It will, as they say in *Mission Impossible*, 'self-destruct.'"

"Spot me the money."

Finally, he saw I was serious. He took a few steps around the garage, shaking his head repeatedly. "This is not good."

"I didn't ask for an opinion. I've made you a great offer, take it or leave it."

"Let me think." He stopped pacing. "I will give you two thousand dollars. But only if you leave Axel."

"What the fuck are you talking about. Give you Ax, for two grand? That's fucking insane."

"I do not want him for myself, he goes to Community Services. At least someone else looking after him will not do something stupid like store stolen goods or run a meth lab."

"Shut the fuck up," I whispered. The landlady was down the

driveway taking out the garbage. "I won't be doing either." I planted my hands on my hips. "Since when do you give a shit about your son?"

"I did not say that I did, but someone needs to."

I got in his face and pushed him with both hands. He hardly budged.

"You're such an asshole, Bash."

"Back off, Hannah, or do you not need me anymore?"

I reached for my smokes.

"Why do you carry Ax around like an unwanted parcel belonging somewhere else? You do not care about him. You only care about yourself. Just take the money. I am sure you can still visit."

"You don't know a thing about me." I sparked up a cigarette and offered him one. "The answer's no. Your deal stinks."

"Hannah, I do know you. I am sorry, I was wrong to say you do not care about him. Heaven help anyone who would lay a finger on your boy, our boy. But you are a runaway train. He is a passenger who did not buy a ticket and must get off. You did it before with the children, you let them take care of them."

"That was after you took off, asshole."

"That is beside the point. You got your life together. They returned both to you. Maybe try it with Axel now. Take a long break. It could be good for both of you."

I folded my hands together and placed them on my head as something dawned on me. "Hang on a sec. You got two grand you've been sitting on instead of helping me out? Meanwhile, I'm working the Double Nightmare every weekend?"

"No, I do not have it now, give me some time. But for this, I can get it. Think about it."

I didn't have to think about it. I'd just lost Faye forever, and every free, sober moment, there was a big hole in my stomach. I wasn't going to lose Ax too. I didn't trust the child warfare Nazis. I didn't trust Bash or anyone else. I gave the garage another look. Two grand would pay for it all. The thought of parking Ax while Tyler and I got the grow-op going—curing our first harvest, selling it all—was tempting. After Ax's fire, child welfare was coming for us anyway.

"How do I know I can trust you? How do I know I'll see the money?"

"Trust? Let us not be naive. There is none. How do I know you will not just take the money? The risk is all mine."

"Bullshit. If Ax goes into care, who knows if I'll ever see him again. The bigger risk is mine, Bash, mine."

He paused. "Maybe you are right, but I will not just give you two thousand dollars on your word."

"Look, Community Services will contact you. They'll want to see if there is any other family member that can take him. You won't, but at least you'll see they're working on putting him somewhere. Things will be happening. That's when you can give me the money."

Ax walked into the garage right at that moment. "Are you going away with Tyler in a new car? Are you sending me away to the CAS?" He turned his pinched face to his dad. "Is it 'cause of the fire?"

Our hesitation confirmed whatever worst-case scenario was in his head. He bolted, almost knocking over the landlady as she stepped into the garage.

"That there lad has quite a head of steam going. So I'll be needing a deposit if you're interested. Seventy-five dollars."

Knowing it was a high-vacancy market, I didn't think anybody was going to take the unit, but I didn't want to take the chance. I bargained her down to fifty.

"Pay the lady," I told Bash. "I'll find Ax."

He raised an eyebrow.

"It's a deposit on our deal."

———

I was so stoked when I told Tyler about the apartment.

He gave me a thumbs-up as he lit the bong.

"It's on Stanley." I waved away the bong when he offered, not really feeling like getting high.

"Stanley? Place or Street?" Tyler asked while holding the smoke in his lungs.

"What's the difference?"

He slowly exhaled. "Not much really, same road. But I know that
'hood. Lots of big old trees. My old man always used to go get his
hair cut down there, some old Italian guy called Enzio. He'd give me
a lolly every time. I remember—"

"I don't give a shit about that right now. Lots of time to go down
memory lane later. I checked out the garage, it's big enough for two
tents, the area looks really quiet—"

"It is."

"And one bus will get you there in thirty-eight minutes. Once you
score me some wheels, it's a nine-minute drive to your place. Dude,
we're gonna own both Halifax and Dartmouth's North Ends."

"Yeah, about the tents. If I'm assembling these from scratch, we
can save a lot of coin. But I have to start slowly getting parts and ma-
terials—the lights, the insulated walls, the fans. It's all legal-like to buy
and everybody else will be gearing up to grow their four-plant quota.
I just don't want to be too obvious about it, ya know what I mean?"

"Me neither."

"Chill babes, I'm saying that's on your dime, remember? I'll be
needing a grand and maybe a few bills more. Nothing flies until you
front me the cash."

I thought of my arrangement with Bash. "I'm working on it."
Suddenly I did want to get high. "Hand me that bong."

Within days of the store-room fire at the Double Happiness, I had
several calls from what looked like a government number. I knew
they were coming, but I ignored them anyway. The child warfare
Nazis would be coming in person. So I spent hours tidying up the
house while Ax was at school. When I heard a knock on the door, I
knew it was them. I sprayed a heavy dose of Lysol to mask the weed
and cigarette smoke. A woman named Diane Khalil showed her ID
and asked to come in. Khalil. Lebanese. Would she cut me a break?
Or bury me for having a Lebanese kid?

She was polite and everything. As she casually scanned the apartment, I scanned her. Chunky necklace that could drown a small child, black polyester slacks that did nothing for her thighs, flower-print blouse, thick dark hair tied back, and same olive complexion as my kids.

I wondered what woulda happened if the CAS had come to my door when I was a kid. Would my father have run them out of the house? Would Steffi have served cake? Would I have been honest? The answers were obvious. I wouldn't have said a thing. I never did when they came just before Jennifer did you-know-what. But what if I had?

Diane got to the point. "We received a call after a small fire at the Double Happiness Restaurant on Saturday. I'm glad no one was hurt."

"So am I."

"We understand Axel set it."

She didn't say it, but I know what she meant: if you were a better mother, this would never have happened.

When Ax was just a baby and Bash had just left, I was completely alone and angry all the time. I was drinking a lot, taking it out on the kids, no longer caring if I ever woke up. Community Services came by one afternoon after an anonymous call. I figure Bash was the one who ratted. They said they'd do anything to help me keep the kids, but they lied. I know they did. After two visits when the kids were screaming for food—one of them in a dirty diaper I'd managed to miss—they gave me a "choice." Either I voluntarily brought the kids into care, or they would take them. The first meant at least I would retain custodial rights, so that's what I went with. It took a while, but I got my shit together long enough to get them back.

Now it was like time hadn't moved. I was still all alone, still had no one to help me. I was down to just Ax, who I was ready to leverage for two grand. How fucked up is that?

"Hannah?"

"Sorry, I was just wondering about the time. Ax forgot his lunch, I have to drop it off at school."

"It's half past ten. He goes to Ocean View?"

"Uh-huh."

"We have time before lunch. Let's get on with things, shall we?"

"Did you know there were two other kids in the restaurant? All I'm saying is just 'cause Matthew and Justine are Chinese doesn't mean they're angels. Ax looks up to older kids, he's easily influenced."

"I'm going on the initial report. There's more than that, Hannah. We did some digging and received an interprovincial request for service from the Ottawa CAS. It looks like you left there while still under a supervision order without notifying your worker and before the request for service to us could be initiated."

"Things happened really fast." I couldn't decide how to play this. They had found me again, they always did. They weren't going to let up until they had Ax for good. Their job was to take kids away, not to protect them. It was all a lie. A child is best protected by their mother. Maybe if I was a mouse like my mom had been, the CAS would never have heard of me, never placed an X beside my name. I wasn't sure now about Bash's plan. The asshole believed I couldn't look after Ax. Giving Ax up even for a few months meant me saying I couldn't properly care for him. That I was *an awful mother*. That's what they thought about me with Faye. I pictured the CAS workers sitting around their staff-room table with their lattes, plotting how to take kids. My kids. It was a performance thing. Every kid they take moves them up the scale, and my kids were a big bump, I'm sure of it.

I wasn't going to let that happen again. I needed to act as though I was in a rough patch, and all we needed was a temporary lifeline. I suddenly realized it wasn't going to be so easy. The lifeline had to be on my terms and when I was ready. It couldn't be obvious that I was gaming the system, trying to get them to lift Ax from me so I could make good on the agreement with Bash. I was an entrepreneur in need of seed money. Who knows, maybe a change of scene would be good for Ax. He wasn't exactly killin' it.

Diane asked how the past four months had been since returning to Dartmouth.

"Great, I'm doing great. Ax and I are in a good spot together. We're getting along, we got a good routine going." I couldn't help it, reverting to the bullshit lines I was used to feeding other workers. "He likes his teacher. I have a steady job, or at least I did until the fire shut the restaurant down. But I think I can find something else. I got my shit together now. I have a boyfriend." *He was ten when my daughter was born and he's putty in my hands so long as I suck his dick and finger his butt.* "And Ax's dad is helping out." *To the tune of two grand if I play this right.* Except this time, it was mostly true and didn't sound as though anyone needed to take my kid.

Diane said she was happy to hear this. She said she didn't have to follow the supervision order as it didn't apply in Nova Scotia. That being said, the Ottawa file information could be used in court to force compliance with their conditions—like taking parenting classes and counselling, and refraining from drugs and "excessive" alcohol use.

"Or Hannah, you could just work voluntarily with us. We could bypass the court. You can prove to *me* instead of the court that you really do have it together. You see, my goal is the same as yours—a happy ending where I close this file and walk out the door because you don't need me. Wouldn't that be awesome?"

I put on a Barbie smile. "Except this is bullshit."

"It seems like that, doesn't it? You're on a roll and a stranger comes in and tells you to take a parenting class, get into counselling, not get high or drunk. Doesn't seem fair, does it?"

"Yeah," I said, but it sounded like a question.

"Hannah, I can't imagine what it's like to have lost Faye, so I know you must be scared silly at me being here and the thought of losing Axel, too."

"Uh-huh."

"So I want to believe you that a change has meant you've landed in a better spot. Let's assume you're being straight-up with me, and together we can make sure you stay on course. I'll start checking things off, go see Axel, speak with the school, come back later with resources, shake, stir, repeat—and then we'll look to wrap this up as quickly as possible."

"You're going to see Ax now?" I hadn't prepared him. He would sugarcoat things the way I'd trained him. I needed Axel to be honest and to tell Diane that I was scary.

I got to the school ahead of Diane. Principal Godin stepped out of his office and saw me with lunch in a KFC bag for Ax.

"Hannah, how's it going?" he asked. I said that things were good. He took me aside and said that in the last few days, Ax had been particularly out of control, especially toward Mr. Spearman, who Ax normally adored and trusted.

I wondered if Ax was pissed about what he heard in the garage and how much he understood.

Mr. Godin called Ax down. He bounded into the office, stopping in his tracks when he saw me, but then smiled once he saw the KFC bag. I took him aside.

"Ax, a woman named Diane from Community Services, that's like the CAS, is coming after lunch to talk to you. This is what I want you to do—"

"I know what to say, Mom," Ax said, nodding. "We're getting along good, there's lots of food in the house, you never yell, you don't have a boyfr—"

"No, I need you to be ... honest, to say that Mom ... can get loud, that we fight, and that sometimes Mom needs a break."

Ax's face scrunched. "I don't get it. Did I mess up? What did I do? I'll never do it again, I'll be good. I promise."

"Because if you can do this for me, Mom finally has a plan that will get us lots of money and we can live in a house where no one will bug us and we can order pizza whenever we want and get as many dipping sauces as you'd like and—"

"You're sending me away, aren't you?"

I shouldn't have hesitated.

At that moment, Diane walked in and stood behind me. Ax smacked the KFC bag out of my hand. "This is bullshit." He pushed me into Diane, knocking us off balance and me onto the floor. I landed on my hand and it felt like something inside shattered. "Fuck!" I yelled.

18

AXEL

MOM LIED TO me. I was going to make her sorry, even if I died.

I didn't mean to push her so hard, but I was mad and since she was now mad too, I was going to get out of there. I was out the front door and onto the street before anybody could catch me. I turned to the busy street with the fast cars. I was going to take the bridge over the street but a bunch of teenagers smoking blocked it. Daddy is going to give Mom two thousand dollars to go on a runaway train to do business and she is going to do it without me because she needs a break and I'm stupid and I keep messing up, now Daddy's mad at me too. I'll never let anybody take me away. I'll just run away, then everybody will be sorry.

I went as fast as I could across the busy street. Cars stopped and honked. One driver yelled at me. I wanted him to shut up but I climbed the fence to get to the other side of the street. I almost made it over when Mr. Spearman grabbed me from behind and pulled me down.

"Leave me alone, I just wanna die, leave me alone." I swung my arms at him until he bended down and pinned them to his body.

"It's okay, Axel," he said. "I've got you."

He tried to rock me. I kicked and head-butted him until he said there was an F-150 and a Silverado. I looked. He wasn't lying. He's not a liar. I stopped fighting and rested against his body.

"I got you, Axel, I got you."

He did have me and all I wanted to do was stay near him.

Mom came running with that woman. Mom called me a stupid shit and grabbed me by the back of neck before Mr. Spearman pulled me back from her. I wished he'd never let go.

19

HANNAH

AX RUINED MY moment. "You stupid little shit. Again, really? This running off stops now." I almost had him by the neck but his teacher got in the way. I showed Ax my sore hand. "If this is busted, you're in so much trouble. No TV for six months and no going outside until next year."

As much as I knew I had to game Diane, I couldn't have faked losing it any better.

Afterward, I paced like a caged lion in the school conference room while Ax ate his lunch with Mr. Godin. "Can you see the shit I have to put up with? I have no idea what's wrong with him, but I need help."

"What did you say to him? What made him run off like that?" Diane asked.

"I told him you were coming, that he had to be honest and tell the truth, even if it made me look bad, I swear to God." It's weird, but that was for real.

"Why would telling the truth be so frightening?"

"He's scared, that's all. So am I. And I don't think I can take this for much longer."

"Really? An hour ago you said you were in a good spot."

I told her I didn't want to look as though I didn't know what I was doing. But Ax running off into traffic had scared me, and that was the truth. I never know what he's going to do. There in the conference room with Diane, it got easier to talk about how he could shut down and get lost in his own world. Yet it was hard to talk about myself, my past.

"How did your parents show you that you mattered, Hannah?"

I had to think about that. "They bought me things." My answer sounded like a question.

"Which parent were you closest to?"

I didn't have to think about that one. "Neither."

"Did they threaten or scare you in any way?"

I'd been asked this many times before and always answered the same way: that I couldn't remember anything.

"How do you think life with your parents impacted you as an adult, and as a mother?"

What kind of bullshit question was that? But I had to give her something. "I learned that the only one covering your back was yourself. I taught Ax and Faye that early on, except I *would* be there for them ... plus if you were weak, you were someone else's bitch. You're always looking over your shoulder and you'll be shit on by people like my father. I pray to God Ax never becomes like him." Fuck, I'd said too much and hoped she'd just back off.

"You make it seem like they weren't very good at it. How have you survived all this?"

I half shrugged. I didn't want to talk about how I could zone out, completely collapse into a wet ball of tissue, in which case Ax would step in for me. Sometimes I went nuclear and probably scared the shit out of my kids. No one had immunity once I got going.

"Not all parents know what they're doing," Diane said. "Good, caring parents who are tuned into their kids don't grow on trees. They grow into it, maybe. Mine sucked at it, real bad. That's probably why I didn't want to have kids."

"Really?"

She nodded. "Yeah, but now we're thinking of adopting. But enough of me. So why now? Why hit the wall now?"

I thought carefully of what to say. I knew I had to sound caring, to say that I was all in for Ax but that I was out of gas. That I needed a hand, a strong hand to take over just for a while so I could truly sort my life out. I was planning on saying exactly that. Instead, I bent over and dropped my elbows onto my knees and rested my face in my open hands. I took a deep breath and sat up. What came out of my mouth wasn't in the program.

"Do you ever feel dead? I mean not dead-dead, but numb, like you can't feel anything. Like the world is in colour but you're just some bleak, weightless grey mass floating above, and everything is spinning around you so fast, and sounds and voices that make no sense come from everywhere, every crack in the floor, and every hole in the wall. But you can't take any of it in 'cause you're just ... dead."

I didn't know if I made any sense. My life's been a shitshow you don't want to watch but can't turn away from. The sounds and voices are scenes of my family—lots of them in fact, a pile of other crap, but especially of Jennifer. The only way to get through it is to turn down the volume and play dead.

Diane reached over and patted my hand, startling me. It was warm, her hand. I let it rest there for a moment, then pulled away.

"What do you really want, Hannah?"

I shook my head and shrugged. I'd practiced for this moment. I was going to talk about how I just couldn't catch a break or get ahead 'cause everyone was against me. Instead, I just let it rip. "I don't know. My life is one bad groundhog day after another with no hope or help in sight. It's been like this ever since I can remember. I get older, same shit. I move, same shit. My kid whines, cries, runs ... I do this, I do that, same shit." I stared off into nothing. "I feel like I have a plan but I honestly don't know. It's like I'm winging everything, and before I know it, I've got my hands on his neck."

Diane let that hang for a few seconds. "That must be frightening for Axel, and for you. I know that's not the kind of mother you want to be."

I nodded and fought back tears.

"Nothing gets better by itself. We can't cut and run from our problems and time doesn't heal all wounds. Those are bad habits and cheap clichés. Looking after yourself can help, so can therapy, and it will give you pride in learning to be the mother you need to be. The mother Axel needs you to be."

I bit my lip. "Yeah."

"We can explore all these things, but to be honest, you're going to keep spinning your wheels because right now you can't look after Axel and yourself at the same time. Maybe we can look after him by having him spend a meaningful amount of time with someone else while you heal and grow."

I could feel excitement churning up. I didn't have to use any of my rehearsed lines. I could be myself, and it was working. I could game a worker by being me. It felt strangely liberating and vulnerable at the same time. "What do you mean?"

Diane suggested I allow her to reach out to Bash to see if he was willing and capable of caring for Ax. What a joke, I almost said. If that didn't work, we could explore the possibility of a voluntary care agreement. She reminded me I'd had one before, and that it worked out.

I was ready to jump off the couch and do a cartwheel but kept myself together. "I don't know about this, I've already lost Faye."

Diane reviewed the benefits. She said I could continue to be a mother in most ways but, more importantly, I could seek the help I needed without the distraction of parenting full-time.

"I'll have to think about it. You have to remember what I said about Bash. He's been pretty useless, but if you think he can be convinced to step up, be my guest."

"Leave that to me. I'll speak with him. In the meantime, don't say anything to Axel until we have a plan finalized."

Diane left. I'd gamed her successfully, but it cost me something that was tearing at me inside. Something about her kindness and seeing into my vulnerability reminded me of Jennifer.

Back in the day, the news of Jennifer killing herself spread around my high school and my parents' neighbourhood in Stittsville like a swarm of hungry locusts. The local newspaper even did a short piece about the sudden death of a Holy Triverius student. It wasn't hard to figure out that it was a suicide, but thankfully Jennifer's name was kept out of it.

I shoulda bawled my eyes out when she died. All I did was shut up about it, stomp around, seethe like an angry bull—even though I wanted to cry. I heard Ivan on the phone the day after it happened, talking to a friend. "Can you believe this shit on my street? You'd think she could've just taken a whack of pills at school or something." I gave him the nastiest look. Hearing that gave me the outlet I needed. I screamed in his face that it was all his fault. That it all started with him ratting me out to Papa about the letters. I dared him to take a run at me, in fact, I wanted it. Instead, he hung up the phone and slipped away.

A lady cop knocked on our door: Constable Tara Lee. Chinese or Korean or something, who can tell? She had come to see me.

I let her in. She said she was sorry for my loss. That stopped me. No one else had acknowledged that Jennifer's death was a huge loss for me. She explained Jennifer had left several suicide letters, including one to me. The police had taken them away to be examined for evidence. The Krohn parents resisted giving the one addressed to me, but Lee apparently told them it may have been one of Jennifer's last wishes, so the parents gave in. I don't know why Lee told me all this. I think she felt sorry for me.

"If you need someone to talk to after going through this, I'll stick around." Lee handed me an envelope. She had to have known the contents of the letter and figured it would mess me up.

I asked her if the rumours of Jenn hanging herself were true. She took a deep breath and nodded.

I knew it. The Krohns had a sailboat, so Jennifer knew a lot about ropes and knots. She could recite useless information about sailing and ropes the way I could about World War Two. She told me once how she knew how to tie the hangman's knot. I thought it was cool at the time.

Papa walked in and told Lee her job was done and asked her to leave.

Lee said she'd return at a later time, as the investigation around Jennifer's alleged assault wasn't over.

"What for, that girl is dead?" he said.

Lee turned around and our eyes met. She looked concerned for me, then turned to him.

"Your daughter's bruises from last week's assault are still visible. It takes a substantial amount of grip strength to leave marks like that on someone. Jennifer Krohn didn't have that. Can you think of anybody in Hannah's life who does?"

He held his breath.

"I'll continue looking. I'll be watchful, vigilant, and patient. We do want to get the right person, don't we, Mr. Belenko?"

"You have no right to come in and treat me like a criminal. You have questions for me, you wait until I have lawyer. You see lawyer here now? *Nyet.* You want to talk to anybody from my family, you do it with my lawyer." He squared his body to her like a bear ready to charge.

Lee was this tiny thing—she shoulda caved and ran off right then and there—but she got into this stare-down with Papa, like she was ready for a takedown and could do it before he even knew what hit him.

Finally, he gave in and said he was going to call his lawyer. Lee backed away but not before giving him a look like, Watch out, motherfucker.

Jenn's envelope was still in my hands, the open side jagged where someone had ripped it open. I figured that the police and the Krohns had gone through it, so whatever was personal was no longer private. Constable Lee most likely knew about the nature of my relationship with Jennifer. Weirdly, it made me feel better to think that someone knew ... but then Papa swooped in and tore the letter from my hands.

He held it high above his head. "You do not get to keep secrets from your papa."

I gasped. Those were Jennifer's last thoughts of me. Who knew what was in that letter? "You can't. It's mine." I lunged at him, but he pushed me off with one hand. "You fucking ass, that's mine. She gave it to me."

Ivan came from behind and ripped the letter out of his hands.

"It's hers, Papa." I just about dropped my mouth and stared at Ivan who, the most ripped of all the high school seniors, stood his ground with his chest puffed. Papa was a hulk. In the past, he woulda crushed Ivan, who would never have chanced a confrontation with him. Now they glared at each other.

"It's hers," Ivan repeated.

Papa looked confused, then walked away.

Ivan handed me the letter, keeping his eyes from mine. I would swear there was, for a split second, a look like he was sorry before he stalked off to the kitchen as though nothing had happened.

I went to my bedroom, closing the door. I gently opened the letter. Jennifer's cursive was neat and compact, unlike my scribble.

To the Hannah I once had.

She wrote that she'd found joy and happiness during our wonderful moment that evening, that for a brief but exciting instant she felt uncaged, unburdened, and truly free. She said it was 'cause she was with me.

> *Since I met you, I dreamed of being with you, but at the same time I was scared. Scared of my feelings, scared of you rejecting me, and scared of someone finding out. Then after you went home that evening, all I could think about was preserving what we had, and protecting you. I swear that was all I was trying to do. I would never, ever hurt you. I swear to God.*
>
> *But when I saw your face flash with rage like you were ready to pound me to the ground, I was banished back to the cage. Except now I was on display and completely naked to the world and alone.*

She said she'd been very down before, feeling worthless and lost, and had been on antidepressants.

> *I don't think I can come back from this. To be honest, I don't have the strength to even try anymore. It always took every ounce to smile when I really wanted to cry, to join in when I wanted to be alone, to be perfect when I felt like a fraud—what a joke. I just don't want to pretend anymore. Please, please forgive me. I'm sorry for hurting you. I'm sorry for loving you, and I'm sorry for any pain I might cause. Love, Jenn.*

I stared at the words without rereading them. I replayed the last moment I saw her, the wide-eyed horror on her face when she saw my hate and rage and thought it was directed at her alone. Knowing I would never forget that memory. Believing I had pushed Jennifer over the edge. Wishing it was me, and not Jennifer, swinging from a rope.

I felt a guttural cry deep in my belly trying to claw its way out. I reached for my headphones instead, cranked my music, and blocked everything out. I crumpled the letter and threw it in the trash.

———

So yeah, something about this Diane woman took me back. But it didn't matter. It was game on, bitches. I had achieved what I wanted in a weird, roundabout way with Community Services. But my triumph came with the gut-wrenching reality of Ax going back into care. Only for a little while. Except that hadn't exactly been the case with Faye.

20

AXEL

MR. SPEARMAN CARRIED me back into school with Mom
and everyone else following. I thought I was going to get whupped.
After Mom stopped yelling she told me to tell the truth to that
woman Diane, but first they were going to talk alone. Maybe they
were planning what to do with me. I don't know what to believe.
She always says they will come for us if I mess up. But I didn't say
anything wrong and I did everything I was supposed to. Something
was wrong.

Just tell the truth.

No.

Just tell the truth, even Mom said so.

I didn't even know what truth to say. That Mom had a new
boyfriend? She told me before to say she didn't. I was supposed to
say we get along. I started a fire and now Mom has no job, Peter has
no job, and Justine and Matthew probably hate me. Daddy almost
got into a fight at the ghost festival 'cause I had an accident. He's
going to give Mom money for her to go away on business. I think
she would be very mad if I said all that to anyone.

I told Mr. Spearman I didn't want to talk to anybody and I
wanted to be by myself. So he put me in the principal's office. Then
Mr. Spearman came in with his lunch. He offered me some of his

ham-and-cheese sandwich on bread that looked like chocolate but was called pimplenickel. He cut me a piece. It was yummy. He did not want any of my KFC, but he took a Skittle.

Mr. Spearman did storytime on the carpet yesterday. We always get down off our chairs into the middle of the classroom and try to sit closest to him. He likes to close the blinds and turn all the lights off except a spotlight on himself when he reads. He read *Pinocchio*. After the story, he said Pinocchio was a good boy who had made bad choices. "Pinocchio was out of control, lazy, and did not always tell the truth. But he was still a good boy," Mr. Spearman said. He said lots of times good people lie for good reasons, and sometimes those lies are okay. But the worst lies are the ones you tell yourself. I didn't get what the story was about. Maybe he lied to himself about being better and staying out of trouble, then kept lying more and more until he learned he had to stop and by stopping he would grow up.

Mr. Spearman asked me to stay in the principal's office with him when everyone else went out for recess. He said it was scary watching me want to die. He said he wasn't sure if he was ready to talk about what happened. He might want to keep it inside for a little bit longer. Except he wasn't sure if keeping things inside was the right thing to do, so he asked me what I thought.

I said I didn't know.

He said it almost feels like you have to poo and you hold it and hold it even more until it's so painful you're ready to burst.

I don't think he knew about my ghost-festival accident but he was right about keeping things inside for too long. It hurts.

I didn't want Mr. Spearman to feel bad 'cause of me. I don't like it when people are sad and mad and hurt. I like to make them laugh and forget about things.

I said I was sorry if I made him scared, but I wasn't ready to talk about it either and I wasn't ready to talk to that woman Diane about the truth.

Mr. Spearman didn't make me. He asked me what I was going to be when I grew up.

I said I want to be a firefighter or a helicopter pilot so I can save people and make Mom proud. He said I would be good at either of them.

I asked him if he always wanted to be a teacher. He said even though his mom was a teacher, it wasn't his first choice. He was a physiotherapist, then a carpenter for a while.

"You mean like Jesus?"

He smiled. "I guess. I was good at it too. But to be honest, something was missing. I wasn't happy. I had a lot of energy and I really liked working with people. So after travelling for a bit, I returned to school for teaching and fell in love with it right away. I guess, Axel, sometimes we don't know what we want even when the answer is right in front of us. Now I can't imagine doing anything else."

"You're a good teacher, Mr. Spearman." That was the truth.

He thanked me and asked what else I wanted when I grew up. I was going to say I could also be a wrestler, but I think he wanted to know other things. I said I wanted a house, a whole house because I never lived in one, only an apartment. I wanted my basement in that house to have a big-screen TV with PlayStation 4 and Xbox 360 and to live with Faye and Mom but not Tyler. I hoped Daddy would come back to live with us.

"Would that be here or back in Ottawa?" Mr. Spearman asked.

I had to think about it. Ottawa has Dedushka and Oma Steffi, but they make Mom really mad. Faye is there, so is Oma Greta and so is Melina, how could I forget her? I'm going to marry her. So I need a bigger house. One with a swimming pool in case we have parties. But Dartmouth has Daddy and Mr. Spearman and Justine and Matthew, if they will still be my friends. So I picked somewhere halfway. "Vancouver," I said.

I could hear students coming in from the yard. Soon Mr. Spearman would have to go back to class and I would have to talk to the lady. I decided I would tell her that today was a bad day because my tummy hurt 'cause I kept something inside for too long. If she asked me what it was, I would say it was my plan about where I was going to live and with who.

And if she asked me how Mom and me get along and if she has a boyfriend and if we have enough to eat, I will say didn't you see my KFC lunch? I'll say Mom loves me. And maybe Daddy will still love me. And if none of that answers her questions, too bad. I am good at telling lies for good reasons. I could do that.

21

HANNAH

THREE DAYS AFTER Diane and I talked about putting Axel in care, Bash called. "I have your money."

My stomach churned.

"Hannah, are you there?"

"Yeah, I'm here."

"What is wrong? I thought you would be jumping with joy, or screaming at me for taking so long."

I had reservations about the deal and didn't know if I could trust him. I knew that working with Community Services to get Ax in care temporarily was a huge gamble and if things didn't work out, I could lose my son for good.

"The only time I ever scream at you is because you're being a dick, and you're getting close. I'm getting close."

"Do you still want to do this? Because I can think of better things to do with two thousand dollars."

"What's better than spending it on your kid's future?"

"That is what I am doing. What will *you* be doing with the money?"

"Give it to me and maybe you'll find out."

"I am still waiting for someone from the child services to call."

"Soon, soon ... Diane said she would."

Diane finally caught up with him. Bash gave me a detailed blow-by-blow. He said I shoulda told him she was Lebanese. I didn't see why it mattered. He was a Leb for sure but she seemed more Canadian.

"I told her you were crazy." He laughed. "But also that I was sorry that I could not take Ax because I was heading back to Lebanon for a bit." Probably 'cause of his other kid.

"Then I told her, 'You have to take Axel away. He starts a fire and runs away from school, almost killing himself. Also, his crazy mother smacks him around like a toy, a dog is treated better. If he dies it is on you.'" He couldn't stop laughing. The fucker was going for an Oscar there.

Diane probably wrote all that shit down. Knowing how smooth Bash could be, I'll bet he made like he was the heroic father who was worried sick about his son and that I was the nut job.

He came over with the money. Tyler opened the door wearing only his Spiderman briefs. They sized each other up. Tyler straightened himself up and puffed out his flat, bare chest. Bash smirked like he was trying to avert his gaze from the two enormous Spiderman eyes peering up from above Tyler's crotch.

"So you're Axel's sperm donor, Bush Hair?" Tyler let him in and lit a joint.

"Bashir, it is Bashir. And you, my friend, are Teddy, like a Teddy bear?"

"It's Tyler, and you really don't want to be fucking with me. I know people who—"

I stepped in. "I thought you were coming at two?" I pulled a sweatshirt over my head.

"It is two o'clock now."

I waved him off. "You have my money?"

"Half. When does he go in?"

"Half? We had a deal."

Bash glanced at Tyler.

"The deal was two grand once she talked to you. That's done, why you pissing around?"

"Half now, the other half when I see the agreement and the address of whoever is looking after him."

"Fuck you, Bash," I said.

"Yes, fuck me. I think I am throwing away good money for something stupid. If Axel is safe then it is worth it, but not until I know he is. Take it or leave it."

I shook my head and started to say something before I stuck my hand out and counted the thousand dollars.

Bash couldn't leave fast enough.

"The guy's a total dick," Tyler said. "Not to mention a loser for not looking after his kid."

"Yeah, well, he's got another kid back in Lebanon. He knocked up an old girlfriend and goes back once in a while."

"So that means he gets to walk from being Axel's father here?"

"Of course not, but don't get me started."

"Okay, I won't." Tyler snatched the money from my hands.

"What the fuck, Tyler—"

"Start-up costs, remember? I can get the grow lights at Canadian Tire, the carbon filters and fans are on sale at Home Hardware, and I can score the tents with the Mylar reflective walls at Home Depot. Gimme a couple of weeks and I'll have the frame and components ready to assemble."

Tyler tucked the wad of bills into his Spiderman briefs. I'd never had a thousand dollars to throw away like that before.

"I laid the rent deposit down," I said. "We move in three weeks. All I have left to do is tell Ax."

"You mean the poor kid doesn't know you're shipping him off?"

"I'm not shipping him off. I'm taking a break."

"So you can be my little bitch gardener." Tyler reached for my butt.

I dodged the grope. "So we can be partners, so you can build out from Granny's basement, so we can run this town, remember, stupid?"

"Damn straight I do. God, how I love when you dream big." He grabbed his Spiderman and pretended to shoot some web.

He's good at reminding me that he's really a boy.

Diane and I signed a six-month voluntary care agreement, which she promised we could review as we went along. I would be able to call and see Ax almost anytime. Bash could also see him, but this had to be pre-arranged. Community Services would see that he'd continue at his same school. He'd be given every chance to join any community programs, and to see a therapist. Diane would push me going into counselling, make me do parent groups, some stupid wellness programs, and help me find a new job. The Double Happiness had to close down to meet fire-and-safety regulations. That made me feel bad for Peter and his family, but I couldn't linger there.

Once the agreement was finalized, I texted Bash and asked him for the other thousand. He said he wouldn't be over until the next day before work, which pissed me off. I also left a bunch of messages with Tyler. All that was left to do was tell Ax.

I picked him up after school and took him to Nena's Breakfast House for one of his favourite meals. Little soldiers, made special for him—soft-boiled eggs in an egg cup with the top of the shell removed, served with thin strips of toast that he liked to dip into the yolks. Once in a while if I was in a good mood, I'd let him get a side of bacon. This time I ordered it for him. I asked about school, if he was getting along with people, and told him how happy I was that we were out eating a nice fancy breakfast together. That musta made him suspicious. It didn't help that I didn't touch my food and slipped out twice for a smoke. When I returned, I'm pretty sure he could tell that my eyes were red and watery.

"Ax, I've been talking with Diane."

He nodded.

"Well, she's taking you to live with a family for a few months. It's a good thing 'cause Mom has a plan, a really good plan this time."

He played with his food.

"I'll be able to get a break, find work, a new place to live and get a car without worrying about you. I'm sorry, Ax, but it's only for a little while. It's a good thing, really. I can visit, we can phone each other, we can Skype, and later you can even spend weekends with me, Christmas too."

"Is this the plan where you get rich and nobody can ever bug us again?"

That threw me back. I looked away but could feel him picking me apart. So many times I had warned him about being taken away if he didn't listen, if he didn't smarten up. Or that someone would rat us out. It could be his best friend, the nice neighbour, Matthew, Justine, or even his dad.

He asked if it was 'cause of the fire, or if it was 'cause he'd run away too many times, or 'cause he made me mad a lot.

"No, Ax. It's not you. Like I said, I'll be able to get a job, a car, money for whatever you want. It's only for a short time. We'll talk or see each other all the time."

His silent stare was killing me.

"Don't be worried, I'll get you back. We'll even have a new apartment in Halifax. It has a garage and maybe we can build a tree house for you. Don't worry, everything's going to be okay."

"Will I have a foster mother?"

"Y-yes ... I'm still your real mother, though."

"Faye's foster mother bought her a *Frozen* lunch box. Can I have one too?"

What was wrong with his *Monsters, Inc.* box? That shit cost me eighteen bucks. "Sure, why not."

"What's her name?"

"Doreen. Diane says she's nice. She better be, 'cause no one mess-es with my Ax." I forced a smile. "We get to meet her in two days."

"Does Doreen know Faye's foster mother?"

"Probably not."

Ax put on his "everything's going to be alright" smile. "That's okay, Mom. Can I get some more bacon?"

———

Ax seemed to take the news very well. He asked what school he'd be going to, and if he'd get his own room, otherwise he ate his little soldiers and bacon and said nothing else.

Everything was coming together. Bash would be dropping off the other thousand dollars in less than a day. I'd be moving into the new apartment in a few weeks, and Tyler was piecing together the grow-op. I did worry that Tyler had not returned any of my texts. I was starting to wonder if he'd been busted, or finally got jacked and was lying in a ditch somewhere.

The next morning, after I got Ax off to school, I detoured to Tyler's grandmother's house. I saw a couple of Harley-Davidsons parked out front. Tyler walked out of the house with two beefcakes wearing Dartmouth North Shore leather jackets.

"Tyler, what up, I've been messaging you since yesterday." I scanned the bikers, who in return mentally undressed me. Fucking pigs.

"I've been busy," Tyler said with a boyish grin.

"Well don't be leaving me hanging like that. I've sunk a ton of coin and hassle into this. We're partners, remember?"

"Yeah, well, babes, about that partnership. You were so right, I was thinking small. It's time to expand. Everyone knows I only grow primo weed, that's my jam. It's a gift, right?"

"What's going on," I whispered, leaning in closer to him. "What are these goons doing here?"

Tyler shrugged. "They're my new partners. Like I said, you were right. I have to think big, and thanks for the idea. These guys are going to take me there. They're going to set up some serious locations, not just a couple of tents. We're talking whole houses, and I'm going to be their grow master. Can you believe that—*me*?"

"You fucking rat bastard. I gave you a thousand bucks, plus I shelled out the deposit on that apartment. You owe me or I'm going to fucking take a bat to your head."

Tyler grinned as though he'd been caught skipping class on the last day of school. "Yeah, well, I figure with all the weed I smoked you up, and the times I played with Axel, we're kind of even. But no hard feelings, right? Maybe sometime when I'm free I'll pop over and we can party."

"You stupid little shit." I reached for his neck, but the bikers saw it coming and grabbed me from behind just before my hands landed.

I kicked at those meatheads, but they vise-gripped my arms.

Tyler took a step forward. "About that place on Stanley. I think we can use that. You're going to walk away from it."

"No way, I've already paid for the first month."

"Consider it a business loss. And this is for old times' sake," he said as he stuffed two fifty-dollar bills in my back pocket. "No need to thank me."

I lunged forward and head-butted him in the nose, knocking him onto the grass.

"My nose, I think you broke my nose," he cried out. Blood gushed down his jaw.

One of the bikers chuckled. "She's feisty, I like that." He got in my grill. "But if we see your face again, it won't be so pretty no more."

———

Bash was waiting outside my apartment. I avoided his look but let him in.

"I was starting to think you did not want my money," he said.

I knew he'd pick up on my bad mood right away. My hands were still shaking with anger. It felt like my whole body was vibrating.

"What happened to you?"

I shook my head and gave him a look like don't ask or I'll bite your head off. He clued in. Still, he couldn't help himself and asked where Tyler was.

"Rotting in hell with a broken nose, I hope."

He couldn't shut up with the self-righteous BS. "Hannah, boys pretending to be men are cheap and disposable these days."

"You don't get it. The fucker was supposed to go in with me on a ... on a partnership."

He raised an eyebrow. "Is that where my money went?"

"It was my money, we had a deal." Just saying that deflated me and I collapsed onto the couch.

"Ax will be gone for six months, probably forever. Don't worry, we're both gonna be out of your life. I'll honour our agreement." I lit a smoke. "So, where's the rest of the money?"

"Your deal with Teddy is gone, and so is my money, it is all over your face." He said. "Why do you still need the rest of my money?"

"It's none of your business and don't go on like you're my therapist now. We had a deal. Go ahead, fuck me over, everybody does." I sank further into the couch.

I know he was thinking about it, knowing how easy it would be to screw me. He'd already thrown away a thousand dollars he probably didn't have, money he coulda sent home. He coulda saved another thousand by walking away then and there.

He got up as if to leave but then went to the kitchen, returning a moment later with a peeled orange. He separated the segments and placed one in my mouth. His unexpected gentleness reminded me of when Jennifer explored my lips, delicately mapping them. I chased that painful memory away and gazed into his eyes.

He returned my gaze, holding it steady.

"You're such an asshole, Bash."

"And Hannah, you are a crazy bitch."

I grasped his ripped bicep with one hand and pulled his face down to me with the other. There was no awkward fumbling or hesitation as our tongues returned to a sensual default, each already knowing every bump and crevice of the other's mouth. In one fluid motion, we slid back onto the couch. He straddled me. Our tongues stayed locked together while I unbuckled his belt and he ran his hand under my top over my breast.

Just as I was about to seize his hard dick, I pulled my hand away and pushed his shoulder back. "Wait one fucking minute. You're here 'cause you owe me money. If you think banging me changes that, get off."

I beat on his chest and shoulder until he grabbed my arms.

"Hannah, Hannah, calm down. The money's on the table." Sure enough, a bundle of bills were there, neatly wrapped together with a rubber band. "It is yours. I will not touch it again. If you still want me out, I will leave now. I'll honour our agreement too."

I took my eyes off the money and buried my face in the couch. "I don't know what the hell I'm doing. Sorry, Bash." A tear trickled down the side of my face, followed by another. Bash wiped them with a finger, then cradled my cheeks and kissed me softly. We melted into one another.

"No, Bash, no pity party for me. Let's just fuck, the way we used to, before the kids. Before life went from crazy to mental. We knew how to do that, we got something right, remember?"

He gave me a look that said, Are you sure?

I nodded and together we travelled back nine years.

———

With Bash in the bathroom, I counted the money, then hid the bundle. The thousand meant I could stay where I was, as I was sure Jimmy hadn't yet rented the apartment. When Bash came back he got dressed, but not before I eyeballed his stacked body one last time. He was nearing fifty, so a slight paunch was expected. But this newfound softer, more mature side ramped up his manliness.

He caught me looking. He flexed his muscles in a mock Schwarzenegger bodybuilding pose and laughed.

"You know, you're still fucking hot. I hate you," I had to say.

"You still have it too, Hannah. No one has ever made me so satisfied."

"No—we—we still have it." I ran my fingers through an opening in his shirt and tugged at his hairy chest.

"This doesn't change anything, Hannah."

I lit a cigarette. "That's up to you. You can still play dad. But yeah, I'm not down for suddenly becoming friends with benefits."

He pulled on his body-hugging T-shirt. "You can call it whatever you want. But I kept my word. When was the last time someone did that for you?"

I exhaled. "I had to give up my kid for you to step up, so you can skip the Saint Lebanon shit. It was so overdue. Besides, I'm still fucked."

156

I had told him why I'd needed the money after boning, while we were still lying next to each other.

"Messing with bikers will get you in big trouble. You are lucky they did not break your fingers. Running a grow-op with someone with bad acne and Spiderman underwear would have been crazy, very crazy. I cannot imagine the trouble you would have been in. What were you thinking?"

"I was thinking each plant yields four hundred and fifty-three grams, ten bucks a gram, times fifteen plants. That's $67,950 a harvest. You have to sell lots of donairs to make that kind of money.

Bash put his coat on. "Sixty-seven thousand dollars, selling one gram at a time? Not only is the math bad, but your plan—"

"Lay off. Did I ask how'd you score your two grand?"

"Did I ask you where you get your drugs?"

"No, but it's not hard to figure out it's from Tyler."

"Yes, from the Teddy bear." We chuckled.

"But now you have nothing to do with a crazy drug operation or bikers or the police or any bullshit. You are a free agent. You can use your time wisely. It is the same plan you signed, but maybe now you will take it seriously."

I thought about what he said. I really needed a toke and asked Bash to join in and keep me company. He declined as he was already late for work and left. I was glad his lecture wasn't any longer than it was, but I missed him as soon as he walked out the door.

22

AXEL

I COULD SMELL Daddy. He was here before. That got me curious but also excited to see him. Mom didn't say anything. She was in a quiet mood but I saw her get Tyler's comic books ready for the pawnshop and she threw his toothbrush out. Booyah!

The next morning when we got ready to meet the new foster mother, Mom was really cranky and I stayed as far away as I could. But in our small apartment there was nowhere to hide from all her complaining.

"You're not wearing those clothes again. I don't want them to think we're trailer trash."

"Can you possibly spill any more of your oatmeal?"

"Where did you put my phone? How many times do I have— Oh, there it is."

"Do I have to do everything around here?"

"Don't give me that look."

"Sometimes you're such a pain in the ass. Why do I put up with this?"

When she found a drawing I made of me on a truck with a monster flying and breathing fire onto my body, she stopped yelling.

I said I was sorry for being a pain in the ass and that she shouldn't have to put up with me and that it's good I am going away. But I don't want to go away.

I wanted her to say that I was talking stupid. She didn't. So I dropped to the kitchen floor and cried and asked for another chance. I promised I'd be better at cleaning up, that I'd listen more and never get in trouble at school again.

"Christ, Ax." She shook her head. "It's not your fault, okay? It's not."

"So do I still have to go?"

Instead of answering, she got quiet and made me breakfast. I knew then she is for-real sending me away.

23

HANNAH

W HEN WE ARRIVED at Diane's office, Doreen, who was the new foster parent, was already there to meet us. I didn't know there was such a thing as a single foster parent and immediately thought she had to be one tough old bitty. Ax smiled at her and said that she looked like Auntie Em from the original *Wizard of Oz*, Ax's all-time favourite movie. He was right.

"Aunt Em? Now there's a classic." Doreen rhymed off one of Auntie Em's lines. "Almira Gulch, just because you own half the county—"

"—doesn't mean that you have the power to run the rest of us," Ax finished it off and smiled.

Fuck.

Diane moved things along with some of the simpler details. "Hannah, you can call Doreen's house anytime, within reason, of course. Visits will be in your home, we'll have a fixed day and time, but you can work out more visits. Just clear it with me first. Axel says he has a good friend named Jimmy and he can visit him too."

I made a point of looking bored, but my insides rumbled as though a deep hollowness was threatening to suck me in. I wished it would.

"You can also see him at school," Diane said. "You can pop in and take him out to lunch. Most kids love that."

"I don't need you to tell me I can take my son to lunch. I already know what he likes." I gave Diane a pissed look.

Ax dug his toe into the carpet. I don't remember ever pulling him out of school and taking him to lunch. Maybe he was thinking the same.

Diane paused for a moment. "We encourage overnights of course, but we recommend everyone get themselves settled first. Maybe after a few weeks. And you, little man," she turned to Ax, "have to remember to pack your favourite toys, clothes, toothbrush … whatever you want to bring, because we want this to be like your home away from home."

"He's not taking anything valuable," I said. "There's no telling if it's safe, know what I mean?"

Ax didn't have many toys besides the few his father had dropped off months ago, just some Play-Doh, two Hero Factory sets (both missing pieces), and a construction truck set given by the food bank. He loved them all, but he'd be alright leaving them behind.

Diane did her best to soften me up. She sucked up to me by asking questions about Ax's routines, likes, and preferences. I didn't appreciate her playing nice. They were taking my child, taking the last thing that was all mine. There was nothing nice or civilized about that. I'd have preferred she got in my face and called me the loser mother she thought I was so I could hammer right back at her. That woulda been a fair fight. Maybe not. I woulda destroyed her and enjoyed it.

Diane seemed to read my mood and said, "This is where Doreen gets to see that you mean business, Hannah. That you are committed to making this work and will help her to recreate the temporary home that your son needs."

I got the hint. "He doesn't like surprises," I said. "If you change plans from something he really wants, expect him to go passive-aggressive or he'll just go nuclear. Sometimes he zones out and says he hears voices. Just ignore it. He'll drive you crazy with questions but it's not hard to shut that down." I wasn't holding back any boastfulness. "He needs his screen time, chocolate, meat. For breakfast he likes oatmeal, but Cap'n Crunch will do if you have nothing else. That's a good dinner for him too, along with a side of Jos Louis." I loved messing with the foster freaks' middle-class sensibilities.

"He's good on his own. He may cry like a baby sometimes when he doesn't get what he wants, but you don't need to baby him, he's a tough kid. I raised him that way."

An awkward silence followed.

"Well, it looks like we're going to have loads of fun, Axel," Doreen said. "I've got a swing set and a tree house in the back. In the winter, I flood the backyard and make a skating rink. Do you know how to skate, Axel?"

"No, but I really wanna learn."

"I'm gonna teach them how to skate," I said.

"Them, who's them?" Ax said.

Ax had been wanting to learn for a long time. Once, he and Faye went through my closet and found some pictures of when I was a girl. There were a bunch of me in figure skating outfits. It was funny for them to see me in a tight, glittery costume. There was a photo of me on the ice with a stick. They couldn't tell at first that it was me 'cause I was wearing a helmet and face mask. There were good days back then, before boyfriends like Kevin came along.

I told them being on the ice and playing ringette was a lot of fun. That my ringette days were, hands down, my best memories as a kid. I let them know how their mom was really good at it, one of the best, and because I was fast and strong, people respected me and it made me feel good.

I didn't tell them I'd hoped it would make Papa feel that way about me too. He valued athletic glory and watched sports even more than his war documentaries and movies. Unfortunately, ringette didn't make that happen. Nothing ever did.

So when Faye asked if she could play ringette and Ax joined in and said that it would be so cool to see his sister dressed as a gladiator, I said no. I took the pictures back. "It's too dangerous." But I said someday I would teach them both how to skate.

I looked at the foster freak. She was probably middle-aged,

couldn't have a kid, or no one wanted to be with her. So she was going to save the world and play Supermom one kid at a time. She'd ply my Ax with ideas and stupid stuff about fairness and compassion so he'd be a wimp and never be ready for life. "You know, maybe this isn't such a good idea after all. Ax is doing great. I'm doing great. Maybe you can find a kid who really needs this."

Diane pivoted and thanked Doreen, sending her off. She asked Ax to sit in the waiting area, while she talked with me in the conference room.

"What's going on, Hannah?"

"I just need a smoke."

"Fine." Diane walked out with me and made me pace the parking lot while I smoked.

"I get it, you're having second thoughts, probably feel like crap about this. Most parents do," Diane said. "But we talked about this. You've got shit to clean up and things to work on."

I took a long drag of my cigarette. Maybe Diane and Bashir were right. Maybe I could use the break. But part of me didn't really believe it. Part of me, more than anything, wanted to kill Tyler for screwing me over, and for putting me on this runaway train. "I'm not sure I need this anymore," I said to her.

"Are you saying you don't want this?"

I stopped walking. "You're gonna keep Ax, and I'll never get him back."

"Six months, Hannah, we signed on the dotted line. You're still in his life, you're still his mother."

"I said no. Weren't you listening?"

She let me catch my breath before going into lecture mode. "I really believe you and Axel need this. I believe it so much that I'm willing to take him into care without an agreement and without your blessing. I'm prepared to let the judge decide within five days. The judge might tell me to piss off and send Axel home. Or the judge might side with us. In which case, you run the risk of losing—for the time being, or maybe longer—the rights you'd have had if you stayed with the agreement."

"You've been fucking with me the whole time." I stepped into her space.

Diane took a deep breath but didn't back down. "I've been straight-up with you, one hundred percent. Can you say the same to me?"

I couldn't. I couldn't say anything. Had she somehow gotten wind of my grow-op? A cold wind blew through me and I zipped up my jacket and looked away. I left Diane standing there and walked back into the building to get Ax. She followed.

"Have Axel here tomorrow at nine as we agreed," she said. "Or we bring him in and we take it before the judge. Your choice."

24

AXEL

WHEN MOM BROUGHT me to Diane's office to give me to Doreen, she gave me a goodbye hug. I asked her how many sleeps six months was. She said not that many.

She said we needed this break and that she needed to get stuff done.

When I need a break, I play outside. I said I could help her get her stuff done, and that Jimmy would help too. She smiled but it was a tired smile. She said everything was going to be alright and that she would call me tomorrow and see me soon. She said something to Diane then ran for the bus. I waited for her to look back but she didn't. I waved anyway.

I didn't want her to go. I already said I was sorry for being a pain in the ass. Maybe she didn't get that it included about the fire, the poo, about running away, about losing Faye, about everything. She didn't believe all the promises I made to be good forever.

Doreen made me take my shoes off before entering the house. I tried to hide the holes in my socks. They were my favourite Hulk socks. Doreen gave me new clothes from Walmart and Value Village and washed my old ones. She said she would keep them safe and sound until I go home. That made me feel better.

I like my new clothes and having a bedroom all to myself every night. But I don't like her cooking: herb-roasted chicken dinner (I asked if she knew how to do McNuggets instead) with sautéed kale (gross), candied beet salad (double gross) and mushroom quinoa (only a pig would eat that)—things I never saw or heard of in my life. I also didn't like her telling me to clean up after myself. I really thought she was a bitch then, but I didn't say that.

Usually, Mom lets me do anything I want unless she's in a bad mood.

When Doreen told me I could choose any bedtime book instead of my tablet or TV, I threw the books on the floor, then hid in my closet so she couldn't smack me. I didn't talk to her until bedtime when she told me to remember to pee.

If Mom doesn't want me, I won't be anybody's. Every day I fight with Doreen. I don't like washing, and she's so picky about wiping my bum, and I have to change my clothes every day. Every night I sneak Fruit Roll-Ups and bars from the pantry even if I'm not hungry. I keep some in my closet too, just in case. Doreen found some of the wrappers. I said it was mice and she should lay glue traps. Then I said the other foster kid, a big girl who's lived here a long time already, made the mess. I also said the girl beat me up when I was left alone with her, but really, she just never talks to me.

One time or maybe more, I trashed my room and said I would kill someone or myself. Usually, that's when my other voice came.

You're safe now, why are you so mad?

"Shut up."

You're crabby. You live in a house now. Isn't that what you wanted? Your own room, no whupping, no yelling—except for you. What else do you want?

"I don't know. Just leave me alone and stop messin' with my head."

Doreen heard this and told Diane the next time she came for a visit.

I sat on the stairs and listened.

"I don't know what else I can do," Doreen said. "I treat him like gold, he gets safe, consistent, predictable routines. I check all the boxes, but he fights me at every turn."

"Doreen, he's been locked into a fight-flight-freeze mode all his life. These are his default settings and they take practically nothing to activate. He knows how to survive, but living is new to him. Took me twenty-five years to quit smoking, I bounce in and out of diets all the time, and we expect an eight-year-old to undergo a personality shift in weeks?"

"Guess that's not realistic." Doreen sighed.

"Has he tried to run away recently?"

Doreen hesitated. "No."

"Then you've done exceptionally well."

The only thing I understood was about me running. It's true. I stopped doing that.

I started to do overnight visits, then weekends with Mom. But then I started to miss Doreen. I know that's weird. But she always has dinner at the same time and never has other people doing sleepovers and parties and never yells, even when I'm bad.

One morning when I was supposed to see Mom, I wouldn't eat my oatmeal. I said it was like glue, that Doreen was fat and mean, and I would not go to school because my tummy hurt—which was true. I said if they made me go, I would run away.

"If you don't go to school, your mother will be disappointed when she comes to pick you up, only to find that you've run off. Is that what you want?"

I looked up at her and said I wanted to see Mom.

But that's a lie.

Shut up. It's not a lie if no one hears it.

You can hear it, so that counts as a lie.

Shut up.

I didn't want to make Mom sad, so I went to school so she could see me after.

25

HANNAH

THE DAY AFTER Ax went into care, Diane didn't waste any time and drove me to a parenting group at the Dartmouth North Community Centre. I rolled my eyes as we pulled up. I'd been there before, when they made me take parenting and child development courses. Under a million watts of fluorescent lights, everyone was so fucking cheery. People working there were always so damned nice, treating me like a valued guest when really I was forced to be there. Other people drop by to chat, to hang, to check the job board, to take out a library book, to kill time. It's really a prison with Friday square dances. Get a life, y'all.

"Don't roll your eyes at me, Hannah, it's not negotiable."

"You know this is gonna be about blaming parents? Ax needs to be in some sort of anger management boot camp, this is dumb."

"Non-negotiable," she repeated as she led me to Iris, the group facilitator, before leaving.

The parents all gathered in one of the meeting rooms. Concrete walls did nothing to muffle the trash talk in the gym beside us during the youth basketball program, or the smells of the seniors' cooking club across the foyer. Curry, I figured. Fart food. You'd think they'd know better and save the old-timers some grief.

Iris, a social worker, described the core objectives of the group then started us off with introductions. She then said that every unwanted behaviour was a child trying to be heard and understood. That cracked me up and I couldn't keep my mouth shut. "That's 'cause the little shits can't shut up." I got a bunch of parents laughing.

Later, Iris talked about engaging our kids in an approach called Collaborative Problem Solving. "That's easy," I said, "the kids go away, I collaborate at the bar, problem solved." More laughter. It was starting to be fun.

One stuck-up parent in a blue sweater started mouthing off at me. "Let Iris talk, or just leave. This is no joke."

Who wears sweater sets? "I can't leave. Why don't you? This Collaborative Problem Solving stuff is a joke. I mean really, do you suggest I just let my Ax solve the problem of his peeing the bed, setting a restaurant on fire, getting into trouble at school, and running away?"

"So you got problems, your kid's got problems, guess what, we all do," Sweater Woman said. "That's why we're here."

"You mean you want to be here? Anybody else?"

Another woman with pearl earrings and dyed blonde hair with black roots raised her hand. Did she and Sweater Woman come together in some chauffeured limo?

"Two out of nine," I said.

"Someone can count," Sweater Woman said.

I glared at that bitch.

Iris finally took back control of the group and got us through the first hour. That was the floor show, I guessed. Outside, while I was smoking, Iris approached me.

"So you're here because you have to be, not because you want to be, as are others."

"Nothing personal, but this is a crock of shit." I exhaled.

"You're honest, I'll give you that. Maybe it is a crock to you. But if just one parent, one parent gets something out of this, and she winds up getting her kids back, or this helps prevent losing them, isn't it worth it?"

I shrugged. "It's still a waste of my time."

"Tell you what," she said. "You can sleep through this with your eyes open, just let me do my job. In return, I'll tell your worker you were a star."

I thought about that. Steffi never did parenting classes. In fact, our family never really talked about Papa's outbursts, not to anybody, not even each other, except to blame whoever got him going. That was usually me, whether I deserved it or not. We kept our mouths shut. It was a survival strategy baked into our Belenko-Braun DNA. It was much easier to shut down whenever the old man detonated than it was to confront or soothe him. Mama had that tactic down like an Olympic athlete. The minefield that was my life before moving out from my parents' was always best manoeuvred with stillness and immobility.

"As long as I keep my mouth shut, I pass?"

"No better deal in town."

"Okay, I can do silence. Just get better coffee, eh."

"You can bring your own coffee and we have a deal." She started to walk back in but then stopped. "One other thing. Why wouldn't you want to be that one parent?"

I had no answer for her. Instead, I took a drag, then crushed my butt beneath my shoe. For some strange reason, the smoke didn't sit well.

———

Weeks later, while volunteering at the food bank, I yelled at one of the members who stuffed a few extra donuts into his coat. I made him empty his pockets, uncovering not only two squashed, stale apple crullers, but a half-smoked cigarette, unwrapped mints crusted with crumbs, dirt, and hair, a used toothpick, and a hairbrush.

"Jesus, bloody Christ, leave the poor lad alone," St. Frances the Potty said.

"But he—"

"He tried to help himself to a couple of stale donuts. I know that. Every time he comes in to warm up, I say fill yer boots. I save them crullers and put them out when I see him coming. We don't need no bouncer, Hannah."

I straightened the man's coat out and mumbled an apology, then handed him another cruller.

Not having to care for Ax meant I didn't need a part-time job. I had already agreed to therapy and parenting classes, but Diane knew I wasn't going to structure the rest of my day around no stupid pilates or meditation. That was for Sweater Woman. Sitting around and boredom were trouble for me. With that in mind, Diane had made me choose to either work or volunteer. I picked volunteering, two days a week at the food bank. Since I was younger and stronger than most of the other volunteers, Frances gave me the loading job as well as the task of keeping the coffee and snacks going. I also unpacked and sorted larger, heavier donations and purchases.

"Go take a break, things are quiet at the moment," Frances suggested.

"I don't need a break." What I really wanted was a cigarette. I'd quit smoking for the first time ever only a week before. Diane sat me down and added up all that I had spent on smoking. Once she got past twenty-five thousand, she said, "That could've been an SUV, a down payment on a house, or a luxury cruise around the world. Plus, judges hate smokers. They see them as weak and desperate." I'm sure she was bullshitting, but she made her point. I stopped.

Still, I missed the way the harsh smoke itched the back of my throat and flooded my lungs, providing both punishment and relief. Since quitting, I could smell how disgusting the apartment was. I was enjoying chili, omelettes, Chinese food, and donairs like never before. And Bash said I smelled better, which made me playfully punch him in the shoulder.

"Take the break," Frances repeated.

I stepped out into the cool autumn air, away from the smokers. I opened Candy Crush and saw that Jimmy was now ten levels ahead after trailing me for days. That pissed me off. I played for a bit but then lost a level, which forced me to either wait to play again, beg for more lives from friends, or buy more. I bought more. I ignored a bunch of phone calls before I realized I'd been playing for an hour. I rushed back into the church.

"There you are. Your ride's been waiting," Frances pointed at Diane, who was on the phone but waved me over then hung up.

"You forgot, didn't you?"

Normally, I'd have made up an excuse, deflected my screw-up, or blamed someone else. Instead, I owned up. "Candy Crush."

"I've been trying to call you for the last half hour." Diane glared at me. "You've got your parenting class in like ten minutes. Get your things."

My parenting course, my anger management class, and individual therapy had all started off bad. They tried to get me to "take emotional risks" and "show vulnerability." Sure, I could say what a brute Papa was, but no more. I'd missed several sessions until word got back to Diane, who then started driving me to some of them.

"Can't you just chill for once and stop breaking my balls? It's like four minutes away," I said as we got into her car.

"One, you're a woman, you haven't got any balls, so don't make like you do. It's self-demeaning. Two, I'll chill when Axel is back with you. Three, what level are you at?"

"Huh?"

"Anything less than fifteen hundred on Jelly means you're a total loser. Give it up and play chess or checkers or something."

"I'm up for chess. Let's play. There's a board at the drop-in centre."

"You're stalling."

"That's 'cause this stupid parent group is filled with Stepford wives. They're like prissy suburban house-bitches bending over for their husbands." I pictured Mama, and my stomach stirred with rage. I couldn't tell if it was resentment or pity that I had for her. For the first time in decades, I thought of the time I'd walked in on Father, piss drunk on top of Mama, whose eyes were popping out.

"We go through this every week, you're being ridiculous." Diane brought me back to the present, for which I was grateful. "There are parents from all walks of life. Every one of them has a story, not one of them is a perfect parent or comes from a neat bungalow with a backyard pool."

"Not that it makes any difference." I fought against drifting images pulling me back to Stittsville, to the golf-and-country club, to Napoli's, to my family, and to Jennifer …

"This is bullshit." I banged on Diane's dashboard.

She kept driving, fully calm. "Seems that way, doesn't it? Sitting in a room full of strangers practicing parenting strategies when you've single-handedly raised Axel and Faye all these years?"

"Fuck, yeah."

"Then having to go see a therapist who's digging into your insides like a backhoe."

"It's such bullshit."

"Counselling and parenting class can seem that way at first. You're being challenged. Everything you did, everything you learned, everything you ran from is staring back at you. You're vulnerable and exposed in a way you've never allowed yourself to be. It's scary, isn't it?"

I watched some kids playing by the road as we drove by. "Yeah, and I can't say I'm enjoying this."

"But you've made real progress."

"I'm glad you think so. But don't go thinking I'm happy Ax set that fire, or that the fire department called you."

Diane stayed quiet. She doesn't usually do silence. She was hiding something.

"Hang on a second, it wasn't the firefighter who called you on me, was it?"

She bit her lip. "You know I can't discuss it, so let's drop it."

"Who, then?" Doubtful a firefighter would hide behind an anonymous report. Someone I knew had ratted me out. I went through some potential snitches: Peter, the kitchen guys or servers at the Double Happiness, literally anyone at the school, Bash. It had to be Bash, except that didn't make sense. Tyler, that little shit.

"*Who* doesn't change anything. If anything, this has given you an opportunity, remember?"

"I need a smoke."

"And I want a glass of wine the size of a fish tank every fricking day. But I made a pledge." Diane showed off her gold ring. I noticed for the first time it had the Alcoholics Anonymous symbol on it. "My wife gave it to me last week. Ten years dry."

Jimmy had the same ring.

"What the—You're a ..."

"Dyke? Drunk? Whatever. It was worth everything I went through." Diane pulled into the community centre. "You don't get a gold ring here. You get to be a better parent. You get your son back, and you get some dignity. Now get out of my car," she said with a wink.

I looked back at Diane with an appreciative nod before rushing into the building. The group hadn't started, other parents were still settling in. She was right, there were parents from all over.

Sweater Woman dropped out of the course. Hahaha. Or maybe her cleaning woman ran off with her man and the kids. The only dude in attendance was young and ripped. I figured he either had to be here like me or he was gay and didn't have a clue about kids. He coulda been a young Bash. Hell, if not for Bash and I working things out now, I'd have hooked up with him. He was cute enough.

As our group talked about our different parenting issues, it became obvious to me that a couple of other moms babied their kids. And they wondered why their kids were whiners who never listened. Then there was a mother who said very little, like really uptight. When she did talk, it was about her husband. She reminded me of my mom. She said her daughter stopped talking to her years ago and she wanted to make it right. I wanted to tell her it was probably too late, 'cause it certainly felt that way for me and Steffi. I kept my mouth shut, though. Didn't want to jinx things. What if someday, it was too late for Ax and me?

SPRING 2019

26

AXEL

E VERY TIME I come home for sleepovers, I smell Daddy again. I asked Mom if he visited when I was away. She didn't answer at first. Finally, she said sometimes Daddy drops things off and has been hanging around more. She said it like she was making a wish. I checked to see if her fingers were crossed. They weren't, but her shoes were tied so that counts.

Then, one visit, Daddy was already there waiting for me. He bought me a LEGO muscle car. It has two hundred and fifty-eight pieces and is for seven-plus-year-olds. It took the whole visit to build, but we took breaks and he took me to Burger King. The next time I had a sleepover, he was there again and he did a sleepover too. I think it means Daddy isn't mad at me anymore. I just hope I don't screw up and get him mad and make him go away again.

27

HANNAH

A FEW MONTHS after Ax had been in care, Bash picked me up in his Neon after my parenting group. He asked if all this effort was making any difference.

"Dunno, maybe."

"Really? For what, almost two months you would have a fit when you talked about it and called it a stupid waste of time. It is a miracle, *Alhamdulillah*, praise be to Allah." Bash was mocking me.

"Piss off." I jabbed his shoulder as we turned onto the busy main street. He responded with a playful grab of my neck. For a millisecond, my body seized up.

"The road, watch the fucking road," I yelled. All I could think about was the car accident with my father all those years before.

I transferred high schools after Jennifer died. My three years at St. Paulina were a haze of weed, awful sex with boys, an endless cycle of detentions for skipping, and suspensions for "conduct injurious to the moral tone of the school." The school contacted Papa after I got caught smoking in the washroom. He was royally pissed for being called away from work and tore into me before we even got out of the school parking lot. He grabbed my MP3 player while I was listening to it and threatened to stop the car and crush it under the wheel.

"Give it back," I screamed.

"First you tell me when this bullshit stops."

"When you stop being such a pig."

He shoved my face, pressing my head against the window.

Instead of cowering as I had done in the past, I called him a fucking goon.

"I should kick you out of the house for talking to your papa like that. Go live on the street like other losers. *Da*, maybe I teach you a lesson you will learn."

"Go ahead. I'm seventeen, I can apply for student welfare. And welfare will chase you down, so you'll wind up paying for it."

"Who told you such bullshit?"

Officer Lee, but I wasn't going to tell him that. "My friends at school who wouldn't put up with their parents' shit anymore, that's how I know."

He looked at me with disgust and scorn. With one hand on the steering wheel, he reached for my neck, but I bit his outstretched hand.

"Stupid little bitch," he shouted. Distracted, he drove through the stop sign. Out of the corner of my eye, I caught the blur of a fast-approaching object on his side. By the time I could register that it was an SUV, it slammed into us, causing a sound like a bomb going off. It knocked me around. I was caught in a moment of stunned silence until someone pulled me out of the car. I almost tripped over sharp plastic shards on the ground—our headlights. It wasn't until I sniffed the heated metal and sulphur from the crushed exhaust that I realized I'd been in an accident. I looked back at the car. All the windows on the driver's side were smashed. The door had collapsed onto Papa. He was slumped to one side of his seat, motionless. Blood dripping from his head onto bits of glass. I wanted to scream but couldn't move. I only knew for sure he was alive when I heard cursing in Russian.

About a week later, before work at the deli, my freckle-faced co-worker Floyd and I got high and made out at the far end of the parking lot. A high school dropout, he was about my only friend at work. He slaved away in the bakery and could be counted on for weed whenever I was tapped out. I came in early instead of putting up with Papa's moaning and groaning after the accident. I ended up giving Floyd a blow job instead.

Afterward, we leaned on a minivan and had a butt. He said he was quitting the job.

"What?"

"I'm done, today will be my last day."

"Shit, two years here. About time, I guess. But why today?"

"I got a ride to Halifax. It leaves Friday."

"Looky here, aren't we the free spirit? That doesn't give us much time to celebrate your freedom."

"The thing is, Hannah, I want you to come."

"You want me to drop everything and just go with you to Halifax?" I had to laugh.

"This is no joke," he said, pulling his pants back on.

I lit a butt. "We get high, we fuck. It works. What would I do in Halifax? What are *you* going to do in Halifax?"

"I've got an uncle who can set me up with something."

"Oh, well, that sure sounds like a solid plan. Why didn't you say so in the first place?"

He pretended like he didn't hear my sarcasm. "I love you. We can be together. No more sneaking behind vans and the changing room, no more rushing home. We can get our own place and start fresh."

"What the fuck are you talking about?"

"You hate it here even more than me. I want to look after you."

"Yeah, but ..." He had a point. No one had ever said they were in love with me before. I mean actually said it. I didn't even dare to dream that someone would commit themselves to me. I might as well have wished for a solid-gold ringette stick.

I studied him. His freckles popped out where the light hit them. He could use a haircut—the grunge look didn't suit him. His happy-face T-shirt was really dorky. I could do a whole lot worse, though.

"Friday, heh?"

Floyd smiled. "Our new life can begin in three days."

"This is pretty fucked up. I wasn't expecting this." I blew smoke away from his face.

"Yeah, well, do you want to be slicing bologna and living in Shitsville for the rest of your life?"

I needed to think about that and took a deep breath before exhaling. Could I take another day of looking after Papa and being ordered around like a lapdog? Probably not. But I couldn't just go. He'd almost killed himself trying to hurt me. Did I really think things would get better if I stuck around?

"Let me think about it. We'll talk after work."

I was in a daze for the rest of the evening, thinking about Floyd's plan, when a vaguely familiar voice startled me.

"Hello, Hannah."

"Sorry, do I know ... Wait, aren't you the cop at my school?" It was Officer Lee out of uniform. She looked so different with her long, straight black hair, ripped jeans, and a lavender tank top. For a cop, she was smoking hot. Not that I was attracted to Lee like I was to Jennifer. In fact, I hadn't felt interested in another girl since. But then, no one had been a friend like that.

"It's my day off. I want to catch Johnny Depp's new *Pirates of the Caribbean* movie. I forget what it's called, but it doesn't matter. If all he does is read the phone book in Turkish, I'm happy."

I grinned. "*Dead Man's Chest*, it's called *Dead Man's Chest*."

"Great, then I'm going to do *Dead Man's Chest*." Lee ordered some honey ham. "You got a break coming? I thought maybe I could share some information, stuff you'd want to know."

"What kind of stuff?"

"About the accident."

"How do you know about the accident?"

"Because I've been concerned about you for a long time."

That was weird. "You said you were off duty?"

"I am, me and Johnny got a date."

I couldn't hide a smile. For a cop, she was chill. I was curious. "I get a break in an hour. Meet me behind the liquor store where we smoke."

An hour later, Lee was out there sipping a can of Red Bull.

"I'd have made you out for a Starbucks latte mochaccino kind of person," I said, pointing to the can.

"I am, but that's breakfast. Here, have one." She handed me a Red Bull.

I opened it and began sipping, then lit up a smoke.

"Your father has just been served with a summons," she said.

"What's that?"

"It means he got ticketed for running a stop sign."

"What? If you mean that accident, it makes no sense, we got hit. My dad's hip was broken and he got a concussion."

"He ran through a stop sign, you said so yourself. This led to him causing a dangerous accident. The other driver was seriously injured."

"That's bullshit. We got hit."

"Your father lost control of the vehicle. You were interviewed right after. It appears he may have assaulted you, which led to the accident. At least that's what the officer pieced together from the physical evidence and your interview."

I bit into my lip. "No, no way."

"He said you were pretty upset and fully aware of what happened but probably didn't realize where your words would lead. Right now, your father probably doesn't know how damaging your statement is to him. But if he fights the ticket, or if the other driver sues, he will eventually find out what you told the officer."

"I'll deny it, or I'll just say that cop lied, the other driver lied, I hallucinated, whatever."

"Do what you have to do. But you should also know that this assault is a chargeable offence."

"That's bullshit, I'd never make a charge or whatever you call it."

"Of course you wouldn't, he'd kill you."

I crushed my smoke beneath my shoe. "Then why are you doing this?"

"So you'll be ready."

"What are you talking about, be ready? Like I'm gonna hire some goons to protect me?"

"You make a statement, we lay a charge, you file a restraining order, we find you somewhere safe, set you up."

"This is stupid. My break is over, and so is this conversation." I turned away.

Lee grabbed my hand. "Maybe not now, maybe not for a while. But you can always come back on this. No one deserves to be treated like that."

She slipped me her card. I looked at it, memorized the number, then tore it in half and threw it into the air. If what she said was true, I could be in big trouble.

As Floyd filled up the day-old tray of bread, I gave him a thumbs-up. I was getting out of town before Papa beat the crap out of me again.

I returned home from work late in the evening hoping that he would be asleep. We'd set up a bed for him in the living room so he didn't have to navigate the stairs with his hip injury. This meant that he was positioned in the centre of the house, aware of and watching everyone coming and going.

"You work late, again? You bring home more kolbassa?" he asked from his La-Z-Boy as I walked in.

"Yes, Papa. How are you feeling?"

"How do you think? Did you forget I have broken hip and concussion?"

All my father ever did was question and command me. He'd even respond with questions to my questions. He'd probably always been that way, but it really pissed me off that day. I was putting an end to it. In three days I was going to Halifax with Floyd.

"Get for me some kolbassa. Put lots of your mother's beet horseradish."

As I went to the kitchen to do what he'd ordered, I wondered whether kolbassa would be good road-trip food. I had no idea how far Halifax was. I placed a plate of the sliced sausage and horseradish beside him. He was engrossed in a World War Two documentary on the siege of Stalingrad, one of the many he'd made me watch as a kid.

He shifted and moaned. "Bullshit hip."

"It's only been a week since the surgery. Did the doctor say—"

"Four weeks to four months, maybe longer." He turned the sound down. "Did you think I was not listening?"

"No, Papa."

"Did you know the police were in our home today?"

I tensed up. Fuck, Lee wasn't bullshitting me. "No, Papa, I was at school, then work. How would I know?"

"You tell me."

I bit my tongue and stared at the images on the screen profiling a Russian sniper named Zaitsev who had killed two hundred and twenty-five Germans at Stalingrad. I had planned to play dumb and not mention anything about Officer Lee visiting me at work today.

I asked what the police officer was after.

"He give me ticket, he say I failed to stop. That is bad for insurance, but it is also bullshit. That other driver changed lane and speeded up then hit us, *da*?"

"Is that how you remember it?" I didn't take my eyes off the Russian sniper.

"What you mean is how I remember? What other possible way could this happen to me? I call my lawyer who say be ready for being sued. The best defence is offence. I will sue. Insurance people will see police report. He say you will give report too."

"You're right, Papa, this is bullshit, he hit us. He came out of nowhere."

"Exactly. But policeman saying he has witness. I have witness, you. Why did the police not talk to you before, I do not know. Nobody sues Youri Belenko. We will beat this stupid no-stop ticket."

Fuck. I was that witness. Even if I denied remembering that, it was on record. I was so fucked.

He turned the sound back up and artillery fire and the rumble of tanks filled the living room as we watched the Russian army force the Germans into a humiliating surrender. Papa raised his clenched fists in a silent cheer. He turned the volume down again. "Hannah?"

"Yes."

"Today your papa feel ... old. Very old, and broken."

I dared a long look at him. This was a startling revelation for him to share. For sure, he looked feeble, almost scared. At that moment, I felt guilty for the accident, completely responsible for his pain and downfall.

He continued. "I need you like never before. I need you to look after me. Ivan and your mother will have to take over business until I come back. It is very busy now that I have contracts in Nova Scotia. I want you to quit your job, come home every day after school. I trust no one else to do this. This is the best plan for the family." He wiped away a tear. A tear. I had only ever seen Papa cry when Russia beat Canada for gold at the hockey world championships, and I was just little then.

I realized that despite walking out on his country, he was a proud Russian. He would die defending Mother Russia, and yet he'd never been back, never even spoken of returning to see his parents, his extended family, or his friends. I wondered if he considered himself an outcast. If those back home would now see him as a sad, pathetic traitor who had once rolled the dice and came up snake eyes. I actually felt sorry for him. He was pathetic.

He handed me the empty plate. "More, please."

"More" and "please?" *More* of him wasn't something I could take for much longer. But it was exactly what I was going to get every day. *Please*? He never used language like that with me. People who dominate and control don't ask nicely. Was he becoming desperate, or had the accident softened him? No, he was still that Russian sniper: cold, calculating, strategic.

"Yes, Papa." I went into the kitchen, thinking of Floyd and our new life together. As much as it sounded great, I couldn't imagine abandoning Papa at this time. More than ever, I felt trapped.

"Hann, Hannah? You disappeared again. Where did you go this time?" Bash asked.

I shook my head. "You know you were such an asshole after Faye was born?"

"*Ya sharmouta.*"

"No, you're the bitch."

He banged the steering wheel, but then took a deep breath. "Stop. Let's not go there. Yes, maybe, maybe I was an asshole. I was very stressed. But you, you were scary."

I shrugged. "Maybe I was scary."

"Maybe?" we said in unison before laughing.

"Hey, Ax loves the Wii U, I can't get him off it. I'm not sure that was a good thing in the long run, but thanks for coming to see Ax again. It means a lot to him, and to me. I never thought it would help me get my shit together, but it has."

Bash looked at me as though I were a stranger. "Who is this woman beside me that is suddenly calm and polite, thanking me when she would have bitten my head off before? You are an imposter. Help, police, help, get out of my car. No, wait, I like this. Come to Papa."

"You know I don't like it when you call yourself Papa. It creeps me out."

"Brad Pitt, come to your Brad Pitt, then."

I broke out laughing. "Brad Pitt? Man, are you old. Gimme Kit Harington."

"You want to be with a woman?"

"No, stupid, Kit Harington ... *Game of Thrones* ... 'You know nothing, Jon Snow.'" I gave him a sexy look and a smile. "I could show you."

We pulled into the building's parking lot and my good mood quickly dipped—a Halifax Regional Police cruiser with two officers sat waiting.

"Fuck," I said. My first thought was that Tyler had told them some story about his grow-op and put it on me. I wasn't going to put up with his bullshit. I got out of the car, walked straight toward them and asked, "Did you check his grandmother's basement?"

"I don't know what you're talking about, lady. But we're here to execute a warrant."

"That's what I'm saying. He's a lying, double-crossing, petty punk."

"Are you Bashir Malik?" one of the officers asked Bash as he walked up beside me.

"I am. What is the problem, officer?"

"We need you to come with us, sir. You're under arrest. Please put your hands on the roof of the car."

"Bash, what the fuck's going on?"

Bash complied. They searched him, then cuffed him. One of the officers read him his rights and led him toward the police car.

"It is a small misunderstanding at work. I will get it all sorted out," he said. "Do not worry. Tell Axel I will see him soon. Next visit we will go to the Discovery Centre."

"This is bullshit, he hasn't done shit, he was with me, let him go." I jumped within an arm's length of one of the officers, who recoiled and reached for something.

"Ma'am, I'm asking you to step back. I'm only asking you once." She pulled out a small canister—pepper spray.

I didn't budge. "What's he being charged with? Somebody tell me what the fuck is going on."

"Theft under five thousand dollars," one of the officers said.

"That's a lie." I thought of Tyler. "You can't believe a con who can't even drive. How much did he say he took, how much?" I yelled at the officer in front of me.

"Ma'am, you take two big breaths and two steps back and I'll explain."

I took the steps but not the breaths.

"Just under two thousand. If he has a half-decent lawyer, the Crown will treat it as a summary offence, like shoplifting. Like I say, not a big deal. We need to book him but he'll be out before you know it."

"Two thousand, two thousand?" I bent over, stared at the pavement, and covered my head with my arms. I began to seethe and shouted, "I made him do it, he did it for me, I took the money." I stepped toward the officer and the other one standing a few steps away lost it. She had to have just got her kiddy-cop papers. She shot a short spray into my face, just as Ax and his foster mother pulled up for his visit.

I heard Ax screaming as I keeled over blind and gasped for air, face on fire.

When one of the cops threw Bash into the back of the cruiser, Ax went ballistic and banged on the window. He rushed out of the car before it had completely stopped and ran to me. He can be pretty strong once he gets going and tried to lift me up off the ground by the arm as I groped around and, between coughs, begged for water.

"Stop, Ax, don't touch her," Doreen cried out, but it was too late. My hands gripped his.

"Water ... get me some fucking water. Ax, run inside and get me some water." Then I swore at the officer still standing nearby, also partially blinded and coughing.

Ax scooped into a small snowbank and rubbed a handful of snow in my face. The cold provided some relief. Several other police cars arrived with sirens screeching. Then he started to wail and said his eyes hurt, and his nose and face and a paper cut on his finger were burning. Bash was crying inside the police car and kicked at the door.

"Fucking asshole newbie cop," I said to the other officer who handed us some special medicated wipes, meaning his partner. But his attention quickly turned toward Bash still kicking at the inside of the door.

"Stay away from my son," Bash yelled.

The officer politely asked him to calm down or a public mischief charge would be levelled. Bash stopped but could still be heard swearing.

I continued swearing at the cops too, but they didn't charge me.

Doreen took my hand and said, "I got sprayed at the G20 protests in Toronto, it's nasty. Let me get you inside your apartment and soaped down. I hesitated, then surrendered and allowed her to lead me and Ax. She was totally at home in my apartment as she washed our hands and faces. "It might sting for a bit, but it should go away. Just wash up real good and keep your eyes moist. Blinking helps. And change your clothes too." She came out of my bedroom with a towel for each of us from the closet. The bitch knew what she was doing. I mumbled a thank you.

"Shit, I wanna smoke," I said.

Ax looked around for my smokes.

"I quit, remember? I'm sorry now."

He still had a hard time recognizing the apartment. It smelled clean and things were put away. Our last few visits had been different than before. I yelled less, made sure not to blame him for things, and wasn't mad all the time. Best of all, Bash had been coming around.

Not long ago, he wouldn't have dared to ask me about his dad at a time like this. But things were more chill recently and he was ready to test my limits, as Diane would say.

"Mom, why did the police take Daddy away?"

"Because they're pigs."

Doreen shot me a disapproving look.

"But what did he do?"

I didn't want to get into details. Bash meant well. "He was doing what fathers are supposed to do, he tried to protect you."

"Protect me from what?"

Usually, I tell him how the world is filled with people who wouldn't hesitate to lie, cheat, deceive, and hurt him, and that you always had to be on guard. I thought of my own father and how he was more interested in protecting the family through collective silence—which allowed him to preserve his grip on everyone. "Your daddy was putting you first. Not all dads get that. But yours finally did. I've got to get him out of jail. Come on, Ax, we're going to the cop shop. We're gonna go get him."

"You think that's a good idea, especially with what he just experienced?" Doreen said.

"I don't have a choice."

"I can take him back with me. Or is there someone else who can look after him while you go? If so, I'll drive you."

"Jimmy can watch him," I said.

Maybe Ax was disappointed he couldn't come, but life sucks sometimes. I've told him that a million times and he has to get used to it. He also knew I had to save his dad. I phoned Jimmy to ask if he'd look after Ax while Doreen dropped me off at the station. I started to explain why.

He said to save him the explanation—the whole neighbourhood saw that shit show. He was in the garage, and he always had time for Ax.

⸻

By the time I arrived at the police station, Bash had already spoken to a lawyer and been released. "I have a court date in three months. This is not like shoplifting," he said with his head down, lips pursed.

"What are you saying?"

"This lawyer," Bash showed me his business card, "says the court could go for an indictable offence. They hate people who take from their boss. I could get a criminal record, maybe travel restrictions. Who will hire me now?"

"That's bullshit, this lawyer is gaming you, he just wants the job."

"Maybe, but he also said my previous arrest would not help me."

"You've been in Lebanon, what arrest?"

Bash glared at me.

"Oh, that," I said, wanting to disappear. "It was so long ago," referring to his domestic assault arrest years ago—my doing, after I'd whaled on him and claimed that I was the victim. I guess the cops still had him on file.

We went for a strong cup of coffee at Nena's.

Bash rested his chin in his hands, which were clasped on the table. "What was I thinking?" he said quietly.

"Of Ax, probably," I answered.

"I'm supposed to be in Lebanon at the same time I am in court. Now I do not think I can even afford to go."

I felt a familiar sharp twinge inside. I couldn't locate it exactly, but it stung, the way it usually does when people I care about suffer 'cause of me. Mackenzie, Jennifer, even Papa after the car accident, and now Bash.

"How much do you need?" I asked.

Bash hooted with laughter, but there was no humour behind it.

"How much do you need? I'm serious." I figured I could work for Tyler. It wouldn't be hard to make him feel like the man he wasn't. I could still learn the trade and make some serious money.

"No, just stay away. I just know you have another stupid idea in your head. Forget it. Everything you touch turns to shit." He shook his head. "Why can I not see that until it's too late?"

"Fuck, Bash, I didn't make you skim the till, don't put that on me."

"No, you didn't, I am the stupid one. Stupid, stupid, stupid." He banged his head with his closed fists the same way I'd seen Ax do a thousand times. "I had a good job. I was looking after my mother and sending money to my son. Now you think I will take money from you?" He hooted again. "Like I said, everything you touch turns to shit, including me."

My son. He'd stepped up for his boy back in Lebanon, so why had it taken so long to step up for Ax? Now it had gone to shit, probably for both sons.

He got up and left his coffee untouched. I couldn't handle watching him go. I wondered if I'd see him again.

28

AXEL

MY EYES WERE still sore, but the burning from the cut on my hand was better. I don't know what Daddy did wrong. Mom said he was trying to protect me. From what?

I wanted to go with her to the police station because I could rescue Daddy. Doreen had put me in karate lessons every week. I even learned some moves and was ready to use them on the police if they were mean to Daddy.

And why did they attack Mom but not take her away too? Maybe she didn't put me first like he did.

Jimmy was in the garage working on a canoe when we got there. Mom hugged me hard before leaving. I wanted to tell her to go for their balls if they were rough on Daddy but said nothing. I seen inside Jimmy's apartment before, but this was my first time in his garage. He caught me staring at everything and laughed. In the middle of the floor was an upside-down canoe skeleton he was building. He had lots of tools hanging on a wall and on a long table, and a machine to cut wood. On another wall were cans and brushes and a small canoe. Different sizes and shapes of wood hung from the ceiling and against another wall. A small wood-burning stove kept us warm and made the garage smell like the fireplace at Oma Greta's. Beside the stove was a tiny fridge with a faded picture on it. Jimmy looked younger and a lot skinnier in it. He was with a woman who I think was his girlfriend, and a boy smaller than me. The boy was on Jimmy's shoulders and Jimmy was smiling at the boy and holding his arm like he was saying, Don't worry, I got you.

He gave me the only stool in the room. That made me think that he doesn't have a lot of people go in there and that I must be special.

"My daddy got arrested today for protecting me."

"I saw, and your mother got pepper-sprayed. Nasty stuff. Are you okay?"

"I got some on me when I rescued Mom, but I'm okay. How are you?"

Jimmy smiled. "That's one of many things I like about you, Axel. You care about people. You would run in front of a truck to save anybody."

"Yep."

"Anyway, enough talking. Your timing is perfect, buddy, I could use the free labour." Jimmy got me to hold a thin cedar strip in place while he stapled it to the canoe mould. Then he showed me how to use the small brushes to slowly apply carpenter's glue on the strips.

We stapled on another cedar strip, then carefully brushed on the glue.

Jimmy went to the fridge and pulled out two cans of Pepsi. He opened both and gave me one. It was yummy.

"Parents, if they're doing their job right, do a million things for their kids without their kids ever knowing it," Jimmy said.

"Why would the police take him away if he's just doing his job?"

Jimmy pulled out another cedar strip and told me to hold the far end so he could staple it. "Sometimes we have good intentions but bad ideas. And sometimes we need more than parents to protect us."

"Yeah, from bad guys like the police and CAS."

Jimmy handed me more glue and the brush but didn't say anything.

"This is so much work. How long does it take to make a canoe?"

"With your help, it'll speed things up. Without it, you could probably watch that *Scooby-Doo!* movie a hundred times before I'm done. But sometimes it's worth taking things slowly. Slows the bees down, remember?" He pointed to his head and made a *bzzz* sound.

I started to get tired. "Can't we just nail some plastic together?"

"We probably could, but I like working with cedar. You have to handle it just right, but it's forgiving if you're careful in putting it all together. The paddling is better, the canoe is fast, light, strong, and they'll last a long time if you care for it."

"What are you going to do, feed it water and let it lie in the sun like a turtle?"

Jimmy chuckled. "Actually, moisture and sun are the worst things for it when you're not using it. Sometimes it seems obvious what's good for something, but then we get it all wrong. Maybe that's what happened to your parents. But Axel," Jimmy stopped working and put a hand on me, "you always got to hope they'll get enough things right."

We worked and drank our Pepsi. He pulled down some cookies from a shelf, but they were stale. He asked me how school was and if I'd made any friends. I told him I had forty or fifty friends and I got to pick one for an indoor recess to play in the gym with Mr. Spearman once a week.

"That's a lucky friend," Jimmy said.

I did some more gluing. "Jimmy?"

"Yeah, Axel."

"Is that your family?" I pointed to the picture on the fridge.

He stopped what he was doing and curled his lips in. He nodded and whispered, "Yes."

It was like I could see the bees flying in and out of his head. Like someone invaded the hive and that someone was me. The garage is his private place and I did a bad thing asking him something I should not have. I wanted to quiet his bees down. So I said I really liked hanging with him and asked if he and Mom could go out, then we could hang even more.

He burst out in laughter and kept laughing and laughing until he had to put his brush down and hold his sides and sit down. "Too funny, my man, too funny."

I didn't think it was that funny. It was a good idea. More importantly, I settled his bees down. Now I know to never ask him about his family unless he can put the bees somewhere they won't hurt him anymore.

29

HANNAH

DIANE SAT ON my couch, waiting for Doreen to bring Ax back to me for good after six long months. I paced my apartment, stopping to pop another piece of Nicorette gum.

"Have you heard from Bashir?" Diane asked.

"No, I tried a million times. Jimmy says his apartment's empty. He probably got evicted, maybe missed rent. Apparently, Bash tried to hit him up for some money. He thinks he skipped town."

"It's really too bad. To be honest, for all his faults, I always felt he had a big heart. I guess you two had something going still?"

"What are you, my therapist now too?"

"It's a legit question. You and Axel need stability. Not knowing where Bashir stands in your life, or even where he is, must be a major distraction. You can't let that unravel you."

I was glad she didn't press me on why he was up on theft charges. "He's outta my mind, and outta my life. Okay? Can we move on?"

She nodded. "I'll just say I'm not going to let that setback define this agreement, nor should you. It's Easter and Axel's coming home for good. Show him what you've learned and let's close this file."

I heard a knock and Ax charged in with Doreen behind. He gave me a hug and I said I was making nachos, one of his favourite dinners. Ax said "yummy" and looked back at Doreen. Then he told me they'd just made nachos the day before and he even helped grate the cheese and stir the beef. Mine came out of a box and would be vegetarian. Beef is expensive. The kid was annoying me before he even got his coat off.

For the first few days, we gave each other lots of space and made an effort to be nice and respectful to one another. I really was happy to have him home. But at times it felt like my own childhood, in that no mistakes were allowed, except now I was the parent.

30

AXEL

I CAME HOME for good on Easter. Mom smiled and said nice things, like she was glad to have me all to herself and planted Easter eggs all over the apartment. But I could tell she was using every super power in the world to not blow. And all the super powers in the world could not stop her for long. I wished Daddy was around. She was in a better mood when he was visiting too. Now I don't know where he is.

I asked if she would take me to the Discovery Centre like Daddy said he would. She tried phoning him.

"Fucker." She threw the phone against a pillow. "He said he would take you, so he should man up and keep his word." She wasn't loud when she said it. But it was like her powers were running out and the old Mom was coming back.

That night, the voice came back.

Better watch out.

The voice sounded like me but older. It used to sound younger and was always mad, telling me I did a stupid thing, that I was going to get whupped. Sometimes I heard Mom's voice too.

"Why do I need to watch out?" I said out loud.

You know why. The old Mom's back.

"Mom's better now, everyone knows that."

Who's everyone? Do they know that for sure?

"Shut up."

Is everyone there when you're home alone, with Mom?

"Diane said she's proud of Mom. Doreen said so too."

Are they there when Mom is whupping you?

"Mom is better now, she hasn't whupped me in a long time, so shut up."

Don't be mad at me, I'm just saying, watch out.

"Shuuut up."

If Mom's better, what happened to Daddy?

I banged my fist into my forehead.

"Shut up, shut up, shut up. Why don't you leave me alone?"

Mom came into the bedroom. "Who you talking to, Ax?"

"Nobody."

"Well it better be nobody, I haven't got time for you to go crazy on me."

I know Diane and Doreen talked to her about my voices. She thought it was all dumb. But Mom used to think whatever was wrong with Faye was also dumb. And then bad things happened.

31

HANNAH

———

I FORGOT HOW wet and windy Halifax springs were. One day we were walking out of the Atlantic Superstore in search of a taxi. I stopped. At the far end of the supermarket, an eighteen-wheeler marked Belenko Transport slowly backed into the delivery bay. I tried to look into the cab—I swore the driver looked like Papa.

A gust of cold wind blasted through the parking lot, sending shoppers rushing to their cars. I dragged Ax and all our groceries toward the truck. The driver, a huge man, slowly climbed from the cab. I dropped our bags, unleashing a bunch of red grapes onto the pavement.

Papa?

Ax, urgently pulling on me, was trying to sheepdog me into a taxi.

I ignored him. My eyes tracked the truck driver as he limped into the loading dock. Papa had a limp after the accident.

"What are you looking at?" Ax squeezed my cold, ungloved hand. "I'm scared."

We reached the front of the truck and stared into the darkness. I could see the outline of that enormous man. He turned around and limped toward us.

I stepped back and watched the silhouette grow. "Papa?"

The man emerged from the dark. "Are you alright, madam?" He asked, in a thick South Asian accent.

I sunk into myself and shook my head, offering a weak apology.

"Taxi, Mom, let's go." He waved it down, and we rode home in silence.

The next day, I saw my therapist and spent much of the session edgy, fidgeting constantly, and pacing the small office.

"Why aren't you just a little bit more relaxed, Hannah?" she asked. "Axel's home, the supervision order terminates soon, and you've even quit smoking, the hardest thing anyone ever does."

"You're the therapist, why are you asking me?" I hate it when they ask you something when they already have the answer.

"We've discussed this," she said. "From what I've gathered in our sessions, your parents were not only emotionally absent, but they were also your primary threat."

"There you go again, I've got daddy issues."

"Attachment issues, I'd prefer to say. Yours have left you in a chronic state of hypervigilance brought on by, I'm guessing, a lifetime of physical and emotional trauma. In other words, the alarm bell is always on."

"You guess?"

"Well, you're not really helping me fill in the blanks."

"You do it anyway with a crock of shit that I don't even understand."

"You do, Hannah. I know you understand, deep down inside."

The condescending bitch. I was so tired of people trying to get me to rip the Band-Aids off.

Once the supervision order expired, I skipped the next therapy appointment. When the therapist emailed me, I said I didn't have money for the bus or to pay a sitter, which was true. But the real reason was I didn't see any point. Blah, blah, blah. Talking wasn't going to make past stuff go away or get any better. I no longer had to play this and stopped going.

Both the parenting group and the in-home child management training had ended. I no longer had to keep up with that bullshit either. I let the apartment slide. It made me feel gross, I didn't like it, but the worse it got, the less I wanted to clean up and fix things.

To be honest, it got back to pre-CAS days with unwashed dishes, stained tub and toilet, clean clothes piled up with the dirty ones, and smelly garbage collecting in a corner. So what, eh?

One day after I got Axel to school on time, I came home, snuggled into bed, and didn't leave again until it was almost time to pick him up once the after-school program ended. I heated up some Chef Boyardee mini ravioli for his dinner and gave him the whole can while I munched on crackers. We ate in silence until I noticed him fiddling with a new Ant-Man pencil case.

"That's not yours," I said.

"Yes, it is." He unzipped the case and pulled out markers that he examined as though he'd never seen them before.

I snatched them from his hand.

"That's mine," he whined.

"You little thief, you stole this, didn't you?"

"They're mine," he yelled. "Give it back."

I thought of Bash. If only he hadn't been so stupid, he'd be here now, with us, and I wouldn't be alone again. Stupid ass.

"You're just like your daddy, aren't you. A stupid-ass, a two-bit thief."

Ax flipped his plate of ravioli off the table. "That's mine, Doreen gave it to me."

"You little shit, you're gonna clean that up even if I have to rub your nose in it."

He ran from the table into the bathroom and yelled behind the closed door, "I hate you. I wish you would die. Die, die, die!" He banged on the door with each word.

I was jamming markers back into the case when I noticed a card. *To my Ant-Man, small, smart, mighty, and adorable. Love, Doreen.*

"Fuck," I said out loud.

Before I could go apologize to Ax, the phone rang. I put it on speakerphone and grabbed a rag to clean up the ravioli.

"Hannah?" A familiar voice. Steffi. My footstool of a mother.

"Mama? How'd you get my number?"

"It wasn't easy, you keep changing it. But your Oma said you'd headed east. I called everyone I could think of."

"Who gave you my number?" I wanted to know who the rat fink was.

"Oh, I don't remember. Somebody who knew somebody who knew somebody, which led to Axel's father's WhatsApp, then his phone number."

"Bash? You spoke to Bash?"

Ax continued banging.

"Yes, he's in Lebanon. For a deadbeat dad, he's pretty nice."

"Lebanon? Fucking ass, took off again, didn't even say goodbye to Ax. Why are you calling?"

"Watch your tone, please."

"Oh, you're gonna treat me like I'm twelve again? Did you ever check Papa's language, Ivan's language, eh?"

"I didn't call to fight with you."

"Then why did you call?"

Ax's banging got louder.

"Oma's dying and she might have a couple of days, at most."

I caught my breath.

Mama spoke about how the cancer had come hard, and quickly. "She wants to see you and Axel. Will you come?"

The banging stopped.

Ax knew I listened to Oma and looked up to her like no one else. He told me he once tried on her fake teeth, that the skin on her face sagged like a baby elephant's, and that he thought her big, arthritic knuckles were secret spy weapons. We had spent quite a bit of time there.

I asked Mama for more details, but the word *funeral* triggered me. "She's not even dead yet, how can you be planning a funeral?"

Ax opened the bathroom door and crept toward me.

"Hannah, we have to. These things don't plan themselves. Besides, she had already made many of the arrangements and was pretty specific about what she wants."

"What do you mean?"

Mama sighed. "Well, she wants an open-casket viewing and a small service at Kelly Funeral Home followed by cremation. She has asked about you many times, so I know she wants you to be there. You can stay at her house."

"Did she want anything else?"

Mama remained silent.

"Mama?"

"She said she doesn't want your father there, but she was getting very old, her thinking was not straight, and—"

"So you have to respect it, that's what she wanted, legit."

"Your father will behave, no need to worry."

"Behave? Since when does he behave?" I couldn't help but laugh. "No need to worry? That's all I ever did, fuck knows you never did. You spent thirty years singing, 'Don't worry, be happy,' and looked the other way until he needed a footstool to put his feet up."

"That's not fair. He is not an easy man."

I hadn't expected her to acknowledge that. It was huge, more than she'd ever said. I gave another sarcastic laugh, but this time it was mixed with tears. "What the fuck is fair about anything? My kid's dad takes off to Lebanon again for the second time now. I live in a shithole basement apartment. The only family member I ever got a scrap of respect or support from is dying, and you wanna talk about fair?"

"Fine, you be the drama queen again. Your Oma is dying, it's up to you to do what you want. It always is."

I wanted to tell her to shut the fuck up. Instead, I lowered my head onto the counter and into my bent arms.

"Hi, Oma," Ax said into the phone as he pulled up a chair and started rubbing my back.

"Axel? How's my Spiderman?" Mama said, switching her tone up completely.

"I'm Ant-Man now, Oma." His tone changed as well.

"Ant-Man? Does that mean you like picnics?"

Ax chuckled. That was funny, I'll give her that. Although it bothered me that they got along so easily. I don't remember ever getting that kind of attention.

I reached for his pencil case and handed it to him. "We'll be there." I hung up the phone. I just had to work out how I could afford it.

I microwaved another bowl of ravioli from the can.

"Are we going to Ottawa to see Oma's Oma?"

"It's your Oma's mom. It's your great-grandmother Greta who's dying."

He scrunched his face, unable to figure out the family tree or what dying meant.

"Maybe Oma Greta will change her mind?"

"No, Ax, she has cancer, it's inside her." I began a search for trains to Ottawa. "She doesn't get to decide." The twenty-five-hour train journey only ran three times a week to Ottawa. We'd just missed one.

I Googled return flights while Ax stacked the ravioli I'd picked up from the floor before skewering them with a knife. There were daily flights, but they were almost thirteen hundred bucks for two return tickets. It might as well have been a million. Two one-way tickets came in at half that. I reviewed my money situation. Fortunately, it was cheque day. Five hundred of that $862 cheque automatically went to Jimmy. My cellphone, cable, and Netflix were another $105. That left $257 to cover food, bus fare, and anything else that came up, like these plane tickets to Ottawa. I could pawn the bong and get forty bucks. An old cellphone might net fifty. I had another $125 stashed away. I was still short—big time. Getting home from Ottawa was something I wasn't going to think about until the time came.

I dropped Ax off at school then went to Capital Pawn on Windmill where I badgered the owner into forty-five dollars for the bong and $175 for the Wii U Ax's dad had recently given him. I knew he'd freak, but I wasn't going to dodge the truth that I had to hock it for the plane tickets. I decided to tell him that I'd buy it back once we returned, along with a new game, plus he got to fly for the first time. But it still wasn't enough to afford the tickets.

I made it in time for my shift at the food bank, and early enough to set up my own food supply for when we returned.

"You're looking a wee bit frantic. Everything alright?" Frances the Potty asked.

I told her about Oma and that we'd be gone for a few days, maybe a week. She said she'd say a prayer for her. I wanted to hug Frances, but that woulda been strange since I wasn't exactly a hugger. For a second, though, I just wanted to be accepted like everyone else who shot the shit with her. The moment passed and I drifted to the loading area and started moving boxes.

Cheque days were the quietest at the food bank, but Kim could always be counted on to come in with her stroller every other Wednesday, even if it fell on baby-bonus day.

"How's my honeybee, Axel?" Kim asked.

"He's Ax, what can I say?"

"You can thank the Lord he's home with you. That's what I say about my Shaquille. He's in the science club. That's my boy. Every wonderful day I thank the Lord I still gots him."

I planted a box of dry goods beside her stroller and started to load.

"That's alright, honeybee." She waved me away. "The exercise is good for me."

As she bent over to pick up and stack each and every item, the corner of her wallet stuck out from her coat pocket. My heart went into overdrive. Cheque day. She'd be flush with cash.

"Here, let me help you with that." I bent down with Kim and handed her a 2.5 kg bag of flour with one hand. My other hand slipped into her left pocket and came out with the wallet. I stuffed it down the back of my jeans. I couldn't believe how easy it was.

"Wait, I forgot something." She padded her coat, checking her right pocket and then the inside one.

I held my breath and looked away. Her wallet now felt radio-active tucked in my jeans, ready to explode.

"Something's not right here," she said. "Wait, here it is." She pulled out a bag of black licorice. "On sale at the GT Boutique. For Axel."

I exhaled. "For Ax, thanks."

Kim said her goodbyes and I went on a bathroom break where I went through the wallet. I counted almost four hundred, her child tax benefit for the month. I also found pictures of her three children. The most recent were of her alone with Shaquille, the only child still with her. I was having second thoughts and knew she couldn't have gone far. I could tell her that I'd found it on the floor. For the first time, *I* could be someone's hero.

I looked at her family pictures again. I closed the wallet and fondled the faux leather skin. I knew Kim needed the money, her kid depended on it. Without it, she'd be short. He'd go hungry, get cranky. They might get booted from their apartment. Shaq and Kim might be so revved up one or both of them would lose it. The school or neighbours might notice and speed-dial the child warfare Nazis.

She'd be fucked. Shaq would be fucked. It sounded too much like Ax and me.

But I needed it too. I had to see Oma one last time. I would never have this opportunity again, whereas Kim would have another cheque rolling in next month. Maybe her worker would cut her a break. My stomach started turning over. Knowing I was gonna keep the money, I coulda thrown up. More than anything, I needed a hit of something.

I left my shift early and bought a pack of smokes at the Circle K. Then I walked to the liquor store for a cheap bottle of white rum. I thought of taking the bus for the fifteen-minute ride to the Mic Mac Mall. Instead, I cabbed it. Once there, I booked two one-way tickets to Ottawa.

I came home and ran into Jimmy coming out of his garage.

"You look like you're on a mission." He nodded at the rum.

"Yeah, a very delicate operation." I unscrewed the bottle and offered him a drink.

"You know I don't. But I can fix that drip in your showerhead now."

"Well, it's about time. Come on in." I unlocked the door and we entered.

He noticed the mess. The garbage bags piled up in a corner were especially embarrassing.

"Well, I can't say I like what you've done with the place. You went OCD with cleaning for a while back there."

"That's 'cause I had Community Services on me. With Ax home and them gone, there's no point in busting my ass, right?" I pulled an overnight bag out of the closet. "Hey, can you give us a ride to the airport tomorrow? I gotta go home for a few days."

"Axel too?"

I turned around. "Of course, stupid. Why would I leave him behind? I just got him back."

"I would've taken him," he said without hesitation.

"That woulda been great, he does love you. Woulda saved me some serious coin. But I don't want anyone else looking after him but me. Anyway, he should come for this."

"Why? You're stressed. He's going to get stressed. All you're going to do is yell at him."

"Christ, Jimmy, you're sounding like Diane did. Thank God that shit's over with."

"You mean they really blew you off?"

"The supervision order's expiring. I'm walking and there's nothing they can do about it until someone else rats me out again."

Jimmy looked away and shifted uneasily as though he were hiding something. What was up with him? That made me think of the few times he got close to being judgy about the way I looked after Ax. Had he called them on me? No way, Ax loves him, Jimmy wouldn't hurt him. Unless he was making a play for my boy.

"Wait a sec … It was you." I got in his grill. "What the fuck, I thought you were my friend, and Ax's friend."

"I am, that's why I got you both help. I love that boy." Jimmy's voice almost cracked.

"You call that help? Suppose they kept him. Suppose that foster freak diddled him. Did you consider that? You know what that woulda done to me?"

"It's about you, eh? When is it about Axel? He walks around you like you're ready to blow. Plus if you would only open your heart and see that. Can you imagine what it's like for him? No kid should lose their childhood like that."

"So says the childless wonder. What the fuck do you know? I don't see you trying to raise a kid." I knew that one hit him hard. I never got the full story about his family but he never asked about mine. I respected him for that, even if he was now dead to me. "Just get out, get the fuck out, and stay away from my son." I slammed the door behind him and cursed his name and what he had said. *Can you imagine what it's like for him? No kid should lose their childhood like that.* What the fuck? Ax can handle anything. I did. The times Papa smacked me around, I took it and handled it then and every time. Ax has got it good compared to that.

Except it did scare me. I had never known what it was not to be afraid. I didn't like how that thought got into my head because it had nothing to do with Ax. Still, Jimmy was out of line.

I poured a rum and Coke and had a cigarette before packing.

32

AXEL

WHEN **MOM PICKED** me up from school, she said we were going to Ottawa. Only for a few days 'cause we had to say goodbye to Oma Greta. She tried to make it sound fun because we were going on an airplane. My first time on a plane, she said. But because she already looked very sad, it was hard to feel like it was going to be a good time. When we got home I wanted to rub her back and tell her not to be sad and that maybe Oma would be okay. But I knew it wouldn't help. Instead, she smoked a lot and drank alcohol with Coke.

I put on my boots to go over to say goodbye to Jimmy and ask him to guard our house, but Mom got really mad and told me to stay away from him forever 'cause he was a snitch, which is the worst thing Mom can say. "He called the CAS on us. He can't be trusted."

"No, he's not. He's my best friend," I said.

"He called the CAS on us. He can't be trusted."

Jimmy? But he's our friend. "Why?"

"How the hell should I know? But he's the reason you got taken away. He's the reason you had to stay with Doreen and why I had to take all those stupid courses and counselling. Just stay away from him. Never mind."

But I thought I went to Doreen's 'cause Mom had a plan. We were going to live in a house with a tree house and no one was going to bug us anymore. Jimmy's my best friend. I wanted to ask him what happened. I just couldn't believe that he was a liar. It was almost like Mom read my mind about going to sneak out to Jimmy's garage. She told me to stay put and pack my bag with things that I needed. We had a plane to catch.

33

HANNAH

———

A FREAK SPRING storm rocked Eastern Ontario, delaying our plane's arrival in Ottawa. By the time we landed, snow and ice blanketed the city. Ax musta loaded his backpack with his rock collection, 'cause it was heavy as shit. We stomped our feet to keep warm the whole forty minutes waiting for the goddamned bus.

When we finally got to Oma's, exhausted and frozen, I pulled out the key to the house and worked the lock, but it wouldn't turn. I phoned Mama and put her on speaker while I fiddled with the lock and key.

"Your father changed the locks yesterday. I only just found out," Mama said.

"Why the hell didn't you tell me? Ax can't feel his toes."

"I didn't know when you were coming. You don't tell me anything," she said.

We stared at the heavy falling snow. I could hear Papa in the background telling Mama what to say.

"As the power of attorney, we have to protect your Oma's assets."

"What the fuck does that mean? Your daughter and grandson are half-frozen. You said we could stay here."

She didn't answer me right away—but I heard him raise his voice at her. "I may have misspoken. I'm sorry, Hannah. You'll have to find somewhere else. But if you want to drop Axel here, we'd love to have him."

"What the fuck, are you serious, leave Ax with you? You told me to come and that I could stay here. Oma would never fucking stand for this. I'm gonna tell her—"

Papa took the phone. "You go and tell her, go. You cannot scare me. She is crazy and almost dead. She hears nothing. She can do nothing for you. You cannot run and hide to her like before. We control that little shithouse now."

"Mommy, I'm cold." Ax whispered as he leaned into me for warmth.

I hung up and stomped on the ground. The snow started coming down even harder. "Wait here," I told Axel.

"No, Mom! Please don't leave me!"

"I'm just going around the back. There's a small window I can open. Wait here."

Ax was relieved when he saw I was true to my word. I unlocked the front door from the inside and let him in. I told him to leave his coat on while I adjusted the thermostat. The place hadn't changed much since I was a kid. Clocks still covered every wall. She still had a million spoons from around the world and enough Royal Doulton to feed the entire Royal fucking Family.

I led Ax into the bathroom and ran a hot bath.

A noise at the front door startled us. I hadn't locked up.

"Don't leave me, I'm scared," he begged, tugging at my coat, then cramming himself into the space between the toilet and the bath.

I wondered if it was Papa and reached for the nearest weapon. A plunger. Ax quietly followed at a distance as I went to investigate. I raised the plunger over my head, rounded the corner, and was halfway through a swing when I came face to face with a police officer.

The officer had his hand on a baton—and was also in mid-swing.

"Drop your weapon and get against the wall."

"This is my grandmother's house, I used to live here."

Ax started bawling.

"Do we look like we're doing a B-and-E? C'mon," I pleaded, then asked him if I could attend to Ax.

He nodded, then identified himself as Constable Malik.

I rubbed Ax's hands and told him everything was okay. I tried to explain to Malik why we were there and asked if Papa had been the one who called him.

Malik put his baton away and called off the backup. "I can't say. We got a call about suspicious activity. There have been a number of prowlers in the area. The neighbourhood is very alert."

"It was my father, I know it."

Ax tapped the constable on the elbow and pointed to a picture of himself, Faye, and me on the wall. "See, Mom used to live here."

The officer peered closer. "Cute, where's the girl?"

Ax turned away and banged his head on the wall.

"Stop that, Ax." I turned to the cop. "It's a long fucking story. Look, we're cold and we're tired. We just need to crash, okay?"

He examined my ID. "I don't see anything with this address."

"I said it's a long fucking story."

"Do you have a key for the premises or anything that would suggest you have permission to be here?"

"Shit, we'll be bouncing in just a few days. We came home for her funeral."

"Oma's funeral. It's my first ever. Mom teached me how to spell it. Did you know it's spelled like 'fun' and 'real' except it's not going to be?"

The officer winked at Ax, then handed back my ID. "I'm sorry. You can't stay. If it was up to me, I'd let you. But the owners may see this as trespassing."

"That's bullshit." I said. "This is still my grandmother's house."

"My daddy's name is Malik too. Do you know him?" Ax asked.

"I know lots of Maliks, it's a popular name."

"My daddy's the King of Donair. He lives in Fartmouth." Ax giggled.

"Dartmouth, Nova Scotia," I corrected and smirked, suddenly missing how straight-up Dartmouth is.

"That's a long way away." Malik bent down to Ax's level. "What's your name, buddy?"

"Axel."

"Well, Axel, I'm sorry I don't know your dad. But I'm sure he's a good guy."

I interrupted: "Look, we have nowhere to go."

"No friends, family …?"

I shook my head.

"Remain here, please." Malik took back my ID and made some calls.

Ax asked me what was going on and if we were going to jail.

I said I didn't think so, but I wasn't convincing.

Malik was gone a full ten minutes before returning. "Have you got somewhere else you can stay?"

"No. Does that mean you won't charge us?"

Malik shrugged. "That depends. Anyone see you enter the premises?"

This time it was me who shrugged. "There's a storm out there. Who can see shit?"

"Well, that's good. I have some discretion. To me, I'll log this as a trip down memory lane. No harm, no damage."

Ax and I high-fived.

"But," Malik said, "your name's in our system with a flag. It went directly to my sergeant, who I just spoke with. She's saying the same thing as me. If the owner or whoever has power of attorney won't allow you to stay, you can't."

"Fuck."

"But she suggested I reach out to the housing crisis worker, so I called. Your name hasn't been red-flagged there, and they have a room at the Carling Family Shelter."

Ax asked if the shelter was like his fort when he had thrown a blanket over two chairs and made a tent.

"No, Ax."

I pleaded with Malik. "I thought you were gonna give me a break."

"The owners are supposed to be notified," he said. "They could try to lay a charge later, but my sergeant wants me to let this go, and I agree. Believe me, you did catch a break."

"Why does your sergeant care what happens?"

"You'll have to ask her yourself."

Ax tugged at me. "Is she a friend of yours, Mom?"

"No, Ax, she's a cop, weren't you listening? Wait—*her*?"

"Yeah, Sergeant Tara Lee."

———

The family shelter was a big four-storey building of concrete, glass, and metal. Directly across the street was a Tim Hortons. On the other side of Carling Avenue was a motel, Apple Auto Glass, and a Payday loan store with a sign that said Cash in a Flash. I used to go to the one near the Double Happiness in Dartmouth and say really fast, "Cash in a flash, let's dash and mash our hash," which always sent Ax into stitches.

Malik led us inside and spoke to the intake worker. Then he bent down, removed a pin from his lapel, and put it on Ax's coat.

"What is it?" Ax asked.

"It's the flag of Lebanon. That's a cedar tree. They smell great, it's a beautiful country. Maybe you'll go someday." Malik high-fived Ax on his way out.

The intake worker had me fill out a form and went over some of the rules as she walked us around. She showed us the kitchen with the communal fridges and dining room.

"You can stay for as long as you need so long as you're looking or waiting for something more permanent. Women usually take turns cooking, but if no one does, then you're on your own. We teach practical skills every weekend, like how to cook and how to sew. There are two beds to a room, and a couple of lockers to put your things in. Every room has two keys, only you and the staff have them. If you do drugs, engage in any illegal activity, or create a disturbance, even once, you're out."

"Wait, didn't the cop tell you? We only need a few days, a week at most."

She said she was sorry to hear that and added that the average stay was thirteen months. She continued with the orientation. She showed us the common room with an old projector TV, a cracked foosball table, shelves of books, tables with board games, and a separate room for children, filled with broken toys. The residents eye-balled me suspiciously.

"You're expected to clean your own room and tidy up after your-selves in common areas. You are allowed to remain in the shelter all day if you want, but we expect you to actively work on getting a plan in place for permanent housing. Your son will have to be registered for school and we can give you a list of three schools in this area."

The intake worker finally led us to our room, which smelled of fresh bleach and old sweat. There was a bunk bed and a double ready to be made, a small table, and a single hard plastic chair. She pulled out a handful of garbage bags. "You'll have to bag all your clothes, every piece. We have a lice-and-bedbug policy. The washer and dryers are downstairs. We'll have to spray your bags."

"Is this really necessary? We really just need to sleep and we're outta here in a few days."

"It's to keep the bugs out and you in. The laundry room closes at ten. I'll come back in an hour to see how you're doing. Curfew is at ten. Doors will be locked. This is no holiday."

34

AXEL

WE WENT TO the hospital with the big H. It was my first time in one not counting when I was born. I know people die there, and it's where ghosts get their start. I once saw a Halloween movie where the bad guy pushed a girl's head into hot water and her face melted off. I had nightmares after that.

I didn't want to go, but Mom said it was my last chance to say goodbye to Oma. She said she didn't have anybody to leave me with. She even tried Melina's mom but she was busy. So I would have to see Oma one more time before she becomes a ghost.

After breakfast we bussed and walked to an old stone building. I squeezed Mom's hand when we got off at the fourth floor.

"Mom, it smells."

"Quiet, Ax. People are dying here."

The smell was worse than the washroom at Peter's restaurant. There was pee, plus bleach and grass mixed together. But everything looked clean and the hallways were quiet, even with people coming in and out of rooms. A nurse pointed us to Oma's. We saw Oma Steffi down the hall, talking to another nurse. My hands got sweaty and I squeezed Mom's hand even more. I wondered if Dedushka and Uncle Ivan would also be here. Oma Steffi saw us and waved. She gave me a great big hug.

"Why didn't you call? I would've picked you up," she said.

"Pick us up? That sounds like an offer of help, the way a mother might help her daughter, unlike yesterday when you locked us out in a fucking snowstorm."

"I told you I had nothing to do with it. That was your father, and I said I was sorry. You know how he is."

"I know how you are too, so let's cut the bullshit."

"Language, Hannah."

"Language, Hannah, language, Hannah. Sorry, was that you trying to parent again? It didn't happen too much so I don't recognize it. By the way, we're staying in a dungeon of a shelter, in case you're interested."

"Are we going to do this here, now?"

"It's as good a place as any. It's not like we've ever talked about anything other than not upsetting Papa before. Yeah, great family sit-downs they were."

"You were not the easiest child. Now that you're a mother, I hoped you'd see that parenting isn't so easy, especially with a child as energetic as Axel."

I didn't want to hear them fight. So instead of being scared, I got brave and left them for Oma Greta's room.

"It's me, Oma Greta, Axel." I always liked how she pronounced my name in her German accent so it sounded like Ax-sir. Her bony face and hands were scary, but they didn't slow me from going right up to her.

She had her own room. On the wall was a whiteboard with a bunch of names and a picture of a sailboat. I was glad she wasn't going to die surrounded by other dying strangers.

"Axel? Axel? Thank God, you're here, child." She could hardly raise her hands for a hug.

"I'm so happy to see you, Axel." Her thin cracked lips called out for lip balm.

Instead, I helped her drink some juice.

"Do you have any money?" she asked.

I emptied my pockets and showed her fifteen cents.

"That is good, very good." She waved her skinny hands and arms like she was swatting mosquitos. "I need to get out of here. All

I need is enough to get on the Baseline bus. It'll take me home, I'll be safe there."

"Uh, but aren't you sick, Oma Greta?"

"Nonsense. What I am is in danger. They're drugging me here. There are bad people in the basement, in a cave hot enough to melt steel. Every night I hear good people being taken away. They cry, they beg for their life."

She coughed then took a long breath. "These bad people are like monsters but they look just like us. When the good people go into the hot cave, loud banging follows. And then it belches out fire and hot air. I can hear it. I can feel it."

I knew what she was talking about and wanted to save her. "There is a monster like that at our place too. It's so scary. Maybe they're related."

I gave Oma my money and my new Lebanon pin.

She took many short breaths before talking again. "Must be, there are monsters everywhere."

"What else can I do, Oma Greta?"

"*Ja*, find out where the garbage chute is. I will slide down the chute into the garbage bin. It will be messy, but from there I will get the bus, and I will be safe."

I told her that even though she looked bad, she was being brave. I said I wished I could be like her.

"But you are. You're the bravest boy alive. Thank you so much for coming, dear Axel."

She started to moan. Talking looked hard for her. I wanted to stop and go away and not make her feel worse. But she told me to come closer.

"Yes, Oma Greta?"

"You are the last hope. You are the only one with a chance still. But you must leave. You know this, do you not?"

The voice in my head had said the same thing. Was she connected to them? Did she know something secret? "Yes, Oma Greta, I think I know this."

"*Gut.* I also knew you were brave. Your mother is also brave, but she cannot leave, not now, maybe later, someday ..."

35

HANNAH

"**A**x, don't tire her out," I said as Mama and I entered the room together.

I said hello to Oma, but almost freaked as I got a closer look at her gaunt, helpless face.

When I was a kid, she was the only one there for me. She was tiny, old world, old school, and nobody fucked with her.

Her small house was a shrine to old shit. She had cabinets and shelves of Toby Jugs and doilies under every fucking thing. The place was always spotless—she pursued dust, dirt, and stray crumbs relentlessly. Oddly enough, she let us roam free. I could go up and down her electric La-Z-Boy all day, or slide down the banister and she'd let me. She and Opa, before he died, used to let us reset all the clocks so they'd ring at the same time. It sounds dumb, but every moment there was an escape.

When I walked out on my family for good a few months after Papa's accident, I had ten bucks on me, my ID, bus pass, MP3 player, and my work clothes. I autopiloted my way to the safest place I could think of: Oma Greta's.

She bitched me out at first and said any mother would be worried sick if their teenaged daughter was missing and then insisted I tell Mama where I was. So I texted her: *I'm done. Keep my shit.*

Oma did not agree with me when I said it was best not to tell my parents where I was. But she was cool about staying quiet until I had a plan, though she insisted the plan had to include me finishing school.

"Like, can I just stay registered?"

"*Nein*. Under my roof you go to school until you can go no more, then you work, then you are retired. You are on step one. Also in my house, you learn to cook, clean, and whatever else I can think of."

"Oma, you're such a Nazi."

"Not funny. You do not know what a Nazi is. And you do not know that thousands of good Germans resisted them and died for it. Besides, compared to me, the Nazis were too disorganized." She cracked a thin smile.

"Oma, how did Mama ever put up with you?"

Oma put the kettle on. "Steffi was an easy child. Good at school, no back talk, no trouble whatsoever. I thought I had a dream child."

"But some Russian dude came along."

"*Ja*. I did not see that behind her obedience was no self-confidence and no personality of her own. She bent to the first man to flash her a smile. I saw that too late. I regret that and take full responsibility. You, however, have some fire. You still have a chance. Your mother was twenty-four, a virgin still. I know this, living at home and working in the back room of the gym when she met your father."

"But Oma, how do you know I've done it? Maybe I'm still a—"

"Stop. I am old, not stupid."

I cracked up.

"Steffi worked the same gym as Youri. She was a bookkeeper. He would coach, then exercise and close the gym. One day as she turned the lights off, he startled her by playing that Swedish song everyone was gaga about—"Dancing Queen.""

"By ABBA."

"*Ja*, whatever. For a big man, he was a good dancer. My Steffi loved this. The charm offensive repeated itself the next three nights until he took her for a Greek dinner. She would hear everything about his life, his near Olympic glory, his plans to open a gym. He didn't ask about her, but she didn't notice. In fairness to Youri, she probably offered nothing, for she always believed that she had nothing worth offering. In the dance of life, she finally found a partner. But he would have to lead and on his terms. It was understood.

"Two years after they married, your brother was born. For a while, Youri was a proud papa. He danced and toasted when he saw how far little Ivan could fling his soother out of the crib. He believed he had another shot putter in the making, one who could compensate for his failures.

"Then you came. Your first Easter here, he and my Adler tried to watch a Premier League game, but your ear-splitting crying— sorry, but you were a colicky baby—interrupted them. Your father yelled for her to settle you. Your mother cringed. She tried soothing, burping, and feeding you, but you kept wailing. She was close to tears. She thought maybe it was an ear infection. He ripped you from her arms and tried to sing you a lullaby. When that failed, he rocked you as though he were winding you up for a throw. Your screams got worse *und* worse. He yelled in your face. 'Stoy—Stop!' It was awful to see.

"I tried to help, but he paced the house with you like a wild animal with eyes almost jumping out. He punched the wall while he was still carrying you over his shoulder, and he made a big hole. So I took you and Ivan at every chance. But I could not keep silent. I confronted him on his parenting, which meant your Opa and I were shut out from your life except for holidays."

I pulled out the tea bags. "Do I still have a chance?"

"*Ja*. If I did not think so, I would not have opened my door to you. But first, there are many practical issues. You need clothes, personal items ..."

"A computer, money ..."

"I do not have much money. And I cannot help you with the computer. I know nothing about them. But I can help in other ways. First, we drink tea, then we go to the mall."

We were sipping our tea when I remembered someone from a few years back who might be able to help.

After deleting a ton of emails and voicemails from my parents, I tracked down Constable Tara Lee, who agreed to meet me at school the next morning.

The next day, I met her in the school conference room. Lee's easy smile surprised me. I wasn't sure why she remembered me. I hadn't seen her since the day she gave me Jennifer's suicide note about five years before that.

She asked if I had left on my own or was asked to leave, and whether an assault was involved.

I sighed then shook my head. "I had enough of my parents and just had to get out."

"Hannah, let's cut the bullshit, alright? He nearly twisted your head off once, I'd bet my badge it wasn't the only time, and just a matter of time before it would've happened again, right?

I kept my head down and mouth shut, which probably said a lot.

"Do you want to file charges?"

"No, and don't ask me again."

Lee sighed. "Okay. Let's at least get you set up with student welfare."

I agreed.

Lee called a social worker while I checked my phone to discover many missed calls and messages from my parents.

The social worker came in, sat down, and introduced himself before asking me a ton of questions. "It's always a bit dodgy to apply for student welfare when a student has left home by choice. To some welfare workers, it might look like an opportunistic adolescent just tired of following reasonable rules," he explained.

"There's nothing reasonable about my father."

"Maybe so, but every cranky teen wants to blow their evil parents off at one point or another. Why should we pay for this, is what the welfare people might think."

"Fuck this." I got up to leave. "I'll just stay at my Oma's."

"How long before he comes for you?" Lee asked.

I paused. "I'll just go. He won't find me."

"Student welfare's $604 a month. I know of a way," the social worker said. "We call to make an intake appointment. Make sure you bring your ID. Our good constable here will have to provide a third-party letter of support. She will share her concerns with the case-worker, citing that the home is unsafe for you."

"But I never said that, so how can you say that?" I turned to Lee.

Lee hesitated. "Without an official complaint by you ... it's going to need some finessing. You're already out, now it's about staying out and starting over. I'll take my chances and draft you a letter."

I sagged with relief. Lee placed a hand on my shoulder. That weirded me out and made me stiffen up at first.

"You're really brave, Hannah," she said before leaving.

The social worker was walking me through the main office when I suddenly saw my parents step through the doors to the office area.

Papa lifted his cane and pointed at me.

"Go back to my office and wait there," the social worker instructed.

He intercepted my parents, who looked to be on their best behaviour.

"There she is. We were so worried," Mama said.

"Hannah can be dramatic, like many other teenagers," Papa said. "She is normal that way, and she does not like hearing the word *no*. Everything must be her way. We are both slaves to her moods."

Mama nodded and picked it up. "We love her. That is why we worry about her. She has not been home in two nights, we had no idea where she was. Do you have children, can you even imagine?"

Papa stepped toward the office I was hiding in. I could see him through the frosted glass of the window.

The social worker was half Papa's size but he put out his hand to signify *stop*. "Mr. Belenko, maybe if you grab a seat, I'll see what I can do."

"I am her father, you cannot stop me from taking her home. Where is the principal?"

"He's out for the day. I can get him to call you. But to be honest, when a student Hannah's age doesn't want to leave with her parents, neither we nor any police officer is going to compel them to go. The principal will tell you the same thing."

"What kind of bullshit is this? She is my child." Papa moved quickly even with a cane. He strode past the social worker and opened the office door, surprising me. He reached over and grabbed me by the arm and yanked me out into the hallway.

"Jabira, call the police," the social worker barked to one of the office administrators.

I kicked out Papa's cane, sending him crashing into a recycling bin. I fled from the school and ran the length of Cornell Street onto Baseline. Police cars, their lights flashing, sped along Baseline Road toward me.

I thought I was going to be busted for assaulting my father, but the police made a right and sped toward the school.

Oma got quiet when I relayed all this to her. "When you poke a mad dog, it will come." She sighed. "Had I been a younger woman I would have relished the confrontation."

"What are you saying, you're going to make me go back home?"

"*Nein*. I did not say enough when your father came along and flashed his muscles to my Steffi. I will not repeat that now. How do you young people say it, 'Bring it on to me?'"

"No, 'bring it,'" I laughed. "And if you're really pissed, you can say, 'Bring it, bitch.'"

"*Nein*, I can never say that. Can I?"

I shrugged.

She pursed her lips, then scowled and said, "Bring it, bitch."

Papa was not deterred. Two days later he parked his twenty-eight-foot trailer in front of Oma's house. He ignored the bell and banged on the door.

Oma slid the chain lock into place and opened the door.

"Youri, what brings you here?" she said, revealing only her face.

"Is this how you greet the husband of your only daughter, hiding behind a chain?"

"Maybe I am doing you a favour. Maybe I think you would not like to see an old woman's naked body, hmm?"

"Then I wait for you."

"You could be waiting for a long time, I have a bath ready for me."

"At seven-thirty in the morning?"

"I am old, and I am running out of days. Otherwise, time is meaningless."

I watched and listened from an upstairs window. Papa leaned heavily into the door.

"Yesterday Ivan saw Hannah on a bus heading in this direction," he said. "I know she is here."

"This is my house. You are not welcome. Please go away."

Once again he banged on the door, shaking the entire house.

A neighbour walking her Labrador called out. "Is everything okay?"

Papa turned around. "This is nothing, mind your own business."

Oma slammed the door and bolted it.

"Is Greta alright? Greta? You there?" The neighbour reached for her phone.

"Everything is good. I am son-in-law."

A jogger came by and stopped. "What's going on? I heard a loud bang." He looked toward Papa. "Who's that?" he asked the neighbour.

"He says he's Greta's son-in-law, but I haven't seen Greta," the neighbour replied.

Papa turned back to the door. "I will come back for Hannah." He stormed off, climbed into his truck, hit the air horn, and drove away.

Once Oma saw that he'd left, she opened her front door and waved to her neighbours, mouthed a thank you, and gave a thumbs-up.

"My neighbours are like watchdogs, good shepherds, bless them. You can come out now," Oma called up to me.

I came down but stood away from the door. "He'll be back. And he'll keep coming back."

"*Ja, und* we will be ready. I told my neighbours to watch out for his truck."

"How did he look?" I asked.

"How do you say, 'pissed'?" She sighed. "I thought he was going to break the door down. I think I will not answer it if he comes again."

"That's not going to stop him. I'm sorry, Oma, you don't need this. He's gonna ruin your life like he's ruined mine."

"Nonsense. Get your things. I'm driving you to school."

Papa kept coming, at odd hours and days. He'd bang on the door and if I was home, I'd huddle in the kitchen, ready to run out the back way if he got in. Eventually, Oma called the police. He'd always be gone before they came, and I insisted on not pushing things. Other times he would park and phone us, and just idle the truck. I was scared Oma would have a heart attack like Opa did. I'd brought my shit to her and it was going to kill her.

———

Ax told us about the fire-breathing basement monster, Oma needing bus fare, and her garbage-chute escape plan.

Mama stroked Ax's head and cracked a small smile. "It's the morphine that makes her hallucinate. She's not herself anymore."

"Nonsense," Oma exclaimed from her hospital bed. "They are drugging me, yes, but it is so I do not resist. Ax knows this, don't you, Ax?"

Ax pulled at my arm. "There's a monster here and in the shelter, we have to get away."

"Shut up, Ax, don't feed her hallucinations," I said.

Oma pointed a finger at me. "*Nein*, not my dear Hannah. You are one of them now, you work for them. It is too late for you. Stay away from me, stay away ..." She started to cry. "I just want to go home. No one will hurt me there ..."

I fought back my tears. "Why didn't you tell me?" I turned to Mama.

"It's the morphine."

"But this isn't her." I opened a juice box for Oma and brought the straw to her mouth. I kept trying to have a conversation with her, but she'd get all worked up in between lapsing in and out of consciousness.

Mama took us to a late lunch at the hospital cafeteria.

"Any moment now is what the doctor said," Mama said, covering up Ax's ears. "But I'm glad you got to see her."

"As if Ax can't hear you." I pushed aside my untouched sandwich.

"Well, I'm not glad. It's not how I wanted to remember her, and it's not the kind of conversation I wanted."

I thought of the time I stole money from Oma then ran off to Halifax. She never even mentioned it when I returned with the kids. She welcomed them—and me—with open arms.

Mama made a big deal about picking up the lunch tab, which allowed me to ask for enough money to return to Nova Scotia. She gave me all the cash in her wallet, eighty-five dollars, but was stubborn about sending me any more. I tried to guilt her about us being in the shelter, but she lectured me about having to live with my own choices.

"You sound like every CAS worker and therapist I've ever had. Do you all belong to the same fucking book club, or what?"

She ignored my shot.

"Mom, where's Boris?" Ax asked.

"Holy shit, how could I forget." I looked at Mama. "Where is he?"

"With us. Who else was going to look after him? Your father loves him already, too much, I would say."

"We want him back."

"In the shelter? And how will you take him back to Halifax? Your father will have something to say about that."

"More bullshit." I chain-smoked a couple of cigarettes, and went back to the hospital for another visit with Oma. She slept the whole time I was there, which messed me up a bit, so I left in case Papa showed up. I also needed to get some groceries before our return to the shelter.

I let Ax play in the shelter's children's room while I went out for a smoke and tried again to make some calls for a better place to crash. Everyone said no. When I got really desperate, I left messages with my brother, and even my ex Kevin. Then a staff member tapped me.

"Hannah, Axel's out of control. He strangled a child he claims stole his Spiderman shirt. You shouldn't be out here while he's unsupervised."

I sucked the last of my butt. "For fuck's sake, what now?"

36

AXEL

MOM SAID THE shelter was only going to be a few days, but it was longer.

I hate sleeping there. I dreamed of a dark night sky where a new star suddenly came out. In the dream, Mom said a new star means an angel got born to guide you. That's when I knew that Oma Greta died. Mom said it was cancer, but I think the bad people in the basement killed her.

Oma Greta looked so small in a coffin. Her funeral was the first time I ever seen a dead person before. It was cool and sad at the same time. I thought she would be all burned up. Instead, she looked like something took away her lifeforce. I don't know how they got her body out of the cave in the hospital.

I saw my grandparents walk in. They like to be called Dedushka and Oma. I wasn't sure it was them 'cause they looked a lot older. Mom's whole body got tight. She gave them a mean look. Dedushka was always big and wide like the Thing in *Fantastic Four*, but now he lost lots of hair and got wrinkly on his hands and face. He walks bending over with a cane. Dedushka and Mom started to whisper-fight in the church until people started to look and Oma told them to shush.

Dedushka playfighted with me and pretended to use his cane like a lightsaber. I asked to try it and he let me. But then Mom and Oma

Steffi also got into a whisper-fight. Oma Steffi said Mom was being disrespectful to Oma Greta. Mom said she would rather sit on a pile of steaming dog shit than sit beside them at the front of the church. Mom said that Oma Greta always thought Dedushka was a loser.

This made me laugh out loud, and I got some dirty looks.

Mom and me sat a bunch of rows back from Oma Steffi and Dedushka.

"Is that Uncle Ivan?" I asked Mom.

"Yep."

"He looks like Dedushka."

"That's 'cause they're a lot alike."

Uncle Ivan is muscly like John Cena and walked up the aisle with a lady on his arm who looked like she was a teenager. He stopped and stood tall over us.

"Miracles never cease. Is that my nephew, Axel?"

"Hi, Uncle Ivan."

"You should come visit," he said. "I'll make a man of you."

"And how would you know?" Mom said.

Ivan said *Fuck you* without any sound then sat beside Oma and Dedushka.

A man said a prayer, then everybody said one together. I didn't know the words. He asked people to come to the front and talk about Oma Greta. Oma Steffi said what a great mother Oma Greta was to her, and how she taught her courage and determination. Then some of Oma Greta's old-lady friends went up and spoke about her gardening, her baking, her loyalty, and how she was generous and forgiving.

Mom was crying a little.

Then Oma Steffi thanked people for coming and invited them to join the family for a reception.

"Wait!" Mom stood up and said she wanted to say some words. Oma looked back at Dedushka, who shook his head and did a karate chop. Mom saw that and went up anyway. I thought she was going to yell at the neighbour who made a joke about Oma Greta's great baking. But then she said she was Greta Braun's granddaughter.

"She was there when I had no one. She was there when I messed up, and still there when I messed up again, big time." Tears started coming down her face, but her voice just got stronger. "I never got to thank her. Never got to ask her to forgive me for taking her love for granted, for covering my back when I didn't know how to protect myself, and for me being such a shit, although she never held it against me." She started to cry for real. "She was a great gardener to some of you, a great baker to others, a friend to many. But to me, she was the only family who was there for me when I needed someone." She looked at Oma, Dedushka, and Uncle Ivan before stepping down.

I seen Mom bawl many times. Like when she was crazy mad, really sad, even sometimes when she can't stop laughing. But this time she was shaking like her insides were in a Dairy Queen Blizzard. When she sat down, I held her hand.

People were moving into another room for sandwiches when Oma went up to Mom. "Hannah, your words rang true and were from the heart. We're both going to miss her." She reached out to Mom. "I just wish you—"

Dedushka jumped in and cut her off. "That was disgraceful." He made a sour face at Mom. "At your Oma's funeral, you shame her daughter, our family."

I heard Mom say many times that Dedushka was a complete loser and a total asshole who doesn't deserve to have me or Faye in his life, and that someday she planned to screw him over. I hardly ever saw him, but when I did, he was nice and gave me presents. He even secretly asked if I wanted to live with them someday. I said yes 'cause I didn't want to make him sad. The last time he did that was before Faye was taken away.

Mom told me to grab some cookies like she wanted me to go away. Something was going to happen. The fudge was on a nearby table and I wanted to go get some, but Mom looked scared and I didn't want to leave her.

She said to Dedushka, "Oma was the kindest person in my world. She was what you shoulda been. She gave a shit. Think about what I coulda said, Papa. Like how you were absolutely evil to me, how you drank until you pissed yourself. How you drove away all the friends who gave a shit about me."

"I am your father. I did everything for you."

Mom's voice went quiet so only me, Dedushka, and Oma Steffi could hear. "Was almost strangling me to death *for me*? Was raping Mama *for me*?"

She said *rape* so soft it was hard to hear. I wanted to know what that was. It sounded like the worst swear word or the worst thing you can do to Oma.

"Lies!" Dedushka slammed his cane. "How can you say such lies?"

"I covered for you and for everybody else. Even today I covered for you. I coulda said how you kept me from Oma 'cause she saw you for what you were. I coulda gone on for days up there."

Dedushka's big hand grabbed Mom's arm. "You do not get to walk away after saying such lies in front of my grandson." He got close to her ear. "Know this. I will destroy you."

Mom looked like a little girl about to get whupped but who was ready for it. "Bring it."

Dedushka stepped in front of us. "Your mother tells me you are in a shelter, like homeless people, like welfare bums, like always. You belong there. My grandson does not." He put a hand on my back. "What kind of mother are you to do this to your son, my grandson?"

Mom wound up like she was going to whup Dedushka. I pulled her arm to drag her away, but she snapped her arm back and I fell. My head hit something hard. It felt weird and I touched a sore spot on my head and saw blood, flashy red like Iron Man. It started dripping onto my shirt. I freaked out and screamed and kicked when people came closer.

Mom raised her voice. "Ax, settle down now ... shhh, settle down." People crowded around us, which made me feel like I was trapped. I screamed even more.

"See what you have done to your son?" Dedushka said. "That is child abuse. You do not deserve to be a mother."

"You know all about child abuse, don't you?" Mom said as she bended down to me. But I was mad at her 'cause she made me fall when I tried to rescue her, so I pushed her face and got blood on her.

"Settle down," she said again.

"If you cannot help your son, I will," Dedushka said.

Two men in fancy suits came with a first aid kit. One of them told everybody that they were managing the situation. "Go get something to eat and drink. We've got this covered."

That worked.

One of the funeral men asked me lots of questions about being dizzy and if I wanted to throw up. I said no to everything, but also, all of a sudden, just seeing food made me a bit sick.

When we got back to the shelter, the staff asked about the Band-Aid on me. Usually, I like to talk about my boo-boos, especially the bloody ones. But I couldn't get my words out. Mom explained what happened and said we were fine. I felt a bit wobbly, though, like water.

"Maybe you want to get him checked out by a doctor?" somebody said.

"We just need to sleep," Mom said. "We don't need any help."

I heard the word *sleep* and that sounded really good.

But then I couldn't. I slept really bad again. I knew the Basement Beast was chomping on kids like me and breathing fire all night long. I got up to check the locks. Then my inside voice came.

They're already locked, but they won't keep it out.

Then what do I do? I asked.

I already told you, you have to leave.

But where, to Dedushka's?

Hmm, never thought of that.

Mom will never let me.

You're right.

Maybe I should just go?

Maybe.

Jimmy ran away, now he builds canoes. My daddy ran away, now— I really don't know what he's doing. But yeah, maybe I can do that.

That's right, Jimmy ran away a bunch of times as a kid, didn't he? But didn't he say it was a bad idea? He said if you wanted to run away you should go to him.

Yeah. But I don't know how to get there.

Your dad, he's a runner. He ran from Lebanon to Halifax, now he's somewhere good, I bet.

Mom said he's probably back in Lebanon. But I don't know how to get there either.

Maybe you can run to Faye?

Hey, that's a great idea. But I don't know where she is.

Yes, you do, CAS. But your mother will fight them to her death on that. She'll never give you up. You're all she has left.

Yeah, I know.

The Basement Beast roared. I put my boots on but couldn't find my outdoor clothes in the dark. I looked back at Mom, who was snoring. I unlocked the door and walked down the hall. With all my muscles I pushed the emergency exit door. An alarm went off, so loud that I had to cover my ears and jump out. I could hear talking. Was it the Basement Beast? I ran outside where it was dark and climbed a snowbank and raced across the big street. A car missed me and went on the curb. It squealed like a Super Mario Kart. I went past the motel with the blue-and-white sign and down another street. I could see a long, dark snake that was the river. Far away, lights on the river snake shone like stars. I wanted to go where there would be no Basement Beast, no yelling, no whupping, and maybe, maybe Oma Greta. But my head started to hurt, and a bad wind went through my T-shirt. I bent over and covered my head.

Someone was coming for me. But the cold hurt so much I didn't notice the lights on the police car.

37

HANNAH

I WAS CALLING out for my Ax down Carling Avenue when I saw the cruiser pull into the shelter with a blanket around him. I'd been so freaked out that I hadn't realized I was in a T-shirt. I ran to him. He said something about the stars, but I just hugged him so tight and said I'd never let him out of my sight again.

The shelter staff insisted I take Ax to emerg, but he was tired, I know he was. They got pretty bitchy about it too. Him running off had to have been one of his nightmares. He'd had this thing going on in his head about a basement beast. It was my fault for us staying in the shelter as long as we had. All he needed was to get some rest and we could leave the next day. Sitting in emerg for eight hours woulda just messed the both of us up.

I settled him and me back into bed. Two hours later, some big Black dude from the CAS knocked on my door. I got pretty riled up once I saw the police behind him.

He said there was a report from earlier in the day from Ax's grandfather alleging that I was negligent, and one from that shelter staff that I'd failed to take Ax to a doctor after a bloody head injury with untreated concussion symptoms. Bullshit. Then Ax running off and me refusing to take him to emerg afterward got me this fucking visit. I said Ax was fine or was until they woke him up, thanks a lot, assholes.

He handed me a document. *Warrant to Apprehend*, it said. They were taking my Ax.

38

AXEL

THE CAS MAN, Amari, waited with me in a big room in a big
hospital with lots of chairs and other children and parents. Except I
did not have my mom. There were games, toys, and a TV with vid-
eos playing, but I just wanted Mom. Then they put us in a small
room with a really high bed and nothing to do. Amari asked me lots
of questions and tried to be funny, but he was stupid and I was still
sleepy. A doctor came into my hospital room and made me look at
his moving finger, then asked me to spell my name backward. I
think he thought I was a kindergarten student. X-A. Who can't do
that? He asked if my head hurt. I said yes. I wanted to say it was
'cause of all the stupid questions. But I did not.

After a long time, it was daytime and they said I could leave.

He said I was going to stay with a really fun foster family for a
bit. He tried to make it sound like a sleepover, but I didn't believe
him. I asked for how long. He said that depended on Mom.

I was so tired and mad once Amari dropped me at the foster
parents' house, I had a meltdown and said I would kill anyone who
came near me and that I wanted Mom. I threw the blanket and pillow across the room and kicked over a chair, then tried to open the
window. The foster parents pulled me off the window ledge and sat
me on the bed and squeezed me between them. They held my hands
and talked about how happy they were to have me. I said I was

going to burn their house down and stab them in their sleep. I tried to head-butt them and stomp on their feet. I scored a few times.

I didn't want them to see me crying, but I couldn't stop it. My nose started to run and my head hurt, then my body just felt like a stuffy. The foster parents laid me down and dried me off because I was sweating a lot. They put the blanket on me, kissed my cheeks, and left the room, leaving the door open.

My inside voice came back. *Feel better?*

"Shut up."

Crying usually makes you feel better. Maybe they have some peanut butter cups?

"I don't want any peanut butter cups."

You're worried about Mom, I am too, really.

"You think she's okay?"

What do you think?

"Fuck."

Exactly. But what can you do?

"I'll kill everybody then I'll kill myself."

Not a good idea.

"Yes, it is."

All you needed was to get out, and now you're out.

I slammed my bed with my fists. "But ... but ... maybe that wasn't a good idea."

No more yelling, no more whupping, there will always be food, you get a clean home with no parties ... You're in a house again, a whole house. It's what you wanted."

"I want my Mom," I yelled. "If I can't go home, I'm gonna kill everybody and then I'm going to die, die, die ..." I didn't care if they heard me on the other side of the door.

But you said you wanted to leave.

"I didn't. You said, not me. You told me I had to leave. You did."

It doesn't matter, Mom will never let you go.

I started to cry again and let tears fall down the side of my face without wiping them off.

The foster parents were whispering by the door outside my room.

The next day they took me back to the hospital. This time I got to stay.

———

I got to see Mom two days later. She brought me Pokémon cards and a pepperoni stick. Mig, my helper, let Mom into my room. I got my very own room like at Doreen's. Mig left the door open and stood nearby. Next door, a teenaged boy was locked in. I could hear him yelling and swearing at everybody. He said he was going to fuck them up. He banged the walls and things were breaking, then there was more yelling and people moving. Then quiet.

I hoped Mig didn't get sweared at.

"You see, they don't know what they're doing," Mom told me. "They put you in this loony bin 'cause they think we're both crazy." Mom's knee shook like she had ants in her pants. "But what they really want is to separate us and take you away from me." Mom started to get red. She was more tired and sad than I ever seen, like she was crying all night. Worse than the time we found out Faye was gone for good. "Don't listen to them, you hear me?"

I wanted to look after her, but then I started to get nervous and just wanted to go.

I remembered what she taught me to say. We get along, there's lots of food, things are good, she has no boyfriend.

I looked to see if Mig was listening, but she was across the hall. I wanted Mom to feel better, so I hugged her.

She cried. "Who loves you more than anybody?"

"You do, Mom, you do."

"Who's been there for you always, Ax?"

"You, Mom. You always been there." Except when you put me with Doreen.

I told her what my days were like. I talked about the food, which was good. There's always someone to talk to and something to do. I

239

shoulda lied, 'cause she got madder and said she was gonna talk to Dr. Patel. The way she said *talk*, it wasn't good. It was a long time before he came.

"Is this a goddamned hotel you're running here?"

Dr. Patel looked at me and said to her, "Maybe we can take this into the meeting room, just you and I."

"I've waited an hour for you already and I've missed the next bus, so you're not gonna drag this out by making me go to some stupid meeting room."

"Fine. Axel, would you be so kind as to allow your mom and I to have a private moment in your room?"

I nodded and went into the hall, close enough so I could hear them.

"You put my son beside a whack-job teenager so he can learn to be mental too. You ply him with a pile of medication that I was *not* asked about, and you spoil him like he's on an all-inclusive cruise. A good way to ruin him. He should be snatched from you guys, such bullshit."

Dr. Patel said that he was unsure what he could share with her, given that the CAS had taken over care and custody.

That got her going. She raised her voice, and some people in the hallway turned their heads to listen.

I was about to pull the fire alarm when he said she was right to be concerned and to ask questions. He promised to get the CAS worker in as soon as possible so that they could all meet and address her concerns.

She backed off and I took my hand off the fire alarm.

Mom left after that. I was kind of glad 'cause it was Taco Tuesday and Mig said they make good ones. I was liking CHEO a lot. Because of Mig, I like mornings now. She wakes me up every morning at exactly the same time with an Ojibwe song that she plays on a wooden recorder she made. She helps me pick out my clothes for the day, get dressed, and take my medication. Then I get to have breakfast in the schoolroom along with the other twenty kids.

The school is in one room. I'm the youngest by a lot and I got

Mig all to myself. She helps the teacher by starting the class with morning boosters. Simon Says is my favourite.

One time I made fun of her name by calling her "Big Mig the Jig." I called her that a bunch of times with different combos: dig, fig, rig, and wig. She laughed and told me she'd heard worse, much worse.

"Like what? Stupid head? Penis breath?"

She laughed. "Never mind. But my real name is Migizi."

"Magoosa? What's that?"

She giggled. "No, I'm definitely not a Magoosa. It's Migizi. Migizi means bald eagle."

"Cool, except you're not bald. Axel means Ant-Man in German." This time *I* giggled.

After the hour and a half of school in the morning, I ask Mig for chocolate milk and cookies. Mig would do almost anything for me.

"Can we bake cookies again?" I asked. "Or pizza?"

"Maybe after school, but you're meeting with Dr. Patel and your CAS worker, Laura, and your mom after rounds, remember?"

"Another meeting?" I was in the hospital for five or six or seven or ten days and every day people asked how I was feeling, if I wanted to die, about the voice inside my head, and about Mom. What I really want is to play with the therapy dogs. I heard there's a clown downstairs, but it's only for the other kind of sick kids. I thought of sneaking down but knew the alarm on the door would go off. Last time I went through a locked door, the police came.

It's okay to just hang out in the playroom, also known as the lounge, even without a clown. It has crafts, books, movies, and some toys and games.

Dr. Patel and Laura came to say hello. I was surprised but happy to see Laura again. I sat down across from her and looked around for a way out, just in case. Migizi left to get me a fidget spinner. They said Mom was a bit late so they'd wait. "But you don't need to be here, Axel. In fact, this is a meeting for grown-ups," she said.

"Like my mom?"

They nodded.

I asked if they were going to talk about me.

Dr. Patel and Laura smiled. "Yes, Axel. We always meet when we have a new patient, regularly in fact. Usually, we have the parents in, but in your case, it's Laura. We have so many children here that, with more hands and minds working together, we can help children feel better sooner so that they can go home."

I already felt better. No more headaches. I thought I would hate the hospital but it's what I thought a hotel was like. I wonder what going home will be like. To Dartmouth, to the shelter with Mom, or with foster parents? I would have liked my choices more if Faye was there too. Laura says my sister now has three mothers who love her. That sounded strange at first but then I got it. Maybe she got a new brother too.

Dr. Patel looked at his watch. "We can wait for your mother a little longer."

I started to drift off until Dr. Patel snapped his fingers. "We lost you for a moment, Axel."

"Huh, uh, me? I was just thinking. When do I have to go home?"

Everyone paused, until Laura said, "We'd like to send you home, but we need to know how you're doing."

"Uh, me ... I'm doing really good, thank you. How are you?"

She smiled. "I'm great, great thanks ... You're so sweet."

Mig came in with a fidget spinner for me. I had that spinning on the table right away. I'm really good at it.

"How's the head feeling?" Dr. Patel asked. "Any pain?"

"Nope." I had the spinner going between a thumb and my first finger.

He asked if the medication made me feel any more relaxed and calm.

"Huh ... yeah, very relaxed and calm. It's good medicine, especially with chocolate milk. Have you tried it?" I snuck at look at Mig.

Dr. Patel kind of grinned and I knew he thought I was funny. "Tell me about the voices again. Were you hearing them just now?"

"No, I was just thinking about my Mom."

"And what were you thinking?" Laura asked.

"Just that maybe she misses me."

Dr. Patel jumped back in. "When the voices come, are they telling you to kill yourself or anybody else?"

"You asked me that before." I placed the spinner onto the table and it went around and around like if Boris was a Superdog chasing his own tail.

"Yes, well, today it might be different?"

"Not really. It's only just sometimes I wanna die, don't you?"

He started to say something, but I guess forgot his words.

"We all get sad," Laura said, "and sometimes the pain inside is so bad that we just want to hit the reset button. But dying isn't something we come back from. It means giving up—forever. Most of us don't want to do that. I hear you laughing and having fun with Mig, I see you play in the lounge … That's the sound of someone who has lots of life to live."

I thought of Oma Greta, who would never come back for Mom, and how sad that made her feel. I looked at the fuzzy slippers on my feet. "I guess."

I didn't want to make Mom any sadder.

39

HANNAH

T HE STUPID TAXI driver made a wrong turn, then he had no change. I wasn't going to tip him seven dollars on a thirteen-dollar fare, so we had to find somewhere to get change—unbelievable. I gave my Ax a big hug when I finally got there. It wasn't my fault for rushing in late, but I still felt like shit about it.

Ax hugged me back. Man, that felt good.

The doctor said hello and the social worker introduced herself. I recognized Laura instantly. Glinda the Good Witch. Glinda the Evil Rat. She still had that ugly, thick ginger hair and those goody-goody eyes. The last time I saw her, she testified against me and lost me Faye. Now instead of being a visitation supervisor stooge, she was my social worker. Fuck. For sure she was going for Ax. They were clearly already pissed at me, looking at the clock like that.

She said it was good to see me again, then suggested Ax and his bodyguard go to the playroom while the grown-ups talk, but that I could visit with him later. The bitch wasted no time showing us who was running the show. Ax took his fidget spinner and looked back at me, then quietly left. I know he missed me, I just know it.

"Thanks for coming in, Hannah." She took out her notepad. "This is a chance for us to update you on what Dr. Patel and his team have been doing."

"I know what they've been doing." I listed my concerns about how soft and spoiled Ax was getting, how he was being exposed to out-of-control teenagers, and how he'd been medicated without my consent.

The doc couldn't have been more than twenty-four and I'll bet he was still popping zits, his own. He admitted that the floor could be "colourful" and "energetic" at times. Then he got high and mighty: "Based on our observations, and our discussions with you—thank you for your cooperation, by the way—we feel he meets the criteria for ADHD. Attention deficit hyperactivity disorder. He also meets the criteria for a generalized anxiety disorder."

"No shit, Sherlock, he's hyper. Especially when he's away from me. And that anxiety bullshit—it's 2019, everybody's got it." Just then my phone rang, my lawyer. I declined the call.

Doctor Whatever looked at Laura, who nodded for him to continue.

"We also talked with Axel many times and reviewed data from previous child welfare files. I'm inclined to believe he has an attachment disorder."

"What?"

He went on to explain how some children don't feel valued or safe, and they don't feel they can safely explore the world. "All kids need emotional reassurance, and for their parents to be tuned into them. If not, they're hesitant to turn to them when they're distressed or become reluctant to accept comfort from them. Yet they're fearless with complete strangers. They can look as though they lack boundaries and can come across as open books."

"That's my Ax, he could make friends with a serial killer. You're wrong about us, though. Did you see the way he hugged me? Did you see the way he looked at me when he left?"

"We did," Laura said. "And we've also noted that he doesn't turn to you when he has emotional needs. In fact, he's more likely to shut himself down, even while he tries to protect you. The problem is, his needs don't get acknowledged or met, and he never really learns to turn off the alarm."

"He's a tough kid, I raised him that way." My phone rang again. Damn, Manon couldn't have picked a worse time.

"Do you need to get that?"

I hesitated. "No, let's get on with this."

"This isn't news to you," Laura said. "Community Services went through much of this with you in Dartmouth."

Glinda was thorough. Bitch.

"Which is why you taking him from me and sticking him in here is such bullshit."

"Don't you think it's worth figuring out what's going on with him? He could've died when he ran from the shelter. And we need to get a handle on him hearing voices, don't you agree?"

"Sure, but it's normal for people to have their own angel inside. I did my research. I'm not completely clueless." I'd gotten a good shot in.

"You're not wrong about people having a conscience, an inner critic, or even a cheerleader inside," Dr. Know-It-All said. "But his voices only appear when he is in an especially vulnerable, distressed place. We have been able to identify that these episodes come after a major event, like being in the shelter, going into foster care, or when he's afraid of repercussions from you. I think that says a lot."

"So he's not crazy, see." And neither am I.

"Of course not. With some children, voices can not only be protective and guiding but a cry for help, even a deflection from trauma," she said.

"We call it dissociation," Dr. Full-of-Himself said. I didn't know what he was talking about and he was loving it. The bigger the words, the bigger the bullshit.

"What Dr. Patel is saying," Laura said, "is that voices can be something very real in a child's mind. They can be conjured up to withstand something very, very distressing. Or it can be to let us know that they have needs. I just feel that Axel's are worth exploring, especially when considered in conjunction with his anxiety, his attentional and behavioural challenges, as well as his attachment issues."

"So you still don't really know. It could be this, it could be that. But in the meantime, let's take him away from his mother." I got up. "My lawyer's gonna hear about this."

"Axel's lawyer will get a full report, as will all legal reps," she said. "I'm just glad the court felt that Axel should have his own legal representation."

"Well, that was dumb. I've got Manon to look after the both of us. She's not gonna let you get away with anything. You guys have been coming after me ever since I became a mother. It's discrimination because he's half Lebanese. Manon's gonna fry you in court, just wait and see."

"Well, the judge ultimately decides, but because the potential outcomes aren't so cut-and-dried anymore, it only makes sense that Axel also has his own lawyer. Eventually, all four lawyers will sit down and do their legal thing.

"What do you mean, 'all four' lawyers?"

Laura hesitated. "Did you not know? Your parents have filed for a party-status motion to be part of the court proceedings."

"What are you talking about?"

"Your parents are requesting the court make an access order and will put forward a plan of care for Axel. As his kin, we'll have to take a look at that."

So my parents were going to take Axel from me. They hadn't bothered stepping up for Faye. I know why. She'd have been too much work 'cause of her seizures. And she was a girl. As if I couldn't have seen that Papa would try and screw me over. No better way than to take my Ax. I reached my lawyer, Manon, as the elevator arrived, suddenly realizing I hadn't finished my visit with Ax. I turned back to the locked doors of his unit.

"Hannah, Hannah? Are you still there? I've been trying to reach you. I left a trail of messages at the shelter. I just got something from legal reps for your parents. We need to talk," Manon said.

The people inside the elevator eyed me like I was holding them up.

I stepped back in. I didn't want Axel hearing this conversation.

"Your parents have hired Cheryl Solomon. They're going after Axel."

"Fuck me," I roared, despite the crowded, confined space. And so what if I was loud. I could smell some guy's breath on my shoulder. "I just found out. Why didn't you tell me, why didn't you stop it?"

"I just got through telling you that I've been trying to get a hold of you. I can't control what your parents do."

"They don't know Ax, and they couldn't care less!" My phone cut out when the elevator doors closed, and no amount of yelling could change that.

I got off the main floor and called her back. "Where were we?"

"Your parents. They may not have been active in his life, but grandparents have the right to argue for access or custody. And I'm not going to lie to you. Where the parent is unable or unwilling to provide the necessary care for a child, most judges would prefer to send the child to kin than to put it on the state. Your parents don't have to be perfect. Solomon will paint them as able and willing to provide for your son's needs."

"Bullshit, bullshit, bullshit. They treated me like garbage."

"Is anything documented? Any CAS or police red flags?"

I thought of the opportunities lost, years ago, when I shoulda spat out the truth about my family to Tara Lee. "No."

"I was hoping you'd say there's a thick file on them. Listen, Solomon doesn't have to convince you. It's the judge who decides what's in Axel's best interests."

"You're supposed to be on my side. I'm in his best interest. I'm willing and able. When I wasn't, I agreed to temporary care. Diane Khalil said it was a sign of strength that I did that. Ask her."

"I'm not saying you're not," she said. "But—"

"You're fucking useless, Manon. My father comes after me and you take his side, unbelievable. No wonder I lost Faye with you representing me. What was I thinking running a losing hand, again?"

"You do have a choice here ..."

"Stop." All my life, the same fucking line. My mom, school staff, CAS workers, therapists, and now my own lawyer telling me I had a choice. "The only real choice I've ever had was chicken or beef. No, wait, I can also choose who my lawyer is, and I choose to lose you. You're fired." I hung up and squeezed my fists. I'd lost track of where I was and looked around. Still on the main floor. I stormed outside, lit a smoke, and kept walking. When it was half-done, I was still steamed but then realized I still had my visit with Ax.

I scrambled back in.

40

AXEL

I SAT ON my bed while Mom walked back and forth in my room.

"Everybody's against us," she said. "We need to stand together."

I nodded. "Like before?"

"Yes," she said. "But no, this is worse, way worse. I heard your Dedushka might want you. He's way worse than the CAS."

At least he's my family, I thought. I hoped Mom couldn't read my mind anymore.

"Your Dedushka is a complete asshole, and your Oma is a spineless footstool to him."

I heard snakes don't have spines. Was she saying Oma was like a snake? A good snake or bad one? Probably a bad one.

Mom says a complete asshole is worse than just a stupid asshole, like most of her boyfriends were. Sometimes her boyfriends were nice to me. But Dedushka and Oma are *always* nice to me when I see them. Oma always looks at me like she feels sorry for me and one time she gave me a toonie and made me promise not to tell Mom. Dedushka is never mean to me either. He always playfights with me and never swears at me or calls me stupid or a loser. Once, he gave me an Optimus Prime Transformer.

I asked her why he was a complete asshole.

She thought really hard about my question but didn't answer.

She looked away. "Ax, he's a bad man, that's all I can say. You remember what I told you to say before?"

"Uh-huh. Mom is home all the time, no parties, she doesn't have a boyfriend, we get along real good—"

"But you have to say more."

I didn't know what she meant.

"You have to say how creepy your Dedushka made you feel. You have to say how he scared you, how he smacked you around, grabbed you by the neck. And you have to say how your Oma Steffi never did anything about it. If you don't, you might have to live with them."

But Dedushka never did any of those things. One time he did a full nelson on me, but we were playfighting and I think if it was for-real wrestling he would probably beat me even though I know karate because he's very strong. The CAS are evil, for sure. They took Faye away, so Mom was right about them. But they made me live with Doreen and now my new foster parents, and that's not so bad. Living with Oma and Dedushka doesn't sound so bad either.

———

Dr. Patel said I was getting better. They gave me some pills that would help me relax. But I'm already relaxed. I was sad to leave Mig and the hospital. I liked everything there. Okay, maybe not everything. The teenager beside me swore more than Mom and was always throwing things. Even after he left, another older boy came in just like him. They made the staff mad. I didn't like that. The staff treated me really good. I could tell they weren't used to having little boys around. I didn't like how the medicine made my stomach burn and blocked me from pooing. But I liked telling Mig that I was full of shit. On the last day, Mig gave me a dream catcher. I started to make one when I first got to the hospital, but it was too hard, so I gave up. She finished it for me with wooden beads and three long white-and-black feathers.

"Remember how dream catchers are supposed to trap bad dreams and let the good ones through?"

I nodded.

"Well, this not only does that but also traps the bad thoughts and grows the good ones."

That sounded like a miracle, because I've always had bad dreams, and bad thoughts too. "Really?"

"Well, they're eagle feathers, imitation ones anyway. I believe the strength and courage of eagles will help you turn those bad thoughts and dreams into courage and peace. It works for me, anyway, so I wanted you to have this."

I took the dream catcher and held it up. I gave Mig a big hug and she helped me pack the rest of my things.

At my foster parents' house, I got really popular. Everyone wanted to visit all the time. Laura kept coming to see me, plus I got to see my grandparents, and Mom too.

Mom is living in a different shelter that doesn't allow visitors. She said she doesn't have money to take me out anyway. I woulda been okay just going to the park, but our visits had to be at the CAS head office, like before with Faye.

The first time I was alone with Dedushka and Oma, I was worried. He took me to his work and showed me his fleet of trucks and even let me climb up into the driver's seat. He explained that there were different kinds of trucks to carry different things. Some of them were called dry vans and some were called semis. The semis are the coolest 'cause they have a bed and TV in them. Then there were flatbeds, then reefers, but not the kind you smoke. He even let me blow the air horn.

He said when I get older, he'll teach me how to drive them. And maybe someday they'll all be mine because my uncle is too irresponsible to handle the family business.

We went to McDonald's after every visit and I got to have anything but stayed with the McNuggets. He even let me order ten instead of four. Mom only lets me have four. She says that's all I can eat.

He gave me a dollar for every Russian word I could remember. He started me off with a loonie because I already knew *dedushka*. But then I remembered *nyet* for no, *spaseeba* for thank you and *glupyy* for stupid. That's what he calls everybody who gets in his way while driving. The first time I said it, I got an extra dollar and a high-five.

Dedushka and Oma said I could do anything I wanted. I picked Funhaven. I heard other kids talk about it all the time and wanted to go.

It was like heaven, even more fun than the hospital. There were a million other kids there and they were even louder than me. I ran through the jungle gym and rock wall and the arcade. Dedushka and Oma tried to keep up with me but no way could they do the rock wall. Oma was pretty good in the arcade and crushed the shooting games. Dedushka loved the racing simulator, but he was pretty bad even though his job is driving trucks.

I pulled them into the bumper cars with Dedushka and me squeezing into one. I let him drive. The music and all the blinking lights came on and other kids screamed and laughed when the cars started. He couldn't get too comfortable and had a hard time controlling it. We were rammed from behind by Oma, who laughed and waved before chasing other cars.

"Let's go, Dedushka, quick. Oma's coming back."

But he could only move in circles. Just when he figured out how to turn, Oma hit us head on.

"Get her, get her back!" I yelled to him.

Oma drove off but then another car slammed into our rear and we stopped.

"Hit the pedal, Dedushka, hit the pedal. Let's get out of here!"

He looked at me like Mom does sometimes when she gets quiet then goes crazy.

Just then I could see out of the corner of my eye Oma crashing into Dedushka's side. He covered his head like it was a for-real accident, like he was hurt. He looked super scared. "It's okay, it's only a game."

Dedushka looked tired after the bumper cars and shoved Oma away. I didn't like that. She told me to go through the ball cannons and obstacle courses by myself. Once I did that, I looked back and saw them sitting on a bench. He looked sick and his head was on her shoulder, but she smiled and waved at me. I guess everything was okay, but the way he and Mom can be the same is weird.

I nosedived down the slides and screamed on the roller coaster and started all over again from the beginning until it was time to go. Oma drove this time. They have a big new SUV with a screen all to myself. It is like an airplane from Halifax to Ottawa except I could take the screen off and finish watching it inside their house.

On the drive home, Dedushka kept asking me how Mom was. "She is still in a shelter?" Then he said stuff like, "A mother should have a proper home and a good job to buy things to show love." "Your poor mother having to ride the bus, I cannot imagine it." "And who will be your father next week?" "Your Oma and I have been together for almost forty years. You will always have a place with us."

I'm glad Oma never asks questions because I don't like it when he does that. I think he really loves me but doesn't like Mom. I don't want them to be mad at me, so I just say, "I don't know ... Yes, Dedushka ... Yes, Oma ... Thank you," so that way no one can get madder. They asked about Mom's new Costco job and apartment too. I said I didn't know anything and that's the truth. Mom said she would have benefits soon, which made her happy, so I think benefits are like free food at the Double Happiness. I miss Justine and Matthew. I hope they fixed the restaurant. I feel bad that I started the fire. I'm so stupid.

So even though Mom thinks Dedushka is a complete asshole, he is not to me. He said it was his wish that I could live with them forever and they would give me the life I deserve. He asked if I would like that. Oma told him to not pressure me, that I was just a boy and it wasn't up to me.

That made me think. Could Mom be wrong about Dedushka Youri and Oma Steffi?

41

HANNAH

————

Back when I first ran to Halifax with Floyd at the age of eighteen, I told Oma I loved Floyd. I legit just didn't want the stress of me staying with her to kill her.

She scoffed. "Love is supposed to inspire you to do wonderful things, not be stupid. You do not even know the boy." I didn't like her calling me stupid.

"So you exchanged kisses during breaks, *wunderbar*. He leaves his family so he can collect welfare in another province, how inspiring. He tells you every night he loves you, that he will look after you, *ja*? Do not be like your mother. You can do better."

I didn't need to hear that. It was one more reason for me and Oma to fight, along with me having to go to school, about my smoking, me not getting a job, and the cost of the internet. All of it made me want to disappear. I had eight dollars in my bank account.

Most nights after that, after Oma fell asleep, I'd go into her purse and take out a bill—starting with the fives but soon getting bolder. After about a month, I took her credit card and booked the train tickets to Halifax.

Oma was right, of course, about Floyd. But she didn't know anything about Uncle Jack. Unlike Floyd, Jack was a real man, and a player.

He showed me how to apply for welfare, listing himself as a

landlord so that he could get both Floyd's and my housing rate deposited directly. That meant a thousand bucks in his pocket monthly, leaving Floyd and me only sixty-eight dollars each. In exchange, he shared his three-bedroom bungalow with us. It was one of two properties he managed for his pops. It had a rec room with a big-screen TV, laundry, backyard, and a gas fireplace.

He threw in beer, weed, salad kits, cans of soup, frozen pizza, and a bag of tobacco, and he paid for the cable and internet. His protein shakes and anything dedicated to building muscle mass were off-limits and marked in capital letters on a label from his prized label maker. On cheque day he'd bring home dinner from the King of Donair. Occasionally he'd drop me some makeup or a new outfit, take me out to lunch downtown, or slip me a tenner. When he was really horny he'd share his coke, but only with me. And yes, I had to pay for it, if you know what I mean.

Yeah, Jack and I had something going, even if it was transactional, but we were upfront about it and I never bullshitted Floyd, who, let's face it, was out of his league with me. One time Floyd walked in on us doing a Swedish bike ride, your basic standing anal. He freaked out and huffed and puffed. We made like he wasn't there and kept going. I guess that was a bit insensitive. Serves him right for not knocking, though, right? It's not like we'd left the door open. Anyway, the next day he bounced with a couple of ounces of Jack's weed. Enough to fly back to Ottawa and party it up. It was the ballsiest thing I'd ever seen him do, but good for him.

Two days later, Jack came home with a new roommate to replace Floyd as a tenant: Lilly, a waif of a teenager who'd recently run away from her parents in St. John's. She had a constellation of freckles that reminded me of Mackenzie's. He reeked of sweat and sex and had a wild look in his bloodshot eyes. He demanded to know where I'd been.

"Ahh ... work, Finnegan's Pub, where else?" I could tell he'd forgotten I'd landed some cash-only shifts. He'd been the one gone for a couple of days.

I could hear Lilly vomiting in the bathroom. I felt bad for her but was happy it wasn't me.

"Come on, it's about time for some trigonometry, let's get a three-way going," Jack said, chest heaving, his one nostril visibly lined with white powder.

"Maybe another night. She doesn't look like she's doing too good."

"Nothing another line won't fix." He smiled like a little boy caught licking icing sugar.

Lilly's retching intensified. "Uhhh, maybe you could use some rest."

"Don't tell me what I need." Jack scrunched his face, clenched both fists, and shook like he was about to have a tantrum. "Take your jeans off, Daddy wants to go to magic mountain, *now*. Woooeee."

"Jack, I just had a shit, gimme a chance to shower and get some lube."

"Like I care." He pushed me onto the couch and started to un-buckle my jeans.

'No— Wait, Jack."

When he was done, he smacked my butt, knocking me onto my side. He went back to his room and, from what I could tell, woke Lilly—but silence followed. I figured he'd finally burned himself out. I stumbled into my bedroom, closing the door behind me. I rolled onto my bed and ignored the pain from Jack having just done me. I pulled my hidden money out from under a loose floorboard and counted. I had almost enough to follow Floyd back home, if that's where he'd gone. Or maybe Toronto. Or I could pay Oma back.

———

For a few weeks, Jack was really sweet. He stuck to us girls like glue and took us out for dinner and long drives. One day he came home with some tube-top rompers and skater dresses from Stitches. I re-member 'cause the sale prices were still on. End-of-season clearance. He made a big deal of the chintzy earrings and bracelets, and some

Maybelline. "I love you girls so much. Maybe I don't say it, or show it enough, but I feel blessed by the Big Guy himself, who gave me two wonderful women. God, I'd do anything for you two." He paused, looking at us with sad, vulnerable eyes until Lilly said she loved him too and would also do anything for him.

"Really?" Jack said with a little too much enthusiasm. "Let's celebrate. Let's go for a drive and get some Dairy Queen."

Hard to say no to a Blizzard. But first, he wanted us to try on the new makeup and clothes and jewellery.

Lilly sat in the front seat beside Jack with her hand on his thigh, and his on hers. Lilly didn't seem to think anything about him driving them across the bridge into Halifax for Dairy Queen when there were already three nearby in Dartmouth. But I did.

While at the DQ, Jack dropped his head into his hands. "Girls, I have to be real with you for a second. This is embarrassing for me to admit. I may lose the house, both houses, in fact, the car, everything."

"Shit, no, what happened?"

He looked up at me. "My old man fell behind on mortgage payments. I should've known. He lost his marbles years ago. That's why he left everything up to me. Anyway, the bank said I had a week to come up with some serious coin, or we're out on the street."

He drove back toward the bridge. We stopped by a small park and he sat us on a bench and pulled out some killer weed. Pretty soon we girls were all vibing and giggly. We got back into the car and Jack turned onto Agricola Street and then parked.

"Back to what I was saying earlier. There is a solution," he said. "We can save the houses from the bank and keep a good thing going."

He pointed to several women standing on Agricola, who despite the cold, wore short skirts and knee-high boots, waving to cars passing by. Speaking quietly to us, he praised those women for how loyal they were to their man, doing whatever they needed to do out of love. He said that if we could follow their example for just a few nights, we might be able to keep the houses for enough time to come up with a better long-term solution.

I slowly worked my way through my dope fog. "You want to pimp us out?"

"It's not like that. I want us to stay together. You know I'd do anything to make that happen, right?"

My nod was slow and hesitant.

"You know I love you, don't you?" he asked us.

Lilly said she loved him one more time. I mumbled something, but love wasn't in there.

"We're a team, right? Better together, right?"

We nodded, more out of habit than anything.

Jack pointed his nose at one young man, awkwardly hunched over, who kept scanning around as he followed one of the women into an alley. A few minutes later, another woman got into a luxury car with tinted windows that drove off.

"I want you to know, ladies, how much this means to me. The thought that we'd have to split up, lose the house—it would've broken my heart."

He drove us to Jubilee Road and showed us a house. He took us around the side entrance and upstairs to some back rooms, each with a double bed. He marvelled at how clean, quiet, and safe it was. He said he'd always be parked either outside or on Agricola Street. He talked about how to spot a cop, a bad john, and most importantly, told us, "You can haggle, but don't go lower than forty dollars for a hand job, sixty for a blow, eighty for sex. Plus you get to keep half the tips." But all I could think about was the money he had blown on the clothes, jewellery, and everything else over the past few weeks. I knew this was not going to be for a night or two.

"Any questions?" Jack didn't wait for replies as he handed out condoms and then some hand sanitizer wipes. "You can't be too careful, eh, ladies?"

He dropped us back onto Agricola, across the street from the other women already working. He parked, then lit a cigarette and watched. I looked around. "Lilly, whatever happens next, just follow me, okay?"

"What?" Lilly asked.

I got the other women going and waved a fist. "Bring it, bitches, I'm going to fuck you up, nobody's gonna want your slutty, fat asses ... we own this street now."

"What the fuck, Hannah?" Lilly said.

"Just shut up and follow me."

I picked up some rocks and purposely threw wide. The women responded with jeers. I saw another man get out of a car. The women knew him and egged him toward me. He beelined for me. From the other direction, I could see Jack picking up a head of steam. The two men collided in the middle of the street, exchanging blows. All the women crowded around the melee, either swearing and cheering on their respective pimps or just enjoying the spectacle. Other passersby joined in until the police pulled up with lights and sirens on.

I grabbed Lilly's arm and tried to pull her away.

"What are you doing?" Lilly resisted.

"I'm trying to save your ass."

The police arrived and tried to calm the combatants. I gave Lilly another pull, but she wouldn't budge. She drifted toward Jack. Stupid idiot. I let her go and tore out of there.

***

More than a year went by. I sat in Nena's Breakfast House, nursing a coffee and a headache. I'd been up all night partying with Jeanine from work at the Dollarama. My boyfriend, Derek, had just sat down and he needed some attention, but I was too tired to give a shit. I flipped through the *Chronicle Herald*. On the second page of the local news, an article caught my eye. "Jack McDonald of Crichton Park has been convicted of living off the avails of prostitution of persons under eighteen and aggravated assault of a peace officer. The Crown will be seeking the maximum fourteen-year sentence." A fuzzy picture of Jack cuffed and being led away by the police made me shout out, "Fuck, yeah."

"What is it, Hannah Montana?" Derek asked.

I hated that pet name and had told him so many times. "Nothing, just some dude I knew is going to the clink."

"Who?"

"Relax D, just some loser." It annoyed me that Derek was like every man I'd been with since Jack—easily threatened by the mere suggestion that I'd had another life before him. My last boyfriend, DeAndre, used to scowl and shut down if I even looked at a male server for longer than five seconds. But he was gentle compared to JJ, who got into fights when he saw men hitting on me, then exploded when we got back to his place.

I glared at Derek and shook my head. "You're pretty stupid, you know that?"

"I don't like it when you call me that."

I'd heard that before. Was it Floyd, DeAndre, maybe both? I couldn't remember. "Okay, forget I called you stupid. I feel like a donair. Let's bounce."

"No, I'm stupid for staying with you and your bullshit. Why do I stay with you?"

"Didn't you just answer your own question?"

Derek puffed out his linebacker physique.

"So you're gonna hold your breath and count to ten and then blow my house down? You know I'm hungover, I have no patience for your shit. I'm going for a fucking donair. If you want to come, fine, if not, I'll catch you later." I zipped up my coat to leave.

"You leave now and we're done. All your things will be out in the parking lot when you come back."

"What the fuck, over nothing?"

"Your attitude is nothing. In fact, it sucks. And so is your commitment in this relationship."

"That's three. I've never seen you do that before."

"Do what?"

"String three sentences together." I got up and left a toonie for the coffee. "Don't go pinching this. And if you're gonna trash my shit, don't beat off into it first."

A soft rain greeted me as I stepped out of Nena's. I decided to save the bus or cab fare and hoof the twenty minutes up Windmill for my donair. As I walked, the rain picked up. Derek was a loser, I knew that. I had no regrets about continually reminding him of that. I did regret having to return to my mouldy roach factory of a room rental. By the time I arrived at the King of Donair, the rain had broken into a steady downpour and I was soaked.

The restaurant had just opened, but already people were ahead of me lining up in front of the counter.

"Wait, wait." A server behind the counter with a warm smile beneath a well-trimmed moustache waved me to the front of the line. "Ladies and drowned rats first."

I gave a weak smile as I jumped the queue, drawing annoyed looks from the other customers. Screw 'em.

"Why do you look so sad?" the server asked.

"Ahhh ... my boyfriend is a dick. My ex-boyfriend really, as of half an hour ago. But that's okay, he was driving me bananas."

The server's smile widened.

I noticed his guns. The man was stacked and well put-together.

"Ah, then he is the stupid one. Why would anyone dare risk annoying anyone as beautiful as you?"

"Lady, will you just order, already?" the customer behind me said.

I ignored them. "What's your name?" I asked the server.

"Bashir. But my special friends call me Bash."

SUMMER 2019

42

AXEL

WHEN MOM AND me used to go see Faye, Laura was there. When the police and the Children's Aid took me from the shelter, Laura was there too. Now she is my social worker. And now when I get called to the office, I'm not scared that I'm in trouble and have to see the principal because it's to see her. I thought she was going to ask me the same boring questions about me and Mom. But she didn't do that. She brought in a suitcase of games and toys I never played with before, like Hexbugs, Transformers, magnetic blocks, Clixos, and so many flavours of Play-Doh. Plus she always has food. So we just ate and played. It's fun and I get to miss French.

We usually sit in a room with a small table and two chairs. It's where they keep art supplies. There is also a ladder, a mop and pail, a microwave on its side, and a bunch of wires sticking out of a box. The window is covered up, which made me think that if there is a terrorist or a fire like at the Double Happiness, we could be trapped.

One day when Laura was taking out some magnets for us to play with, she looked a bit sad. I asked what was wrong.

She told me she'd just talked with her mom. "I love my mother and can't imagine her not in my life. But then sometimes I just wish she'd leave me alone, you know what I mean?"

I sometimes wished the same thing, but I didn't dare say that in case Mom found out.

"Like, I know if I was surrounded by Doc Ock, Loki, the Joker, and Magneto, she'd bust in and save me," Laura said. "But then there are times she gets on my nerves and I just need to get away from her. I think all children think that way about their mothers, even grown-ups like me. Does that make me evil? Am I a bad daughter?"

"No, I don't think so. I bet you're a great daughter." But I'm a bad son.

"Really, you think so?" she said.

"Uh-huh."

"So I guess it's okay to have mixed feelings about someone you love. But is hate too strong a word?"

I thought about it. "No, sometimes I hate Mom too."

"Really? You are so loving and protective of your mother. When could you possibly hate her?"

I didn't answer right away even though I knew what to say. Then it came out. "Like when she calls me stupid."

"You're so not stupid, Axel. You may not be the best at French, or math. But you're a warrior who has lived through things most kids would never ever understand. You've lived in so many different places, you've looked after your mother, and you've survived it all."

Laura gave me a high-five.

"And Axel, here you are, giving grown-up advice. Thank you, I think I know what to say to my mother now, even though I know it won't be easy."

I thought of Jimmy, who also talked to me like a grown-up. "You're welcome." It felt good to help her. "Why are you fighting?"

Laura sighed. "It's a disagreement, not a fight. I want to buy a house in Kanata, and she's not happy about it. It's far from where she lives in Orleans. Boreleans, I call it. It's not like I'll never see her again. But it's a really nice house, it's safe, and I just want to live my own life, you know?"

I thought about that but said nothing. Living away from Mom forever isn't something I'm supposed to imagine. I'm glad Laura lined up the magnets so we could play instead of talking about this. I spent the rest of our time looking for things to attach the magnets to. Some things look like metal but they are fake.

43

HANNAH

———

IT TOTALLY MESSED me up to hear about Axel's visits to my parents and to see him with a new toy each time. The very idea that Ax was spending time with my parents legit almost made me puke.

How did I know Papa wasn't going to smack Ax for hiding food everywhere, peeing all over the toilet seat, leaving trails of LEGO around?

On the same day I moved into the two-bedroom, I worked my way down to the seventh person on my list of potential new lawyers. Every other lawyer had either turned me down or said they couldn't take on new clients. In other words, they didn't like my attitude. Shabana Ahmedi shared an office with another lawyer above the Colonnade Pizza on Metcalfe Street in Ottawa's Centretown. I had called ahead and she said her only free time was over lunch, but that I was welcome to drop by.

I entered Shabana's office, then stopped. She wore a chestnut-coloured jersey hijab elegantly wrapped around her head. Large black aviator glasses and a smooth, round face gave her the look of a fresh-eyed college student. Her phone was playing some video on her desk in front of her and she was chomping into a shawarma, dripping sauce onto her hijab. First impressions were not her thing.

"Crap," she said as she dabbed at the sauce. "I have court in half an hour."

I knew I was fucked. Even still, I gave her my standard Lebanese Arabic greeting that Bash taught me. *"Marhaba."*

"Sanga yaast," she replied.

I didn't know what she'd said. It musta shown.

"Sanga yaast—'How are you' in Pashto. I'm not an Arab."

I studied her, awkwardly trying to hide my confusion and disappointment.

"It's great that you know some Arabic, but Farsi, Pashto, English, and really bad French are my go-tos, although if you'd have said *kol khara* in Arabic I'd have known enough to also tell you to eat ... shit."

She covered her mouth when she said shit, then invited me to sit down. I did, but I was slow about it.

She said she had twenty minutes to eat and hear me out. I looked at my list of lawyers, which I'd burned through trying to get someone to even consider me. She was the last one. Crap. I told her about my history with child welfare authorities and of Ax's recent apprehension, my parents' visits with him, and them trying to destroy me by taking my last child.

She scribbled a few things, then finished the last of her shawarma. "So you completed all the counselling, parent support, everything that Dartmouth CAS suggested?"

I'd blown off my last counsellor, but answered yes anyway.

"And it was a family crisis that brought you back to Ottawa? Before that, were you and Axel more or less stable?"

I nodded.

"Hmmm." She stared off in thought. "And the next court date is in three months?"

"Yeah."

"It's unfortunate you didn't have a legal rep present for the motion hearing," she said. "Not that the judge was going to disallow your parents from having access anyway."

"Yeah, well, I'm here, aren't I? You know, maybe this isn't the right fit for me, no offence."

She pulled out some hard mints, offering me one. I pocketed a fistful. I had to walk away with something.

"How many other lawyers have you called since you fired Manon Arsenault?"

"A few," I replied.

"How many more are on your list?"

I shook my head. "None."

"But you have a legal aid certificate, right?"

"Right."

"Who are the other lawyers representing Axel, the CAS, and your parents?"

"I don't know, but somebody named Solomon, I think, was hired by my parents."

"Cheryl Solomon?"

"Uh-huh. You know her?"

"Frig, everyone knows Cheryl Solomon. Solomon Family Law Group. They're the largest family law practice in Eastern Ontario. They cater to raging grannies with money to burn. They like to crush small practices like mine."

"Fuck."

She chuckled. "Just kidding." She sucked on her mint and grinned. "Solomon's a player, she'll mean business. We'll have to bring our A game."

"How the hell did you get a law degree? You'd get carded trying to buy booze."

"Would you be saying that to me if I looked just a teeny bit different—was a man, had stunning blue eyes and Nordic blonde hair?"

"I'm no racist, I just thought you look real young, that's all. Can we move on?"

"*Inshallah*. But if you could pick up some Smirnoff coolers for me, that'd be great—I left my ID by my skateboard back in my dorm, and for sure I'll get carded."

"Look, I'm sorry, okay. What do you want me to say?"

Shabana sighed. "I'm the end of your road, so let's stop with the job interview. You need a lawyer, and I think I can help you."

"Really?"

"Yeah, really, I'm just feeling cranky. My bad. I go through this shit every time I meet someone in a professional capacity. They come in looking for a lawyer but see me as the hired help, the oppressed Arab woman, or the foreign-exchange student. So I do have a bit of a chip on my hijab and you walked into it. But yeah, I think I can help."

I settled into my chair and took a breath. "Thank you. How can I say that to you in whatever language—"

"I'm from Toronto. My parents are from Afghanistan. 'Thank you' works."

"How do you say thank you in Afghani?"

"Afghani is when you're dealing with the currency, like a loonie will get you sixty or seventy Afghan Afghani. Confusing, right? Never mind. We speak Pashto, *tasakor is* thank you. *Wabakahi* means sorry, and you're going to need it. Although a tall skim chai latte says the same thing."

———

A week later, Shabana reported back to me. It took her that long to identify and catch up with Emma Connor, Axel's court-appointed lawyer from the Office of the Children's Lawyer. Thankfully, Emma was an old college mate who could leave enough subtle clues for Shabana to read between the lines without betraying confidentiality.

"It's not encouraging news, but it's nothing we can't work with," she said.

"I don't like the sounds of it."

"Well, Emma said Cheryl Solomon pushed all parties to a settlement conference in three months."

"We never agreed to that. I want Ax back now."

"We weren't there in court to argue otherwise. That was after you fired Arsenault and before you hired me. I'm guessing nobody thinks you can get it all together by then. You'll need to show you have stable housing and employment, that you're off drugs, and not associating with losers. Also, that you've been in therapy and have done all the parenting classes. And, that your visits with Axel show that you're a new mother, and—this is very important—you have to work with Laura Catano."

"Blah, blah, blah ... Not a game I haven't played before."

"I can't believe I have to tell you that you need to take this so much more seriously. You've already lost Faye. In three months, the home study of your parents will be complete. Solomon will want to whack you with a one-two-three combination punch. One: she expects you to fail to cooperate with the CAS. Two: she'll come in with a report of how wonderful your parents will be for Axel. And three: she's counting on history, your history, to repeat itself. Solomon knows what she's doing.

"Shit," I said. "So what's this settlement conference?"

"Call it a pre-trial sit-down," she said. "All parties sit down with Judge Benoit. We review the information gathered by all sides. Reports, case history, and any assessments, including what the hospital had to say. The lawyers prepare a brief. It's off the record, very informal. Benoit mediates, and he'd prefer we all agree on something. Otherwise, he makes a summary judgment motion, or calls a trial, though he's loathe to use up his time that way."

"Wait, Benoit? Thinning dandruff hair and a handlebar moustache?"

"Hard to miss," Shabana said.

"Shit, I nicknamed him 'Beeno' back when I lost Faye 'cause I could tell there would 'be no' breaks in his court."

"We'll have to make our own breaks."

44

AXEL

LAURA BROUGHT ME chocolate milk and a board game called Emotional Bingo. To win, you have to spin the wheel of emotions. Where it lands, you have to give an example of when you had that feeling. After that, you get a token until you fill a line.

She let me spin first. It landed on Disappointment.

"So, Axel, when do you feel disappointment?" Laura asked.

"Never?"

"Of course, you feel disappointment, we all do. It's not a nice feeling, but we can learn to live with it. I'll bet when you have rocket fuel in your legs and want to play soccer—but then they suddenly call an indoor recess—you feel disappointed, right?"

That sounded right. "Yep, disappointment. Token for me!"

I scored a few and took the lead before the questions got harder. My next spin landed on Anxious. She asked if I knew what it was.

"Is it like when you have ants in your pants?"

She held up the token. "Could be. It's like when I was about to tell my mother that I was going to move out and buy a house—I was feeling anxious. I didn't know how she would react, I was a bit scared that she'd lose control. So I could feel my muscles get tight, my stomach hurt, and so did my head. My heart sped up, and to be honest, I just wanted to take off and forget about it." She waited. "Can you think of a time you felt anxious?"

"All the time." I said.

"All the time? Like even now?"

"Not now. Just when I'm with Mom."

"I don't get it," Laura said. "You love each other. How is it that you're anxious around her?"

"You don't know my mom like I know her," I said, pointing a thumb at myself. "She can get sooo scary."

"Really?"

"Yep."

"Wow, Axel, that's an example of you being that warrior I was talking about."

"What do you mean?"

"Well, you're always on guard, always ready to battle or run for cover. I've seen most of the *Avengers* and *Spiderman* movies, and even those guys get some down time. But not you. It must be exhausting, yet you've survived."

"This warrior stuff is tiring. Did I win?"

"Nope, you need one more. But it's my turn." She did her turn and then gave me the wheel. "It's hard to say stuff like that about our mothers, isn't it?" She sagged like a stuffy.

I nodded.

My final spin landed on Hope.

"Hope. What are *your* hopes?"

I had to think. "Like I hope to have super powers someday?"

She laughed. "And what kind of super power would you want?"

I said like a mix of Superman and Wolverine. Then Laura asked what I thought Hulk's mom was like.

That was funny. That was easy. "I'll bet she is sooo scary."

"Why do you say that?"

"Because Hulk loses control all the time."

"That's interesting. So what would the Hulk hope for from his mom?"

I thought about it. "That he could get more hugs, not get yelled at all the time, and maybe she could play with him sometimes."

"Is that what you would hope for yourself?"

I pretended to think hard and put a finger to my head, but it was another easy question. "Uh-huh, why not?"

She high-fived me for winning the game. When we were packing up, Laura asked, "What if Hulk figured out his mom couldn't change?"

"What?"

"What if the Hulk knew in his big heart that his mom would always be scary. If she could never be the kind of mother he wanted?"

That one was harder. She let me think about it while we finished packing. "I think then the Hulk would never feel safe. He would think his mama doesn't love him."

Laura patted me on the back. "You're the smartest warrior I know."

45

HANNAH

⎯⎯⎯

Nᴏʀᴍᴀʟʟʏ, Cᴏsᴛᴄᴏ ᴄᴜsᴛᴏᴍᴇʀs are like drones. They know what they want and what needs to be done. They politely queue up and move on. Except with the free samples. Then they're fucking hyenas pouncing on a kill like they haven't eaten since the last time they were in Costco.

But that day, during my shift, the customers lining up at my sample table were orderly. It didn't mean I was enjoying myself. It's a crap job, after all. No tips, no commission, no bonuses. Nothing. But I do get to say, "White cheddar and potato!" "Cheese and bacon!" "Seven-ninety-nine a bag!" "Two dollars off!" all day. I repeat with a different emphasis each time as though it's the deal of the century. Occasionally I get complaints, but I started responding with, "Yes ma'am, thank you for telling me, I'll be sure to let the chef know"— until the manager told me to lose the attitude.

A couple of young kids jumped up to the countertop when a man ragged them out before getting two samples for them.

"Sorry," the man said to me. "You'd think I starve my grand-children."

They were cute as they gobbled up the pierogi halves. "That's okay. Seven-ninety-nine a bag on sale."

He didn't move on but didn't reach into the freezer for a bag either. I could feel his stare. "Did you want more samples? Go ahead." I cut more pierogies, placing them in tiny pleated paper bowls on my counter.

"No, I'm sorry, I know I'm staring."

Other customers were getting irritated 'cause he was blocking their way to the samples. I sensed a regular ol' Costco crowd of hyenas circling.

"I think I know you," the man said. He turned around to the kids, who were climbing all over the cart. He told them to get off and wait quietly.

"Have you got kids?" The man grinned.

I wasn't enjoying his attention and looked away. "Yeah, I got two. Listen, I don't mean to be rude sir, but—"

"You're Hannah Belenko, aren't you?"

I shifted my weight, my body seizing up. "I'm sorry, do I know you?" I was suddenly aware of how sore my feet were from standing in that one spot hours at a time.

"You don't recognize me. How could you? It's been years. I've gotten old, and so much has happened—two grandkids are just the start of it. It's Bill, Bill Krohn."

I dropped my knife and froze. Jennifer's dad. My first instinct was to run, and I came close.

"Well, this is a sign if I ever saw one," he said.

"Mr. Krohn. Ah, I'm working, I'm sorry, I'm not allowed to talk ..."

"Listen," he said, "I know this is crazy, and like everything else in my life, I don't know what I'm doing anymore, but let's get coffee. Audrey's picking us up. I'll have her take the kids home. I'll wait for you at the Starbucks across the street. However long you take to finish your shift, I'll be there."

I started to say no, but customers shoved him aside while reaching for the remaining samples. So much for civility. He waved goodbye and said, "See you soon!" Another customer, impatient, glared at me, waiting for me to slice and dispense more. Vultures.

Mr. Krohn coulda just kept going and pretended not to recognize me. I sure hadn't recognized him. Time had left him with only a few remaining strands of silver hair. He'd also lost pounds, a lot of them, replaced by a mess of wrinkles and age spots. Yet he looked, I don't know, content? Is that the right word for chill? I wondered if he still sailed. The mere thought of sailing knots made me shudder.

I was about to lose my shit. The manager noticed and said the pierogies were salty enough and didn't need my tears added. He said I could leave early if I needed to. To my surprise, he didn't ask questions.

I removed my food-demo whites and hairnet and saw an umbrella in the staff room's garbage. I fished it out.

The spring heat wave had threatened a thunderous downpour all day. I pulled out a smoke and took my time crossing Merivale Road, forcing motorists to wait. I sensed their impatience behind those tinted windows. Something was coming. When I got to the other side, I had to cross through a sea of box-store parking lots. An explosion of thunder made me jump. I picked up the pace as dark, threatening clouds blocked out the remaining sunlight. Drops of rain fell and heavy winds whipped debris from the street in all directions. Flashes of lightning broke through the clouds, followed immediately by thunder. The storm was above us, almost. With Starbucks in sight, I tossed my butt away and opened the umbrella. It had a broken rib. Figures. I started to run. Thunder cracked the sky again, more lightning. Sheets of rain crashed and the wind turned my umbrella inside out just as I grabbed the door and stepped into the dry, air-conditioned Starbucks.

I shook off the rain as I scanned the café for Mr. Krohn. He saw me and waved me over. I took a deep breath and walked toward him.

He stood up and hugged me. I wasn't expecting that and was as stiff and broken as my umbrella.

"I watched you run the last hundred yards," he said. "You'd think you were really looking forward to seeing me."

We smiled awkwardly and averted each other's eyes at first.

He went to get me a coffee. When he came back, a quiet, cumbersome moment for both of us followed. "It's been a long time," he finally said.

"I guess something like fifteen years," I figured.

"Seventeen years, five months, five days."

"Uh—"

"Since Jenn hung herself."

What the fuck. It was like he'd just torn the curtain down. Years of hiding that painful memory, of denying that I made that happen, of forgetting that I pretty much backstabbed and killed her, came back in that one instant. I wanted to run, but that pulled curtain exposed everything. There was nowhere else to run.

"Sorry, that was kind of abrupt. We saw a therapist for many years after Jenn died. She recommended that we name things for what they are. It's kind of like taking charge of the trauma by naming it rather than running from it. Guess not everyone is ready to hear it."

"No, that's okay." I wanted to add that it would be hard to sugarcoat *me* causing Jenn's suicide, but I couldn't spit it out.

"So, how have you been, Hannah?"

I stirred my coffee. "Well, you know, life, eh?"

"I totally know. Up and down, back and forth, in and out—never a dull moment. Heck, I'd love to be bored."

I continued stirring. "Thanks for the coffee, Mr. Krohn, but I'm not very good at this."

"Bill, it's Bill. We're both adults."

"Okay, Bill. I'm still not any good at this."

"What's 'this,' two people having coffee?"

"I don't know what you want and I don't know what I'm doing here. If you need to shit on me, take a number."

He winced. "Is that why you think I'm here?"

I expected him to yell, scream, rant, rave, and humiliate me. Part of me was ready for it. I deserved it. Part of me just wanted to run.

"Yeah, why else? The worst possible shit happened. I was part of it. To be honest, I don't even know what was real or just me being fucked up. Take your best shot. I won't cut and run."

He shook his head. "Audrey and I got pretty messed up too. We separated for a while. And I don't know if you knew, but we left Stittsville. We felt like we had to. You can also throw in my depression, and probably bipolar too. Jenn likely inherited that from me."

I flinched.

"What saved us was Thomas. He met a wonderful woman, and they have those beautiful children."

"They're beautiful." I imagined a likeness to Jennifer.

"Yes. One of them has the middle name Jennifer. Thomas and his wife are braver than us. They showed us how to move on, to live again, even when things looked ugly. Anyway, the kids gave me a second wind on life, one I didn't think I deserved. I was so broken, but I never really blamed you."

He should've. "Really?"

"Okay, that's not true. At first, we did. We felt many things. In fact, I wished it was you hanging from that rope."

Of course. If not for me, she'd be alive. I expected that. Pile it on, please. I wouldn't have put up much resistance.

"That wasn't very Christian of me, I know, but we were devastated. We know better now. That was a dark spot in our hearts talking. God wanted her sooner than we were ready. He may have called you too, if you'd stayed to live in that house with your father. We knew all about him. Jenn told us. And Audrey hadn't meant to pry, but she saw the bruises on you that night. She and I called the Children's Aid. We told the police all about your dad, some lady cop if my memory still holds. You were a victim too."

I pushed my coffee aside. "What? You called? You spoke to them? Not Jenn?"

"Didn't you know?"

My silence meant a hard no.

"Jenn did talk to the Children's Aid, but only after we made the call and pressured her into it. We're sorry that's how it happened. But she was worried sick for you."

You stupid bitch, Hannah. Jenn tried to tell me that, but I wouldn't listen, couldn't listen.

"We weren't clueless. We saw what your father was even before he attacked you. I couldn't speak about it then, but you were obviously trapped, and probably frightened most of the time. I'll bet it took everything you had just to get by."

I glanced at the rain crashing, sending waves of water running into storm drains. Windshield wipers couldn't keep up with the downpour. In suburban Ottawa where the car is king, what few pedestrians were out there scrambled for shelter as though it were fire and not water beating down on them. My eyes welled up. His daughter was dead 'cause of me. And look at him. He shoulda been spitting in my face. But he wasn't. Instead, he was saying I did what I did 'cause I just had to stay alive. Mackenzie said the same thing, years ago.

"Jenn's death isn't on you. She made a choice. So did you—to survive." He nodded. "I had a supportive wife, a son to look after, the Church, and I still took a while to get my life together. I can't imagine you had much of a chance. It's sad how I couldn't see clearly enough to save Jenn, but I could see you needed someone. I can only wonder about your own trauma and what it did to you."

And to Ax, I said to myself. I shook my head at Bill. "It's a long story, and there are no happy endings."

"Hannah, I truly believe as dark as things were for Jenn, you had to have been very special to her. It might've been love. She was loyal to you and very protective. I'm grateful she felt that." He reached for my hand, held it, and smiled.

I tightened up at first. Then I let the gentleness and warmth of his hand track its way up my arm. For a moment, I let my guard down.

"So, you've got a lifetime membership to bend my ear. I mean it. Audrey's got the kids, the coffee's hot, and Dr. Bill is in session, so let's do it."

I looked into Bill's eyes but couldn't think of anything to say. The only people who had ever wanted to speak to me before were paid to do so or wanted to sleep with me. He just wanted to listen.

"You really wanna hear this?" I half hoped he'd say no. But he nodded.

I pulled my hand back and looked out the window at the Burger King and the people huddled by the door of the liquor store.

"Sorry, Mr. Krohn, Bill. I'm not Jenn. You couldn't save her, and you can't save me either. That's just the way it is. I'm really sorry."

He wouldn't let up. "Then why did you come here?"

I hesitated. "You asked me. Why else?"

"Because I'm just a waypoint."

"What?"

"Waypoints—beacons, markers. Our lives are filled with them. Sometimes we stumble onto them without even knowing it. Sometimes we make them happen. You and I were brought together today. I was supposed to take my grandchildren to the park, but the rain that wasn't supposed to happen changed our plans. You could've politely declined coffee, you could've left me waiting. I missed many waypoints with Jenn. And I'll bet there have been many in your life you just completely ignored."

I saw what he'd done and what he was trying to do. He'd ripped the Band-Aid off and instead of adding salt, he offered tea tree oil. It would sting at first, but then it would get better.

"You're sitting here because you've been missing your waypoints."

He was trying to tell me that a waypoint is a sign and that he was a waypoint. To what? What or who were my other waypoints? Jennifer and Mackenzie? Jimmy? What did they mean, and where were they supposed to point? Is there another direction other than lost?

"I know where you're at. You've been a victim all your life, just the way I was for years. I know the look. I can smell it."

"Then I must stink pretty bad."

We shared a laugh.

I proceeded to bare my soul and reveal my shit story, unvarnished and uncensored for the first time. From always feeling scared to freezing when my brother assaulted Mackenzie, to my last indelible memory of Jenn in the school hallway when she thought I wanted her dead, and to Oma. I paused a lot to dry my eyes with my sleeve, then spilled my anger and guilt about Bashir, and all the Tylers and Kevins, to losing Faye, and ending with my parents filing for custody of Ax.

"So there you have it. My latest episode of the Belenko shitshow. No matter how much I try to escape, it just keeps growing. And maybe I created another Youri Belenko in Ax. What a fuckup I am."

"Maybe that's the problem."

"What, that I'm a fuckup?"

"That you keep trying to outrun things. But you never can. I've learned that the hard way."

"Don't I know it. Child welfare is locked onto me wherever I go."

"It's not the CAS you should be escaping from."

"What are you talking about?"

"You can't outrun that frightened little girl inside you." He nodded in a fatherly kind of way. If anybody else had done it, I'd have said it was stupid.

I'd heard shit like that before, but coming from him, at that moment, it sounded different. I felt it in my core. I had always been frightened. And angry and scared. Of Papa, of losing my kids, of being alone, of having no one. Of losing my mind.

We looked out at a ray of sunshine breaking through the thinning clouds. It illuminated a patch of green where a groundhog was sniffing the air, chewing the grass, oblivious to the cars whizzing by on the busy street.

"Looks like the storm's over," he said.

I shrugged. "That one, anyway."

"Hannah, if you're okay with me potentially overstepping a bit, I think I know your next move."

"What?"

Bill clasped his hands and leaned in like he was about to tell me a secret. "That little scared girl inside's going to grow up awfully fast and take a stand."

46

AXEL

L AURA AND ME munched on carrot and celery sticks and dip. We talked about the Hulk again. She asked if I thought the Hulk would have the courage to let his mom know how he felt about her.

I put my carrot down. "Can we have butter tarts again next time? My foster mother always makes me eat carrots and celery for snack."

Laura dropped her carrot stick down and made a sour face and nodded. "Of course. Raisin, if I remember, is your favourite."

"Yes, please! And I know you like pecan, but you can't bring nuts into the school."

"So, about the Hulk ..."

I remembered what we talked about before. "I think the Hulk can be scared and brave with his mom at the same time, right?"

"Is that what you'd like to be with your mother, brave?"

I nodded.

"Remember how being brave also means telling someone what you want, even if it makes them mad?"

"Uh-huh."

"Would you want someone to tell your mother about some of the yucky feelings we all have inside?"

I pushed the carrots to the edge of the table. "I don't know, maybe it's not a good idea."

"If we use the Hulk's example again, if he has to leave his mother in order to feel safe and wanted, is it like that for you too?"

"I'm safe now."

"Yes, that's because you're surrounded by people who care for you, even when you make a mistake."

"I know."

"And because you're such a brave warrior, everybody wants you. We do, your grandparents, and of course, your mother."

"I don't know that Mom wants me," I whispered.

Laura looked confused. I don't think she believed me. "I'm not sure about that, Axel. She's not perfect, but I'm sure she loves you."

"Oh, I know she's not perfect." I peeled some threads off my celery. "But she just wants to get money and take drugs and drink. My birthday's in August but the most important day that month is still cheque day. Her favourite things to do are get a boyfriend and smoke. She's an expert at rolling cigarettes and whupping me."

Laura looked surprised. "Wow, Axel, you sounded a bit mad there, but also brave for saying hard things. Thank you for trusting me."

I knew Laura even before we lost Faye. That was a long time ago. "I trust you, Miss Laura."

"I'll try and use your trust wisely. I want to let the judge know how you feel because I sense you're not ready to go home."

"I said I wanted to be with Mom."

"You said that many times, also when you were with Doreen. But I can tell when a warrior's just saying things to protect his crew. And your crew is your mom. You'll always protect her first, and you come second. You'll go home to her even if you don't want to. Am I right?"

How did she know? "Are you going to tell Mom this?"

"No, not now. But you deserve to feel safe. You deserve to feel wanted. Maybe you should share this with your lawyer, Emma. She'll want to hear it too. That way both she and I can tell the judge how you feel, what happens between you and your mom, and more importantly, what you want."

"What if Mom finds out?"

"She will, eventually. But the warrior in you has already survived many difficult moments with her. I know you'll survive this too."

———

"Miss Laura, can I ask you a question?"

"Of course, Axel."

"Do you ever see Faye?"

"Not anymore. Not since I was a youth worker watching over your visits with her."

"Do you know how she is?"

"No, not really."

"Did she get adopted? Does she have another family?"

"You already know the answer to that. She left her foster parents not long after the judge made his decision."

"I just wanna know, is she safe?"

"Yes, I'm sure she is."

"Was she adopted?"

"Yes, she was."

"Can I see her?"

Laura shook her head. "It's not up to me. What is it you want to say?"

"If I get adopted, can I be with Faye again?"

Laura turned toward me and put a hand on my shoulder. "You really miss her, don't you?"

I squeezed my eyes tight. I didn't want to cry.

"Everybody loves you. Everybody wants you. And even though it's your life, it's up to the judge to decide what's in your best interest. This is a fancy way of saying what's best for you. But you can help by being honest. You have a lawyer, and you have me looking out for you. Let us know what you want and we'll make sure the judge hears and understands it."

I looked at my shoes. They were new from the box. My foster

parents got them for me. They light up. "Mom says you shouldn't be trusted, that all you want is to take me away from her, the way you did with Faye."

She took her hand off my shoulder and put her face close to my face. "Sweetie, what I want is for you to be safe. I also want you to feel loved, to believe that you matter so much to someone that they would do nothing but wonderful things for you. If that's with your mom, your grandparents, or us, it doesn't matter, as long as *you* come first."

"Are you going to tell her that I want to be with Faye?"

"I'll bet deep down inside she already knows because she also wants to be with her, don't you agree?"

She was right. "So if I can't be with Faye, do I have to go back to Mom?"

She sat up. "Don't you want that?"

I looked down. "Mom and me get along. She always picks me up after school … But I'm not stupid."

"That's what I keep saying," she said.

"I just don't want to be yelled at anymore, and I don't want to be whupped anymore."

"I don't think anybody wants that." She gave me a hug.

I told her about Mom's temper, the things she said that scared me, her whuppings, her broken promises. I said a lot more. After a while, it wasn't so hard to say those things.

47

HANNAH

———

O<small>N THE DAY</small> of the settlement conference, I was supposed to first meet Shabana at her office around noon, and then we'd head over to the courthouse together. Instead, I phoned her from the police headquarters at ten. She was not impressed.

"Are you kidding me? This afternoon we go before the judge with a brief I've worked on for weeks, giving us a slim hope for him to toss this out, and you get arrested? Do you want to lose this?"

"You didn't tell me we only had a slim hope."

"Well, I've put together some of the CAS's case. They're going heavy on emotional harm and physical abuse. They have clear disclosures from Axel."

I drew in my breath. "He wouldn't dare."

"Well, he has."

"That's bullshit. He was probably pissed at me at the time."

"His lawyer says she interviewed him many times. I'm reading between the lines, but she's suggesting independent thinking on his part. There was strength and determination in what he wanted, and he was consistent. He stayed on message."

"What does he want?"

She paused.

"Shabana, you there?" My raised voice drew the attention of several police officers.

"He wants to be safe."

"I keep him safe."

"Well, they have a strong case history against you. They also have similar statements Axel gave Laura Catano that say he doesn't feel safe with you. They will argue that you cannot or will not take his mental health seriously, just as you didn't with Faye."

"That's crap, you can't say that. You can't ..." My voice trailed off. I felt fucked.

"Focus, okay? We're fighting a war on two fronts. Solomon's going to use this like a hammer on a fly and argue that Axel's grandparents, as kin, are his best option. And now you go get yourself in trouble with the police."

"It's not what you think."

"Tell me then, I'm your lawyer."

"We have a few hours. I'll be there, I promise. I'm not sure what's going to happen, but I'm sure I'll get out of here in time."

"Wait, you have to be here n—"

I hung up. I tried to think through what I'd just heard, that Ax had betrayed me and wanted out. "Little shit!" I smacked my hand against the wall. I refocused on why I was at police headquarters and stepped in and out of the building a few times, drumming up courage. I hadn't been arrested, but I did wish I'd taken Bill Krohn's offer to come with me.

Just tell a story, a true story. Make like you're just a witness. Let the facts speak for themselves. That's all you have to say.

It was stupid, but his words gave me courage. I fought the impulse to flee, re-entered the building, walked up to one of the police support specialists, and asked for Sergeant Lee.

"Sergeant Lee? You mean Staff Sergeant Lee, Tara Lee?"

"Uh, I guess, yeah."

"Is she expecting you?"

"No."

"Who can I tell her is asking?"

"Hannah Belenko. But she might not remember me."

The support specialist made a call. "Grab a seat, ma'am."

Two minutes later, a locked door opened and Tara Lee stepped through with a smile and an outstretched hand.

We shook without exchanging words. It was almost like this moment had been planned. She led me to a quiet room nearby. She pulled down the blinds. "It's great to see you, Hannah, I kind of hoped you'd turn up after Malik nailed you over the winter."

"I didn't think you'd remember me." I scanned her face. The creases and wrinkles around her eyes hadn't been there years ago. Her long black hair was now short and peppered with grey. Lean, muscular arms made her look like she could be a CrossFit trainer. The bitch.

"I can't find my car keys half the time, but some cases I don't forget. Like Youri and Hannah Belenko."

"That's impressive. Guess that's how you made staff sergeant."

"It took me nineteen years, just under the average for most female officers, but well above average for males. No politics or male bastion here, nope. And I'm not bitter." Lee made an exaggerated face. "More importantly, you're here."

"Yeah, and I've finally got something to say."

Lee fumbled through her pockets for a notebook and a pen. "It's been a while. But I so want to do this for you."

Make like a camera, I said to myself. Just describe the facts, Mr. Krohn had said.

"Did you ever play ringette, Sergeant Lee?"

"It's Staff Sergeant, by the way. In phys-ed, does that count?"

I shook my head. "I was good, scary good. And then my family fucked it all up for me like they fucked up so many things."

Half an hour after I started talking, Lee stopped me. "I don't know where you want to go with this, but I want to personally take this upstairs to the sexual assault and child abuse team. They interviewed you once before, years ago, about your brother after he allegedly assaulted your friend at a party."

That was when I couldn't tell the truth about Ivan having raped Mackenzie. I bit the inside of my mouth and resisted shielding my head.

"Are you ready for this?" Lee asked. "They'll want to record this."

"I don't know." And that was the truth.

⸺

The police kept me there for hours. I lost track of time and couldn't focus on anything but the questions the police threw at me. Shabana left me a pile of messages. It was five o'clock by the time I got to the meeting at the courthouse and I totally expected it would be over, but I caught a break—they were still there, about to wrap up. Benoit's office administrator ushered me in.

"I'm sorry, everybody," I said. I sat in the one empty chair, directly across from Papa.

The judge bitched me out. I apologized once again.

"Your Honour, may we take a break so that I can confer with my client?" Shabana asked.

"No. If the welfare of your client's son can't compel her to appear on time, I can't imagine what will." Benoit turned to me. "You're very late, but you're in time to hear where I think we should go with this."

My parents looked all innocent and loving. Papa wore a tie and jacket and had this fixed smile on, which I'd seen before when he got pulled over by police. Mama was wearing a dress I'd seen in the window at Melanie Lyne. She looked worried, for who or what, I couldn't tell. I smelled mothballs for some reason. They made me want to throw up.

Shabana whispered to me that Benoit had heard briefs from Axel's lawyer, the CAS lawyer, Cheryl Solomon, and herself.

"Your Honour, Ms. Belenko's lack of punctuality speaks volumes," Solomon said. She began by nodding to her clients. "The Belenko grandparents have stepped up and have demonstrated, without fail, their continued commitment to care for their grandson."

"Your Honour," Shabana said. "All these years, Ms. Belenko has single-parented without any support from her family. That doesn't sound like grandparents with continued commitment, more like a short-term interest."

Benoit held his hands up. "Enough, you two. Perhaps the Belenkos are late to the game, but they showed when they had to, unlike your client, Ms. Ahmedi.

"The home study has raised no red flags. Yes, it would probably be easier to keep up with Axel if you were both twenty years younger." Benoit smiled at Mama and Papa. "But it's love and commitment I'm looking for, not world-class sprint times."

Papa smiled and stifled a fist pump.

"Your Honour, my client has secured safe housing and now has a job. She'll soon have benefits," Shabana argued.

"Part-time work and a two-bedroom with a roommate. Where will Axel sleep?" Solomon asked.

"Stop. I've heard enough." Benoit turned to Solomon. "Ms. Solomon, your request for temporary custody of Axel is strong, and it has wide support." He looked at the other lawyers except for Shabana. Then he turned to her. "Ms. Ahmedi, unless you have information that sheds a different light, I'm not sure a trial is necessary. I'm prepared to render a recommendation now. We could save everyone a great deal of time if you and your client agree to it. Axel's grandparents have demonstrated they can rise to the occasion and act in his best interests. I'm hoping we can achieve consensus, as I'm inclined to—"

"No!" I shouted.

Shabana reached for my hand, but I pounded the table.

"No," I repeated.

"Ms. Belenko, I don't appreciate you coming in like this and interrup—"

"He beat the crap out of me." I pointed at Papa. "He scared the shit out of me so I never knew what was coming and when."

"Ms. Belenko, it's a bit late for this," Benoit said.

"The police don't think so. I was just down at the station talking to Staff Sergeant Tara Lee. She remembers me from when he almost strangled me to death. I was too scared to say anything to her at the time, but she knew. She knew. But I'm not scared to say anything now."

Cheryl Solomon jumped in. "Your Honour, it's this kind of theatre that doesn't help Axel. Please, let's end this."

"Theatre, eh?" I pulled out a copy of a police incident report. "Staff Sergeant Lee will be assigning someone from the child abuse unit to arrest him. Don't believe me? Call her, here's her number." I threw down Lee's card.

"You know what's the worst part of this?" I said, turning to Papa. "It's not what you did to me, it's what you taught me, and what you'll teach Ax about messing up people's lives. Maybe I'm not good for him." I unclenched my fists and rested them on the table. "Maybe he deserves a better mother. No, that's not a maybe. He definitely deserves a better mother. But if the only choice I have left is to keep him away from me and both of you," I pointed at them, "then at least I've done one thing right. If I'm gonna lose Ax, I would rather he go into care for good than live through the abuse I had to put up with."

"These are lies." Papa stood up. He glared at me with the same cold, soulless eyes I'd feared all my life. "My grandson should not be raised by a crazy woman."

My knees quaked, but I stood and met his glare. "I agree, Ax deserves to be raised by someone who isn't a crazy woman, or a crazy man. He deserves another chance to be in a safe home. Shit, I don't even know what that looks like, no thanks to you two. So how can I provide it? As long as he doesn't have to be under your influence, I'll live with it."

"Your Honour," Shabana's eyes lit up and she went at Benoit and Solomon, "it goes without saying that sending a child to a man under investigation by the police for child abuse is not in the child's—or the court's—best interests."

"These allegations, Your Honour," Solomon said, "for all we know they've been concocted and the police and the court are being manipulated by a desperate mother who has already lost one child."

"Your Honour, if there's a police investigation underway, at the very least you must consider deferring making any recommendations," Shabana said.

"Does my son not deserve this?" I said.

"Yes, he does." Mama's voice came out of nowhere, stunning us all into silence.

Papa shushed her, but she reached for his arm and yanked it. "Sit down, Youri."

"Steffi!" Papa apologized to everyone and said Mama was tired and on new medication.

"No." She shook her head at him, then looked at me with her mouth quivering. "I'm sorry I didn't fight for you the way you're fighting for your Axel."

I just about lost my shit.

Everyone fell silent and looked at Mama. Papa tried to look defiant as he sat. He glanced at everyone who stared into him, then lowered his head, suddenly looking really old and weak.

"Whatever is best for Axel," Mama said to Benoit.

I caught my breath.

"Your Honour, may I request a break to confer with my clients?" Solomon said.

"No, that won't be necessary," Benoit replied.

48

AXEL

I DON'T KNOW why it's taking the judge so long. When Mom wanted to go to Halifax, we just went. When Mom wanted to say goodbye to Oma Greta, we just went. I guess it's really hard work to decide. Even I can't make up my mind.

If the judge says I can live with Dedushka and Oma, I'll be happy and sad at the same time. If the judge decides I can go back to Mom, same thing. Happy, sad. If there was a way I could live in two places, like with the good parts of Dedushka and Oma and also the good parts of Mom, I would choose that. They would have to shake on it, though, and that will never happen. They have too many bees.

Yesterday Mom gave me a paperweight with bees inside. Jimmy sent it to me with a letter. He said it means he found somewhere to put them so they don't make so much racket in his head and he can think and won't feel like running away anymore. I left it at Mom's apartment on purpose, so maybe it will calm the racket in her head too.

Laura said she hopes that whatever happens, I still get to see whoever is important to me. I'd like that.

FALL 2019

49

HANNAH

———

I STOOD NERVOUSLY by the open window in my apartment, enjoying the cool September air as I blew out cigarette smoke. Three a day was all I was allowing myself. My goal was to quit completely in one month's time. For good. I'm serious.

I straightened Ax's dream catcher on the wall and adjusted the paperweight on the table. I didn't know what it was supposed to mean. Ax said it's a secret he has with Jimmy. Maybe someday one of them will tell me.

Jimmy sent the paperweight after I mailed him Kim's wallet. I had asked him to return it to her, along with an apology I wrote (it doesn't cut it, I know), a small cheque, and promises of more to follow. He and I exchanged a few texts. He said he'd always wanted to see Ottawa and heard the paddling around here was good. I wouldn't know. He asked if he could teach Ax a few strokes as you never know when it might come in handy. I said that was up to Ax. Some things he can decide now. I told Jimmy he could come for a visit anyway. I could always use a friend.

I scrubbed the bathtub and toilet for the second time in three days. You'd think Prince Harry was coming, but it was just my Ax. I looked at my watch and made sure my router was working and that the tablet was charged.

When the buzzer went off, I leapt for the door. I opened it and waited. After what seemed like an eternity, I heard them come up the stairs. Boris also heard and bounded out of the apartment and into the hallway, where he jumped onto Ax.

"Who loves you, Boris, Ax does." He hugged Boris and allowed him to lick his face. Then he got up and hugged me.

"Great to see you, Ax. Come on in, I've got some celery sticks and dip for you."

He grimaced. "Mo-om."

"They're there right beside the raisin butter tarts."

Ax stepped into the kitchen. Laura and I greeted one another.

She smiled at me. "You're nervous."

"Also excited," I said. "I know it's okay to feel a bunch of things at the same time, even if shit-scared is only one of them."

"Language, Mom. That's a loonie," Ax said.

I shook my head. "What have I done?" I sighed at Laura. "I'm gonna go broke this weekend."

"Maybe, but it's a weekend you deserve, something you've earned. Your first overnight since ..."

"The shelter. Shit, I'll never forget that."

"Loonie, loonie." Axel giggled from the kitchen.

"Will you take a cheque?"

"You're on the right path, Hannah."

Benoit extending the supervision order and averting a trial was huge. I'd helped make that happen by getting the police to lay charges on my father.

"In three months we go before Benoit again. He may give you another break, a big one. You may get Axel back for good. You've done lots of heavy, painful lifting."

"Honestly, Laura, I've been here before. The last time I was in Dartmouth, they checked off all the boxes and cut us loose. I still crashed and burned."

"Are you the same person you were six months ago?"

I shrugged.

"Well, you're not. Six months ago you were a runner. You were always on high alert. You still are much of the time. Old patterns are hard to break, after all. But now you're taking a stand, for you and for your son."

I sighed and chewed on my lip.

"Anyway, this weekend belongs to the two of you. I'm out of here."

I had broken our family's code, and remained standing. I gave Laura a hug. "Thanks for ... for not giving up on me."

"Are you kidding me?" Laura curtsied. "I bow to the warrior in both of you for your courage and determination against insurmountable odds."

"You call that a bow?" Ax and I said in unison as he walked in from the kitchen.

"Ax will be picked up around five on Sunday," Laura said. She gave me a thumbs-up as she closed the door behind her.

"Can we call, can we call now?" Ax asked.

I looked at my watch. "It's about nine o'clock over there. Sure, let's do it. He'll be waiting. Oh, before I forget." I pulled out a gift bag and handed it to him.

He took it and looked up at me. "It's not my birthday."

"Do I need a reason to show that I'm thinking of you? Come on, open it."

Ax tore into the bag and pulled out a stuffed dolphin. "Faye's favourite animal!"

"This one's a bottlenose. I know you might be a bit big for stuffed animals, but I remember the last one you had, do you?"

Ax nodded but averted my gaze. I can't blame him.

"I destroyed it. I was mean, I was angry, and I took it out on you. I did a lot of that."

"That's okay, Mom—"

"No, Ax, it wasn't okay. And you shouldn't be trying to make me feel better and trying to protect me. That's not your job. Yours is to have fun and be a kid. Mine is to make you feel special and to protect you. I didn't do a good job of it. Actually, I sucked. I want to do better, for real this time. I don't want to lose you the way I lost Faye."

"But you didn't lose Faye, I did, Mom. I remember what happened. It was when I said Kevin had a broken touch screen. It was all my fault. I'm sorry, please don't be mad."

I recognized fear and anguish in his face. "I remember that day too. But you didn't lose Faye, I did. It was my job to look after her, not yours. And I failed, not you. Kevin was one of many of my mistakes, so stop with this fucked-up thinking. None of this is your fault."

"Loonie!"

I almost let myself get annoyed for a second but caught myself and took a breath and forced a smile, then pulled out some coins from my wallet that Axel deposited into a coffee can.

Faye's name hung in the air for a few seconds. Neither of us felt we needed to say more. We missed her. I hoped she missed us and that she wondered how we were and didn't judge me too harshly. If she did, that would be okay, I deserved it. Maybe, maybe someday she'd come looking for me.

"I love it." Ax hugged the dolphin and then me.

"Come on, he's probably waiting." I opened up my tablet and went to Google Chat and connected. But there was no audio or image.

"Hello?" I said.

"Hellooo," Axel said.

No video came through yet, but we could hear. "Axel, Axel. Can you see me?"

The connection died.

"It's not working." Ax was starting to get revved up.

"Calm down, Ax, just wait."

Ax stomped his foot and clenched his face.

My impulse was to tell him to smarten up and shut up. Instead, I said, "Deep breath, buddy, deep breath."

I tried to connect again but got nothing. One last time, let's go. Then Bashir's beaming image appeared. "Axel, how are you, my son?"

"Daddy!"

As much as I wanted Ax all to myself, I stepped aside, giving them some father-son time. This might be all Ax would get from his dad, and also all I'd get from him. We both understood that. But we could hope.

Acknowledgements

My growth and success as a writer are largely attributable to my muse, my partner, my everything—Trish Lucy.

Many thanks to my Guernica Editions family for their continuing support and belief in me, especially my editor, the magnificent Margo LaPierre who loved this book right away and then boldly told me to blow it up. The eternal gentleman Michael Mirolla, Anna van Valkenburg and Dylan Curran.

My trusted and talented writing group of more than twenty years, Chris Crowder, Amy Tector and Alette Willis.

Doreen Arnoni for her tenacity in editing the early drafts, again and again and again.

Hilary Lucy, for being the second mother everyone should have.

Bianca Marais for her community building and social activism on two continents and whose podcast *The Shit No One Tells You About Writing* inspired me during the bleakness of the pandemic.

Helen Wong and Rose Cortez for sisterly devotion and unconditional support.

The friends, colleagues, acquaintances and professionals who provided their time, support and expertise to ensure the authenticity and accuracy, in particular ... Wendy Appleby, Marc Brown, Emily Comor, Liam Conrad, Dr. Nicholas Costain, Sadia Faqiri, Sandra Fennell, Manon Ferguson and daughters, Mary Gallagher, Larry Gauthier, Ryan Fraser of Alderney Landing, Debbie Frendo, Cindy Gattas, Mark Hecht, Kim Hutchison, Paul Kozak, Karel and Sheridon Nelson, Donna Palmer Dodd, Kathleen Pyke of Stepping Stones, Kelsey Ryan, Katarina S., Laura Sanschagrin, Jill Skinner-Deputy Chief of Police (Ret.), Andrew Spearin, and Laura Valcin.

And finally to YOU, dear reader for picking up my novel!

About the Author

Wayne Ng was born in downtown Toronto to Chinese immigrants who fed him a steady diet of bitter melons and kung fu movies. He works as a school social worker in Ottawa but lives to write, travel, eat and play, preferably all at the same time. He is an award-winning author and traveller who continues to push his boundaries from the Arctic to the Antarctic. Wayne's first novel *Finding The Way: A Novel of Lao Tzu* was released in 2018. He is currently working on a sequel to *Letters From Johnny* (winner of the 2022 Best Crime Novella, Crime Writers of Canada). Connect with Wayne at WayneNgWrites.com.

Printed in January 2023
by Gauvin Press,
Gatineau, Québec